Jane Berman

Unkosher Slaughter

π

Pardes Publishing

PARDES
PUBLISHING

1 Palmer Gate, P.O.Box 33709
Haifa, 3133602, Israel
www.pardes.co.il

Pardes Publishing is a specialist, international publisher of fiction, poetry and non-fiction.

A CIP catalogue record for this book is available from the Israeli National Library.

ISBN 978-1-61838-215-3

Published in Israel

For my children,

Sarai, Rutie and Moshe

Also by Jane Berman:

Death at The Light House

PROLOGUE

Kibbutz Kerem El

A BLAST of wind slammed the door shut as Reb Elijah Lachmann teetered onto the path that led from his cottage to the synagogue. Instinctively, his hand clamped his skullcap down tight. Through veils of dust, the cypresses in his front garden swayed like giants.

Old man, your mind is playing games with you. The lanes were deserted, the neighbors' houses shuttered. Street lamps glimmered through a mustard-colored swirl. Sand choked the Rebbe's nose and mouth and he bent over heaving, wracked by the cough that had taken root in his lungs.

The wind socked into him, plastering his coat against his body and unfurling his sidelocks into silver ribbons. *Old man, your body is rust and old bone. Soon you'll be rid of it, thank God.* Though the prospect of meeting the Creator had lifted his spirits, flesh dragged him earthward and he longed to return to his study and a glass of hot lemon tea.

But the caller had pleaded urgency. *Rebbe, I've searched my heart, and I must confess. The shul, please,* and since the Rebbe knew every nuance of the caller's voice, had touched the void within the caller's soul, and because that soul was so dear to him, he'd laid his volume of Talmud aside and reached for his coat.

Had his sermon that morning made an impact, after all? As always, on the Sabbath before Passover, the synagogue was crammed with worshippers, and so it was that morning despite the heat. From his armchair on the dais, Reb Elijah surveyed his people, third and fourth generation on Kibbutz Kerem El; men in blue-striped prayer shawls flowing from their shoulders, women fanning themselves with prayer books up in the gallery, children toddling down the aisles.

A group of men had rushed in through the back door, whispering apologies. Their pony tails, earrings and embroidered caps marked them as bohemians from the artists' village down the mountain. Most likely they had come by car, a probability that made Reb Elijah feel uncomfortable, Jews violating the Sabbath especially for his sermon.

Wiping sweat from his beard, the Rebbe pulled himself up and trudged over to the lectern. Children were shooed outside; only coughs and the nagging of the wind punctuated the silence.

He'd worked on the sermon all night, but as he began to speak, he abandoned the text. His voice rumbled inside his skull, as if an avalanche brewing within him threatened to flatten the congregation. He swung from side to side, arms striking the air. A murmur rippled through the crowd, then bursts of sound, shouts. Someone—someone he knew well— he couldn't remember who—jumped onto the dais and put an arm around his shoulders, wrapping his prayer shawl around him. He was led out the side door of the synagogue where his daughter, Malkie, had run to meet him, her eyes glazed with fright.

—*Abba, what's happened to you? Those accusations you made....*

—*He who understands, understands.*

Now, struggling to open the door of the synagogue, Reb Elijah realized that his words had struck their target and that here in the house of prayer, please God, justice would be done.

The synagogue was dim, except for the flame that burned above the Ark. The Rebbe inhaled the smells of dust and prayer books and the faint scent of perfume that floated down from the women's gallery. And another scent as well. A figure emerged from one of the pews.

"*Shalom*, Rebbe."

"*Shalom* to you too. May the new week be a favorable one."

"God willing." A nod of the head.

The Rebbe sank down in the pew facing the *bima*, the platform on which the Torah scrolls were read. His leg ached and he felt weariness tug at him like a petulant child. He thought of bed, if only he could lie down...

But he'd been summoned. He lifted his head to meet the familiar gaze of his caller. "There was something you had to tell me. You searched your heart, you said."

When the voice answered, it was dreamlike, mournful. "Yes, Rebbe, I've searched, but truth be told, my heart is absent."

A chill rippled through the Rebbe's chest. He'd sensed the caller's empty heart for years and wondered how his companion would act now that its lack had surfaced to awareness.

The Rebbe got to his feet. He must be resolute despite his pity and love.

"I've told you, restitution must be made to those you've harmed. You must pay the price for your deeds. Otherwise, there is no forgiveness from God or man."

"And if I don't, Rebbe.." The voice was teasing.

" As dear as you are to me, I will destroy you."

He heard his voice echo in the silence that swelled up into the dome of the synagogue and felt foolish. *Old man, who gave you the mandate to destroy?*

There was a sound, a clucking of tongue against teeth. Two lengths of cord were retrieved from beneath the canopy that covered the lectern.

"What in God's name are you doing?" For the first time, he felt the stirrings of fear.

But the voice didn't reply. The figure grabbed his wrists and the Rebbe felt the cord cut into his flesh, then into his ankles. He tried to shout, but coughing smothered his voice, drowning it in bile.

"Rebbe, mount the *bima*, please." *Please. Ever the polite one, even from the beginning.* Reb Elijah stumbled onto the platform and was pressed down by strong hands. He felt the parquet floor beneath him where he had stood thousands of times to chant from the Holy Torah.

Shema, Israel, he murmured together with the humming of the wind. He thought of his daughter, his many grandchildren, what he had done on earth, what he had left undone.

The slaughterer's knife glinted in the upraised hand, and through the rise and fall of the wind, the Rebbe heard a voice.

"Elijah, Elijah."

Here I am.

CHAPTER ONE

Jerusalem

RACHEL Shine raked dust from her hair and cursed the hot wind lashing the city. As she wiped the countertops one last time, she wondered whether God had hurled down the *khamsin* to test her on the eve of Passover when every crevice had to be leaven-free. If so, she'd get an *F* for failure. Again.

She tossed a bucketful of water onto the balcony, the soapy liquid cooling her toes, then squeegeed it down to the courtyard where the scent of jasmine floated up from between cracked stones. Rachel took pride in the home she'd pieced together from a crumbling nineteenth-century stable outside the Old City walls, the kitchen overlooking a courtyard with a lemon tree and the original well. She'd planted begonias and rosemary among the bougainvillea and honeysuckle. On Friday nights, she'd sit on the balcony, wrapped in a quilt against the Jerusalem chill, lulled by the chants from the synagogues tucked into the alleyways that wove through Nahlaot.

Creating a home from rubble, she often thought, was like reassembling herself piece by piece, after the divorce.

Whatever love she and Nahum had shared since their youth movement days had withered throughout the years of childlessness. Stubbornly refusing to undergo fertility tests, Nahum had blamed her. A guru rabbi from Mea Shearim had tightened the strictures that bound their lives, convincing Nahum that it was Rachel's lax observance that prevented them from fulfilling the commandment to be fruitful and multiply. Her husband's piety soared while she inched further and further away from religion.

First she abandoned her headscarf, loosening her wavy amber-colored hair, then dared insert the amber earrings that were her talisman; the prehistoric insects frozen within reminded her of Nahum. She'd never allow herself to feel trapped again.

After the divorce, when she ran into him on Jaffa Road, he'd avert his eyes from her long slim legs and bare arms. Little did he realize that their holy wars battled within Rachel herself. At thirty-four, she still felt guilty about thrusting her orthodox life aside.

So she koshered her kitchen for Passover, though she'd be with her parents for the full eight days and packed a long skirt for *shul*. As for the Eleventh Commandment, *Thou shalt phone thy mother twice a day to reassure her that thou art still breathing*, she dried her bare feet on a clean floor rag, glanced at the clock—it was just after seven—and picked up the phone.

No answer. Strange, since Aviva was obsessively organized, especially at Passover time. It was possible she'd run down to the mini-market for one more jar of horseradish, one more box of *matza* "just in case," though they'd be having a small *seder*—just Rachel, her parents and her old friend, Alona Golan. Her brother, Michael, who lived with his wife and eight children in a West Bank settlement, was spending the holiday with his in-laws.

The floor trembled, trucks rumbling up Agrippas Street to the Mahane Yehuda *shuk* where shoppers would be waiting impatiently for the unloading of fruits and vegetables, thick carcasses of beef and freshly slaughtered chickens.

Rachel's heart skidded and her hands began to shake as images ripped through her head. Butchery. Flayed ribs. Shredded flesh. The odor of charred bodies.

Oh God, not now..

The severed head of the suicide bomber rose in her mind like a livid sun. He'd been no more than sixteen, his hair neatly parted in the middle of his scalp. That had struck her more than anything, more than the body parts strewn around her or the blood on her face. She'd stared at it, murmuring over and over, *Someone once bathed and diapered and kissed you and combed your hair.*

She stumbled to the sofa, where she lay rigid and shut her eyes, visualizing a frozen lake, birch trees bent under snow. Icicles in her hair, her limbs congealing with cold. Frigid silence to help the panic wind down

It'd been shock, of course. After her hospitalization— two weeks in the trauma ward at Hadassah—she felt slightly ashamed of that moment of compassion for the monster that had just blown up fifteen teenagers outside a pizza parlor.

Save your pity for the victims, Aviva had said, flicking the wings of her headscarf over her shoulder. *Besides, look what he did to you—and you're a therapist, for Pete's sake!* As if that had been the ultimate travesty.

Rachel opened her eyes as the attack subsided. On wobbly legs, she walked to the refrigerator and downed cold water straight from the pitcher.

Four sharp raps from Beethoven's *Fifth* sounded at the door, followed by a musical, "*Boker tov, motek!*"

Choking on the last gulp of water, wiping her mouth with the back of her hand, Rachel injected as much normality into her voice as she could muster. "Just a sec."

She unlocked the door and Miri walked in, but froze as she glanced at Rachel's face.

"Hey, you're white as plaster," she said, adding guardedly, "Don't tell me you've heard." Her powder blue eyes widened against dusky skin.

"Heard what?" Rachel barely processed what Miri was saying. Her head felt stuffed with cotton wadding.

Miri avoided her glance and headed for the kitchenette where she reached for the coffee grinder and switched on the electric kettle. As the fog in her brain lifted, Rachel noticed the restraint in her friend's normally fluid movements. Miri belonged to a fringe modern dance troupe, but her main source of income was the embroidered bridal canopies she designed and which sold for thousands of shekels each. For Rachel, their friendship was a canopy, a shelter against the gusts that threatened to topple her equanimity.

"Make the coffee strong," she said, curling her legs beneath her on the couch once again. "I just had an attack. All the snow in Siberia couldn't pull me out of it this time."

Miri poured. "Three sugars. No backtalk now; your body needs it." She blew off the steam and placed the mug into Rachel's cupped hands.

"You're a lifesaver, you know." With the first scalding sip, Rachel felt the earth tilt back on its axis again.

Uncharacteristically silent, Miri eased herself down onto the tile floor, fingers tracing the interlocking patterns of cobalt and yellow. The skin between her eyebrows puckered.

"What?" Rachel prodded.

"I'm not sure I'm such a lifesaver, "Miri muttered, "after I tell you why I came."

Rachel's heart contracted. *Have you heard?* Miri had said.

"I'm not an invalid. Spit it out."

"Look, there might be nothing to it," Miri said rapidly. "Yaniv phoned me a few minutes ago. Something came through from the precinct near your kibbutz." Yaniv was Miri's boyfriend, a policeman on the Jerusalem Police Fraud Squad. A sweet guy, Rachel thought, but with hardly any time for Miri. *Never date a cop*, Miri always warned.

"Get on with it."

She took a sip of coffee, her eyes fastened on Rachel's face. "Someone died up there."

"Died? Why would Yaniv get to hear about that?"

"Because it wasn't a natural death." Miri rose from the floor and sat next to Rachel on the sofa. "Someone was killed…murdered."

"Murdered?" Her thoughts tried desperately to connect. She moistened her lips, which had suddenly dried up. "Who?"

"Your rabbi."

A swell of relief washed over her. It was a mistake; Yaniv had misunderstood, and so had Miri. There was no *rabbi* on Kerem El.

"Rachel?" That cotton wool sensation again. Why was Miri's voice coming from such a distance, though she was right up against her on the sofa?

To her surprise, her own voice rang out clearly. "You've got it all wrong. We don't have a rabbi, we don't need a rabbi. We have the Rebbe, Reb Elijah."

"Put my foot in it again," Miri muttered, gently turning Rachel's face towards her. "But that's who I meant, *motek*. I meant *Rebbe* Elijah."

A gust of wind rattled the window panes. Rachel hugged her arms to her chest. *How chilly it is, when it ought to be so hot.*

"Look at me," Miri was whispering and shouting at the same time. "Rachel, *look* at me!" She was holding the coffee to Rachel's lips. It was cloyingly sweet, but reviving. She felt as though she were swimming to the surface to reach Miri, trying to twist her thoughts around what she had said.

"Good girl," Miri nodded when Rachel had drained the mug.

"Reb Elijah, murdered." Something was wrong with the juxtaposition of the two words. Why would anyone want to murder him?

"It was a terrorist, wasn't it?" Her heart started pounding again. "My God, a terrorist got into Kerem El."

But Miri was shaking her head back and forth, her ebony curls slapping her cheeks like baby fists. She gripped Rachel's shoulders.

"It's not *like* that," she said. "I'll tell you what Yaniv heard and we'll figure out where to take it from there."

Rachel took a deep breath. "I'm okay. Just tell me what you know."

"You sure?"

"Yes. I want to hear the worst, that's all. Don't worry about me." Seized by the need to move, Rachel began pacing, her hands clasped around the back of her neck. Through the kitchen window, she saw that a rust-colored cloud had manteled the city.

Miri eyed her warily. "The Rebbe was found this morning by the woman who cleans the synagogue."

"In the synagogue?" Rachel stopped in her tracks.

"Yes, and what's so strange is that the person kneeling next to the…Rebbe…was that weird son-in-law of his."

"Shmaya?" Her thoughts careened. Shmaya Catz, the husband of the Rebbe's only daughter, her oldest friend. "Poor Malkie!"

"There's more," Miri said dryly.

Rachel clamped down her rampaging thoughts. "Not now. I'll hear it soon enough." Rachel grabbed her hand and marched her off to the small bedroom down the corridor. "I've got to get to Kerem El. What Malkie must be going through!" She pulled clothes from drawers and closets, tossing them helter-skelter on the bed.

Miri stood in the doorway, arms folded. "You'd better hear the whole story before you tear yourself up there."

"So I can have a panic attack while driving?" She stuffed sweaters, jeans, a skirt and matching jacket into the suitcase along with underwear and jewelry. After a moment's hesitation, she threw in her set of whittling knives.

Miri sighed. "What do you need those for?"

"Just in case." She gave her friend a swift hug. "I'll phone you. Make sure to water my plants, take in my mail and… my brain's turned to mush…turn the lights on and off every couple of days."

Hammering pummeled the roof, muffling her final words.

She kneeled on the bed and reached over to unfasten the shutters. "Look!" She motioned for Miri to join her. "The *khamsin's* over. The rain's started."

Rust-colored water sluiced through the alleyways of Nahlaot. "It looks like blood to me," Miri whispered, staring through the glass.

* * *

Chief-Inspector Absalom Brill felt as comfortable in a synagogue as a vegan in a steakhouse. Yet, here he was at seven a.m. with a dead rabbi on his plate, so to speak.

He swallowed the dislike with which he viewed the

haredim, as the black-hatted pious Jews were called. To him, they were insular and fundamentalist, with enough political clout to drag Israel down into an ayatollah state.

Eyeing Shmaya Catz, the victim's son-in-law, who was rocking back and forth in one of the pews and praying from a small *siddur*, psalms maybe—Absalom had skipped most of his Bible classes in high school—he knew his prejudices were getting the best of his professionalism, and not for the first time.

He turned his back on the *haredi*, skirted the blood-splashed *bima* in the center of the large hall, and walked over to the front of the synagogue, where the body waited and the forensics people were packing up. His knowledge of synagogue architecture never got beyond his bar mitzvah lessons with old Rabbi Tessler, who'd taught him that Jews prayed toward Jerusalem, toward the wall against which the Torah Ark stood. Here, the Ark was framed by stained glass, etched with the symbols of the Twelve Tribes of Israel. On most mornings, Absalom figured, the Lion of Judah would blossom into magenta flames with the light of the rising sun, but now the sky outside was leaden, the big cat a tame and lifeless gray.

He glanced up the steep narrow steps leading to the women's gallery and pondered what the point was of having such a magnificent synagogue if religious women, who were constantly pregnant or holding small children and were at least half the population, had to struggle to get second class seats in which to pray.

But what puzzled him most about the place was its opulence. Absalom recognized wealth when he saw it: gold fittings, velvet curtains, chandeliers, the marble floor, smeared now with blood and streaks of mud. And the size. At least four stories high, with turrets and a domed ceiling painted with silver stars. While knowing little about his religion, he knew a lot about kibbutzim and their modest communal way of life. Though this was changing, Kerem El seemed too conservative to be in the vanguard of those changes. He wondered where the money came from. Rich American Jews? *Protekzia* at the Ministry of Religious Affairs? He was ready to place his bets on the latter.

Interrupting his thoughts, the pathologist from Abu Kabir handed him a clipboard with forms to sign. Absalom gazed at the body bag on the gurney.

"Make sure he's given priority. They told me he can't be buried later than noon tomorrow because the holiday comes in at around six."

The other man made a face. "Tell me about it. We're at my in-laws for the *seder*. I bet you never ate *matza* balls like my wife's mother makes. Heavy enough to sink a battleship."

Absalom didn't smile, only stood silently as the body was wheeled through the rear door, accompanied by sobs from the gathering crowd, the whirring of T.V. cameras and the subdued drone of reporters. Word of the murder had raced through the small mountain community and the media, momentarily pushing aside the news of the latest drive-by shooting. Though his precinct was only a few kilometers away, he'd never set foot in Kerem El. A strange hybrid, he thought, a settlement run by religious Jews where the members worked the fields and lived an orthodox life. He'd heard of such places, but had never visited one. *Nothing like murder to broaden one's horizons.*

The *haredi* had wound up his prayers and was settling down in the pew, eyes uplifted to the vaulted dome. In his thirties, bearded, with a fleshy midriff, he wore the black jacket and white shirt of his "trade," but both were caked with blood. So was the hand that clutched the prayer book.

Absalom exchanged looks with his partner, Yossi Gottwein, who was lounging next to the son-in-law, a "now-I've-seen-everything" smirk on his turnip-shaped face. "*Meshugga*," he mouthed, pointing a twirling finger at his head. Ignoring him, Absalom slid into the pew.

"Shmaya," he said softly. No reaction, no sign that the *haredi* had heard him. The man's eyes, dark as charcoal, swept the star-studded ceiling.

Absalom coughed. Revolted by the blood, by the man's butcher-like build and the sweat that oozed from him, he rapped Shmaya's knee sharply with a pen to grab his attention. Flinching, Shmaya stared down at his right hand.

Absalom tried again. "Do you know who I am?"

The *haredi* continued to gaze at his blood-soaked hand, while Yossi shook his head. "We can't get zilch from this guy. Let's take him down to the station."

Absalom had no patience for Yossi's impulsiveness. Shmaya was about ready to crack from tension. Taking him over to the station would be counterproductive. The man needed the right atmosphere, here in the synagogue, surrounded by the ritual props he knew so well.

"A man is dead. Do you know who he is?"

The *haredi* shifted on the hard wooden seat. "The Rebbe. Malkie's father."

Absalom nodded. *We're getting somewhere. At least he's plugged into something that resembles reality.*

"Your hand is covered with blood, Shmaya. Why is that?"

The *haredi* gazed down at his hand. *"A pure bull, without blemish, as a sacrificial offering,"* he mumbled.

Absalom was beginning to understand. "A sacrificial offering? The rabbi, you mean?"

Shmaya faced him, his lips beneath the thick beard pursed in reproof. "The *Rebbe*, Reb Elijah."

Rabbi, rebbe, what difference does it make? Absalom thought, but he said solemnly, "I stand corrected. Why was the Rebbe a sacrificial offering?"

Shmaya groaned and began rocking to and fro. "So that the abomination of the godless one will cease."

Absalom kept his face expressionless, as if they were discussing a traffic ticket. "And who is the godless one whose abominations must cease?"

The meaty shoulders slumped as Shmaya Catz stared at the row of prayer books lined up on the reading stand in front of him.

"I am," he sighed.

Yossi blinked. "Is that a confession, or what?"

"We'll soon see." Drawing a deep breath, Absalom tried to snare the *haredi's* gaze. "Shmaya," he said gently, "are you saying you killed your father-in-law?"

Shmaya's head bowed, then rose, then bowed again. It was the nod of a man whose shoulders sagged under a burden. "God help me, it was me. I killed him."

CHAPTER TWO

O n Route Six traffic was heavy, typical of the holiday rush. Families heading for the Sea of Galilee, roof-racks piled high with camping gear, drivers laughing with their kids, talking on cell phones; Israelis living ordinary lives, except for the *intifada* that had seeped into their routine like poisoned groundwater.

Rachel glanced at an Arab village hidden behind a wall. Only the tip of the minaret was visible. Not long ago, a terrorist from that village had slammed bullets into a family car, gunning down a toddler asleep in the back seat. Instinctively, she stamped down on the gas pedal.

Three times during the trip, her cell phone had bleeped with the strained voices of her mother and father. Their concern was justified, especially now that her Passover holiday was turning into yet another encounter with violence. This morning's panic attack had reminded her how easily she could regress.

Each new day her fight to regain control began, with affirmations, bracing walks through the Jerusalem hills, and most of all, whittling. A guest psychologist from Kentucky had once given a workshop in whittling therapy, which had grabbed Rachel's interest as a tool for treating aggression and anxiety. After the suicide bombing, she craved the soothing rhythm of the knives, the heft of their ridged handles, the wedges of wood, the smell of shavings, curled like a baby's hair.

It was close to nine-thirty and the rain had dwindled to fitful showers. The temperature had dropped by the time she turned off the highway into the Carmel Nature Reserve. Ahead of her the mountains loomed, shrouded in dun-colored mist, while behind her, muddy waves churned up the seashore. Her cell phone rang but she ignored it, absorbing the landscape as though its shapes and smells offered a refuge from the heaviness that gathered inside her.

She lowered the window and let the air pour in, redolent of pine needles and sea salt with the metallic residue from the dust the rain hadn't washed away. In her mind, she traveled back to the bumpy bus climbing the hill after a school trip, Alona and Malkie packed next to her, licking ice cream off each others' faces. Their mothers would be waiting, shooing them into the shower before pulling on freshly ironed tops and shorts. Of the three sets of parents, only Aviva and Nate were left. Alona's had been killed in a car crash in Italy, and Rebbetzin Sarah had died of bone cancer, leaving Reb Elijah and Malkie more dependent on each other than ever.

Now the Rebbe too was dead and Malkie had no one except God, Shmaya, and six kids in that order, at least in Shmaya's view of things. Rachel shuddered at the thought of her good friend's marriage to a man who was suspicious of anyone that might pry open a crack into the wider world. Since when had

Malkie's spark died?

Revving up the Daihatsu for the climb through the mountains, she noticed the emptiness of the road. It was like crossing a shadowy frontier, where the familiar crags and ravines of her childhood were alien to her. The phone bleated again; her parents probably, clawing the phone with anxiety.

"I'm just below Jabal. See you in ten minutes."

There were three communities located within the borders of the Carmel Nature Reserve: the Arab village of Jabal-a-Zeit, the artists' colony of Zeita, and Kibbutz Kerem El. Wildly different in character, the three settlements were bound together by their complex history and mountainous isolation. Rachel rumbled over a narrow bridge and the village of Jabal came into view, the mosque towering above concrete houses and alleyways. Even the olive trees that studded the mountain below the Moslem cemetery were laden with dust from the *khamsin*. Around the bend, on the opposite ridge, Zeita, the artists' village, nestled within bougainvillead walls, awaiting the holiday tourists that would mob its cobblestone lanes to buy arts and crafts. As her hand tightened on the wheel, Rachel wondered whether curiosity seekers, eager for a glimpse of a murder scene, would add Kerem El's synagogue to their itinerary.

As the road wound higher, she shook off the thought and with a thudding heart, focused on the first glimpse of Kerem El—God's Vineyard—perched on the summit, its red-roofed houses leaning into one another like drunken wagoners in a Chagall painting.

The founders had designed the kibbutz as a fortress, in concentric circles with the water tower and synagogue plaza as its center. The mountain top dominated the Nature Reserve on all sides, commanding views of the Mediterranean to the southwest and the Carmel ridge that folded eastward towards the Jezreel Valley. At night, the sky glowed with bands of light from Haifa, sixteen miles away. The Hotel Spa, the kibbutz' chief source of income, marketed the breathtaking landscape to its largely religious clientele.

The Daihatsu gave a slight jolt at the final incline beneath the cypress grove that led to the gate. Despite the nightly patrols, someone with enough determination could scale the mountain, infiltrate the kibbutz and commit almost any crime without being caught. *Did* commit, Rachel realized, not just any crime, but the worst crime of all. What's more, he could escape where the ground leveled off near the cowsheds and the chicken runs. The fortress of her childhood was only a memory, an illusion.

Outside the electronic gate, a police car, a white television van and several private cars sprawled in the parking bay. Reporters huddled together, smoking or taking notes. The Rebbe's death was national news.

She maneuvered the car through the crowd, aware of the curious glances cast in her direction. Straightening her spine and squaring her shoulders, she forced herself to radiate the impression of solidarity she no longer felt.

A policeman roused himself and uncrossed his arms as she approached. Before he could ask for identification, she heard the hum of the gate, then the familiar voice of Gideon Mann, her parents' friend and a member of the kibbutz Secretariat. He was on guard duty, a pistol rammed in his belt.

"It's all right, Officer. She's one of us," he asserted as Rachel felt tears sting her eyelids.

The policeman nodded and drifted away. Gideon motioned her through, and shut the barricade. As he walked over, arms outstretched for a hug, Rachel felt the tension in her limbs drain away. The respite was temporary, she knew. But at least she was safe.

* * *

"Lucky for us he's confessed so quick, eh?" Superintendent Kozma remarked as Absalom tossed the transcripts of the interview with Shmaya on his desk. "And he's local. Who has the manpower these days to hunt for a homicidal maniac?"

Even at two in the afternoon, Ron Kozma's thin face was clean-shaven, his light blue and navy uniform starched and pressed. From his leather chair, he commandeered the desk like a pilot, clicking the battery of telephones, fiddling with the computer mouse and forever rearranging the photographs of Ruth and the children who beamed from silver frames.

Absalom sank into the chair opposite. In the old days, he and Ron Kozma would have kicked off their shoes and shared a beer, but all that was gone.

"Convenient." Absalom reached over and took a paper clip from the ashtray on Kozma's desk. He got a whiff of Ron's aftershave. *Brut.* Brute. Brutal.

"The *haredi* never said why he did it?"

Absalom twisted the paper clip viciously. "Not yet. Just kept talking about sin. Killing the rabbi provided some kind of release. On the way to the lock-up he looked almost happy."

The Chief shrugged. "A nut case. We'll be hearing from forensics in the morning, I hope."

Absalom nodded. The paper clip resembled a praying mantis, supplicating, long legs.

In the silence that followed, they could hear the staccato pips of the news from the squad room, then the sober tones of the radio announcer.

Kozma grimaced and leaned back in his chair. "Two more drive-by shootings since mid-morning."

"I know."

"One near Ramallah, the other one up by…"

"The Acco-Safad road."

"How many were killed in the first shooting? A father and…?"

"Two kids." Absalom realized he was dropping into the habit of completing Ron's sentences again.

Kozma paused, cleared his throat and attempted a laugh. "At least those reporters are chewing on other carcasses now."

Absalom said nothing.

Kozma's mouth twisted, then he waved air with his palm. "I know what that sounds like, but it's this damn *intifada*. They're picking us off like flies. I don't know when it'll ever end." He glanced at a picture of his kids, frowned and altered

29

its position.

Absalom tossed the mangled paper clip onto Kozma's desk. He stood up and went to get his jacket.

"See you tomorrow."

"Right." Kozma opened the Catz file, then looked up. "Hey, Ab."

Absalom turned around, zipping up his jacket. "What?"

"Where'll you be for the *seder*? Your sister's again?"

"Yeah." Absalom said, opening the door.

"And Ab," Kozma called to him again. His voice sounded strained, as if he were coming down with a sore throat.

"What?"

"You can talk to me, you know. You can even use more than one syllable."

Absalom gave him a long look. "Yeah," he said, and left.

* * *

Less than three hours had passed since Rachel had left Jerusalem; only the suitcase in the back seat was a reminder that she'd made the journey at all. From the moment she pulled up next to Malkie's driveway, the relief she'd experienced passing through the gate had dissipated and her sense of time had slipped more deeply into a black hole. The cold mist hanging over the bare trees increased her feeling of desolation.

The slew of cars parked on the lanes converging on Malkie's house was the first sign that the neighbors had gathered to prepare Passover for the bereaved family. Children and dogs slipped through the open front door. Through the kitchen window, Rachel heard her mother yelling in Brooklynese Hebrew. Women were scrubbing, unpacking dishes, chopping and peeling. Their men tramped back and forth from the kibbutz van, carrying stacks of chairs, crates of soft drinks and boxes of *matza*. The cooking smells that permeated the house—*kneidlach* with grated ginger (Aviva's special recipe), chicken soup, *kugel* with fried onions—beguiled Rachel into normal holiday anticipation. But there was nothing normal in her mother's shaky embrace or the red eyes of the neighbors as she went in to greet them.

Then, there was her first sight of Malkie, slumped on the living room couch, holding the baby. The extent to which she'd changed since Rachel's last visit was dramatic and disturbing. The Rebbe's daughter, with her china blue eyes and flaxen hair, had always been the frailest of the Rachel-Alona-Malkie trio, but now she was thin to the point of transparency. Beneath a scraggly head scarf, her porcelain complexion was ghostly, except for a faded bruise on her left cheekbone. Something stirred inside Rachel at the sight of that bruise. She nearly put out her hand to touch it, but instinct warned her not to. Shmaya was nowhere to be seen, praying probably, trying to recover from the trauma of discovering his father-in-law's body.

Rachel took the sleeping baby and sat down next to Malkie. They looked long into each other's eyes without speaking, then hugged. Malkie was like a dry leaf crumbling in her arms.

Sitting cross-legged on the floor, a pad and pencil in her lap, Alona puckered her lips and tossed Rachel a silent kiss. Perfectly coiffed as usual, makeup in place, she was wearing tight jeans embroidered with sparkling beads. Typical Alona. Defiant, armored in her beauty gear.

Widowed at twenty-two when her pilot husband exploded in a helicopter crash, she'd kicked over society's pedestal and, like Rachel, tight-wired the abyss between the sacred and the profane. Living on Kerem El was a convenience she was reluctant to forego, though her job as head receptionist at the religiously rigorous Hotel Spa cramped her dress style.

Straddling a ladder in the center of the room, Mordechai Levy, gardener and synagogue sexton, was repairing the ceiling fixture, his tools neatly arranged on the top rung of the ladder. Rachel was flabbergasted when his gaze drifted south towards Alona's crotch. Not that men in their fifties were immune to women twenty years younger, but Mordechai, gnarled and sinewy as the trees he pruned, had been one of the Rebbe's "projects," a slum teenager from Jaffa whom the pious old man had nurtured along the path to *tshuva*, the return to religion.

The room was claustrophobic, smelling of stale *khamsin*, dirty diapers and gefilte fish. Lego littered the floor. Macaroon globs smeared the carpet. In the dining alcove, teenagers had set up a makeshift nursery. Toddlers swayed on unsteady feet, biscuits in their fists, while the older ones busied themselves with construction paper and magic markers.

Alona threw up her hands in exasperation. She was ticking

off items on her list with a manicured finger. "Try and focus, Malkie, honey. Let's go through it again. Your aunt's on her way, right?"

Malkie nodded like a mannequin.

"Good. What about Shmaya's"—her mouth curled downwards—"family—parents, brothers, sisters?"

Malkie sighed and shook her head. Alona passed her a tissue.

"The funeral. C'mon, Malkie, con-cen-trate!"

Malkie's head wobbled like a balloon on a stick. "I can't," she whispered, "I just can't."

"She's barely conscious," Rachel said. "Leave her alone." She kissed the baby's head. "Besides, I'm sure even Shmaya's capable of notifying his own family." From the kitchen there was the sound of breaking glass.

The ensuing silence stretched out like black canvas, absorbing the sounds of the children in the next room.

"What is it?"

Malkie had closed her eyes and began to weep. Mordechai Levy coughed.

"Is there something I'm not getting?" Rachel called out.

Alona walked over to the breakfront and took out a bottle of brandy, which she poured into a paper cup.

"I'll take the baby, you take this."

Rachel was paralyzed for a moment, holding the baby like a lifeline.

"Come on." Alona's voice was brisk. She's afraid also, Rachel thought, as she handed over the sleeping baby and took the cup from Alona's hand.

"Are you going to tell me what's going on?" Rachel demanded. She took a sip of the liquid. It smelled like gasoline. Malkie bolted from the room, sounds of footsteps from the kitchen running after her. Mordechai was gathering up his tools.

"So you haven't heard," Alona said, easing herself down on the sofa where Malkie had sat. The baby stirred, the pacifier slipping down her chin.

Mordechai climbed down from the ladder and folded it under his arm. His breath came out in a whoosh from his barrel chest. Tears stood in his eyes as he clenched and unclenched his thick fists.

"Shmaya killed the Rebbe, may his soul be avenged." He lumbered out of the room.

"*What?*"

"He confessed, the scum." Alona spat out the words. Rachel sensed a glimmer of satisfaction in her tone, as if her worst opinions of Shmaya had been confirmed.

"I don't believe it," Rachel said flatly. She took another gulp of brandy. It was less foul than before.

"Did you see that bruise on Malkie's cheek?"

"Yes, but…"

The baby whimpered and Alona settled her gently on her shoulder. "That's *his* handiwork. He's been slapping her around for a few months now. And he's more or less stopped sleeping with her."

"Did Reb Elijah know?"

"Could Malkie ever hide anything from him? Could *any* of us?" Her lips tightened into a grimace. "She says her father noticed for a long time that things weren't right. She finally broke down and told him everything—the sex bit, the fists, the fact that Shmaya was never home and spent days and nights hanging out in that yeshiva of his."

"Nights?" Rachel was beginning to feel the effects of the brandy. Slow warmth crept up from her midriff to her head.

"Malkie had her suspicions. She found this among Shmaya's things and gave it to me." Alona positioned the baby on the sofa between them and reached into the back pocket of her jeans. She thrust a wrinkled rectangular card into Rachel's hand. It was decorated with a pencil drawing of a dome and minaret, with *Herod's* printed below in Hebrew and Arabic.

"What's this?"

Alona shrugged. "All I know is that the Rebbe went ballistic when he saw it. Gave Shmaya an ultimatum. If he didn't give Malkie a quick divorce and disappear, he'd go public with whatever he'd discovered about him; finish him off in the *haredi* world for good."

"So the Rebbe checked out *Herod's*?" Rachel turned the card over and over in her hand.

"Yes, but he didn't tell Malkie any details. Only that he'd see to it that Shmaya never bothered her again."

"Is that why he killed the Rebbe?" Rachel's tongue felt thick. Alona took the cup from her and finished the brandy in one swig. "I don't know what he's told the police, but I think it's a reasonable motive, don't you?"

35

CHAPTER THREE

IT was close to three in the afternoon, long past lunch hour, and the Secretariat was holding its emergency meeting in the hotel dining room where the cook had rustled up coffee, cold salads, and rolls. Outside on the great lawn, Mordechai Levy was raking out the ashes from the *matza shmura* oven. Cartons of the specially supervised flatbread were heaped on a sideboard, to be distributed to the *haredi* guests.

Gideon Mann was aware that no matter how terrible the last few hours had been, worse times lay ahead. As kibbutz Secretary and hotel manager, he keenly felt the responsibility that fell on his shoulders. Steering the kibbutz without the Rebbe's guidance was one thing, but ensuring the long term social and economic future of the cooperative was another.

He could have sworn that seventy-two-year-old Lydia di Rossi had aged since this morning. Though she sat erect in her wheelchair, her heavily-ringed hands trembled and wrinkles etched her cheeks like dry riverbeds. Still, her black eyes burned as fiercely as ever. If he succeeded in holding his own in the face of her molten gaze and imperial silence, he would feel a well-earned sense of achievement.

"How many cancellations so far?" Reuven Ozeri, the

kibbutz doctor, leaned his elbows on the table, steepling his slim brown fingers.

Gideon fingered his pipe. He missed the woodsy tobacco smell around him. It was as much a part of him as his wedding ring. "The phone calls haven't stopped." He gazed morosely at the rain clouds that were massing over the sea. "Our most lucrative season is down the drain, *haverim*."

Ozeri eyed the tables elegantly set for tomorrow night's communal *seder*. "You mean, all this…"

"…will be three-quarters empty tomorrow night," Gideon said, "The food, wine and the *matza* will be going straight to soup kitchens."

The three of them knew the damage wasn't limited to *seder* night. The hotel's religious clientele had snapped up every available room for the entire eight days of the holiday, but all that had gone up in smoke. The financial loss was incalculable. In addition, there was the matter of the Kamienski Trust. In a few weeks, Thaddeus Kamienski would be paying his annual visit to check out his investment. What would he find? A community of dysfunctional zombies?

"Before we break for the day, there's something I want to throw out for discussion." He nodded to the doctor. "Reuven?"

Ozeri coughed and rearranged the knitted skullcap on his kinky hair. "Right. You've heard my beeper ringing non-stop. Everyone on the *meshek* is in total shock. What's happened here today is…indescribable." He wiped his face with a napkin.

"The *haverim* are hysterical. No one sent their kids to

kindergarten today. Two women have gone into premature labor, and they're in Carmel Hospital as we speak." He named them. "Finally, there are the old people, particularly the Holocaust survivors: not everyone's as strong as you are, Lydia."

She favored him with a weary, but wry smile. "Ah, if only we had the luxury of discussing the definition of 'strong.'"

"You know very well what he means," Gideon said sharply.

He wasn't in the mood for her verbal jousts. Why did the woman bracket every utterance with invisible quotation marks? Besides, he felt a headache coming on. He motioned to a waiter to bring over a pot of fresh coffee, wondering how much staff he'd have to let go in the coming weeks.

Ozeri took a deep breath and busied himself aligning the silverware. "The brutality of the murder, in the synagogue, for God's sake, reminds them of other places and other times. I don't have to spell it out, do I?"

"No." Lydia had always been mute about her Holocaust background, though Gideon knew that her entire family had been wiped out after the liquidation of the Rome ghetto. Reb Elijah had known everything about her, though the exact nature of their relationship had eluded everyone. He wondered about the long-term effects of the Rebbe's demise. Tough as she was, she must be suffering terribly. And she had no husband or children to lean on.

Tiny hammers pounded inside his temple. Here he was, thinking about the future again. *The story of my life*, he thought, *always thinking way ahead*. His wife complained that his accountant's mentality never allowed him to savor the present moment. He snapped his fingers to get the waiter's attention. Where was that coffee?

"…the sense of personal safety has disappeared in this country," the doctor was saying. "The drive-by shootings this morning, the kidnapping of that teenager last week, then this morning's outrage. It's taking a tremendous toll on everyone."

"Where is this leading?" Lydia asked, shifting in her wheelchair.

"To Rachel Shine. I saw her this morning. She looked good. Upset, but good."

Gideon smiled at the boy who placed the coffee on the table.

Lydia's wrinkled eyelids hooded her gaze. "She's still not well."

"From what Aviva and Nate tell me, she's recovering nicely."

"Her parents have to put up a good front. I happen to know how she feels. Vulnerable."

"Be that as it may," Gideon continued, taking note of Lydia's knee-jerk protectiveness: what those two women had in common, he'd never managed to guess. "She's an expert on trauma after all, and seeing she's on leave from her job, I thought…"

"To ask her to remain here and… what? Be a mother confessor? She's on sick leave because of that suicide bomber. How is she going to take on our troubles?"

Gideon felt a stab of pity for the old woman's attempt to

assume her usual sharp-tongued persona. Grief was closing in on her. Her shoulders sloped and the fiery resonance had vanished from her voice.

"Is it such a bad idea?" Ozeri asked. "There's only so much that can be achieved with drugs. I can't medicate an entire kibbutz. And any social worker the Local Council supplies...if and when the bureaucrats agree to send one... has no understanding of our community's needs." He looked at her earnestly through his glasses. "A religious mindset, an intimate knowledge of the population—no outsider could possibly be as effective."

"Rachel's no longer religious," Lydia said and Gideon could sense her opposition beginning to flag. God willing, he'd push her a bit more and her arguments would collapse like a row of dominoes.

"You're quibbling," he said, rubbing the back of his neck. He felt as though his muscles were permanently frozen from tension. He couldn't wait to take comfort in his pipe. "No one's going to measure her sleeve length. We just want to mobilize her for the emergency." He pulled out his ultimate weapon. "Besides, think of Malkie. Her husband murdered her father, for God's sake! Doesn't she deserve her best friend's support?"

Lydia sat silently, squinting out through the wraparound wall of glass. Beneath the encroaching clouds a strange white light streamed in. Finally, she shot a stern glance at the two men.

"Do what you must," she said. "But I'll be keeping my eye on Rachel. Too many things are happening in this place that I don't like."

* * *

By the time Absalom let himself into the apartment and kicked off his shoes, darkness had settled over Haifa Bay and the lights that spangled the city glittered in the rain-cleansed air.

Once, Christina would have been waiting for him, tanned legs propped on the balcony railing, sketching on her pad, then racing to greet him, running her fingers through his hair and folding her rangy body around him. Together, they would have looked down at the cruise ships docked in the harbor below, weaving fantasy destinations, while the city roared beneath their feet.

It was Christina who'd chosen the apartment, had hung her artwork on the walls, bought teak furniture from Denmark that turned honey-blond in the late afternoon sun. As night blanketed the city, she'd light candles and incense and tease him to bed.

Almost a year had passed since she flew back to Copenhagen for her mother's chemotherapy treatments. Besides, she said, she was sick of the Israeli sun. She missed the dark Danish winters and Christmas, of course. Israel was becoming sinister and dangerous, his job depressing. *He* was becoming depressing.

They'd been together for almost four years and for the first time in his life, he'd experienced something he'd never known while growing up—that it was possible to have fun, to play.

For him, she was a second skin, the scent of her, the feel of her warm flesh next to him. She loved his tongue inside her, she'd always said, but she'd never said she loved *him*. Nor had he ever asked her about the omission, assuming—foolishly, he now realized—that it was so obvious, it didn't need to be said. How could she just toss him aside like yesterday's newspaper? Perhaps he'd never understood her at all.

Once he'd realized she was gone for good, he walked around with a stone in his chest. His colleagues treated him with respectful distance. He threw himself into his work, putting in fourteen-hour shifts and making some headline-grabbing arrests.

He'd given the candles to his teenage niece, removed Christina's drawings from the walls and shipped them back to Copenhagen. He'd comforted himself that he'd always been a loner, recalling that even the bonds between him and the guys in his paratroop unit and afterwards in the Police Academy where he'd first met Ron, had begun to chafe after too much contact.

Pouring a beer, he loosened his shirt and sat down on the sofa that faced the view of the port. He watched the twinkling lights of Acco on the peninsula across the bay, etched against the humps of the Galilee hills.

Restless, he turned on the news and was startled to see a shot of himself escorting Shmaya into the Kishon lock-up. He felt vaguely disappointed that the *haredi* had confessed so readily. Case closed. Limbo time, until the next murder, the next rape.

He sipped his beer, thoughts of the holiday settling upon

him like a suffocating quilt. Tomorrow, he'd buy a Passover cake and drive out to the nursing home. His father would be slumped in a wheelchair, eating *matza* mashed with milk, mouth open like a baby chick. Filipino caretakers would listen politely as a rabbi from the local council led a makeshift *seder* at tables set with paper plates and plastic cups of grape juice instead of wine.

Did memories of *seders* in Poland flicker through the stroke-jolted brain? Absalom had often speculated about this whenever the old man absently smoothed the numbers tattooed on his forearm, his grainy voice humming broken Yiddish. The subject that had remained unspoken throughout his childhood—his parents' experiences at Treblinka—would remain sealed forever.

The phone rang. It was his sister, sounding harried, reminding him to bring two bottles of wine tomorrow night. In the background, the T.V. was blaring and his nieces were fighting.

He smiled grimly to himself. He needn't worry about being in limbo just yet. An evening with his family would provide him with just the dose of chaos he craved.

CHAPTER FOUR

SHROUDED in white, Reb Elijah's corpse slid into the grave. The gravediggers, tassled sidelocks dancing in the breeze, wiped their hands on their trousers and rolled the empty gurney back to the Burial Society van.

Mordechai Levy gouged a foothold in the earth and leaped into the pit to arrange slabs of stone over the body. Clambering out, he tossed in a heap of earth, then passed the shovel to Nate, Gideon and the other men standing in line to fill their Rebbe's grave. The only sound was the drumbeat of soil on rock.

Slipping her arm around Malkie's shoulders, Rachel scanned the mourners that had been bused in from all over the country and overflowed the sun-lashed cemetery; old-timers, Arabs from Jabal-a-Zeit, yeshiva students, knitted-skullcapped soldiers, *haredim*—those whose lives the Rebbe had touched. An ambulance lingered at the cemetery gate where someone was distributing bottles of mineral water. Under the stern eye of a policeman, cameramen crouched on a hill, while the Channel Two crime correspondent mouthed into her microphone.

Rachel's thoughts wandered to the surrealistic hodgepodge of private grief and soap opera the Rebbe's death had become.

A holy man is slaughtered by his son-in-law, a domestic scandal snapped up by an intifada-weary public. Still, she realized, the horror of Shmaya as murderer was yet to seep through the layers of grief for Reb Elijah, the victim. The Kerem El family mourned mightily, bonded to their old Rebbe, a figure so much wiser and more charismatic than the functionary evoked by the word "rabbi." The Rebbe, who had patted Rachel's head and ruled that her divorce from Nahum was good because she deserved someone better; that even though she'd abandoned her religious observance, God meant it to be so.

Across from her, her brother Michael gave a reassuring nod as he fumbled in his shirt pocket for a handkerchief, while huddled in her wheelchair, Lydia di Rossi snared Rachel in her jet-black gaze; it was so bleak yet compelling, that Rachel caught her breath. It held both a signal and a plea, that graveside stare.

As Rachel met her eyes, she knew that she couldn't postpone her decision much longer. She would stay. She owed it to all of them, but especially to Reb Elijah.

As the cantor sobbed out *El Maleh Rahamim*, she felt tears splash her cheeks and Malkie melt beneath her grasp. Insubstantial as water, she swayed over her father's grave, shaking her head from side to side, her lips mouthing *No, no* over and over again.

* * *

At Malkie's house, the post-funeral tumult buzzed alongside pre-holiday hysteria. Alona sliced cake and poured coffee for the guests, while Rachel snatched a few words with Michael before his journey home to the West Bank. Children raced down the hallway, babies wailed, and underneath it all, the screech of chairs and tables being dragged from room to room.

Rachel ducked into the bedroom to check on Malkie, who lay on a narrow bed, adrift in the sedative Ozeri had administered. Approaching the sleeping figure, she felt the weight of the day press her down; lifting her hand to stroke Malkie's hair required gravity-defying strength. "Sleep," she whispered, rubbing the dry strands between her fingers.

The room sealed them in with the dankness of a catacomb. The odor of sweat rose from heaps of unwashed clothes. Screwing up her nose, Rachel creaked open the window, letting in a faint brush of air, chemical-tasting, from yesterday's *khamsin*. Shadows bunched in gloomy corners, which she refrained from scrutinizing too carefully. The mirror above the dresser was hidden beneath a sheet in honor of the dead and to remind the living that life and its vanities were ephemeral. A lugubrious portrait of a sage hung on the wall, as if judging the Catz' marital arrangements, which struck Rachel as drearily familiar; narrow twin beds separated by a night stand.

A raspy cough from the doorway made her jump. Lydia rolled in, her gypsy earrings reflecting the feeble light, then pressed the door shut behind her. Rachel crossed the room, bent down and kissed her cheek, crinkly as raisin skin.

"Why aren't you out there?" she whispered.

"With all those children? I'm not a nanny. Besides, I must hold vigil here; I owe Elijah that much." Lydia jerked her chin in the direction of Malkie's inert figure.

"I know what you mean," Rachel murmured.

Lydia pointed. "Sit down on that creature's bed. We have precious little time and there are urgent things we must discuss."

Rachel felt a twitch of irritation. Shock had trimmed her to the bone, but she braced herself for one of Lydia's philosophical diatribes.

Lydia moistened her lips, the lipstick a dark gash across her face. "I killed Elijah. I sent him to his death."

Shmaya's blanket felt gritty beneath her thin skirt. Rachel closed her eyes and willed herself to be patient. In the tone she used with addled clients, she said, "Do you want to talk about it?"

"Don't patronize me," Lydia snapped. "I need your help. Why do you think I agreed to Gideon and Ozeri's insane plan to bring you here?"

Rachel dug her nails into her palm. "I'm trying to follow you, but you're making it very hard." From the hallway, a thump sounded and a child's voice cried, "*Ima!*"

"Try harder," Lydia hissed, pulling a tissue from her watchband. "Listen carefully; I don't have the strength to repeat myself." She emitted a sigh; her brittleness was starting to sliver.

"On Friday night, Elijah came to see me. Throughout our long friendship, I'd never seen him so agitated. Or so helpless. His hair and beard were wild, his eyes red from sleeplessness. He told me an incredible story that made me doubt his sanity, just as you doubt mine." She shot Rachel a wry smile.

"'My life's work is crumbling,' he told me. 'Immorality and even criminal acts are rife on Kerem El.' My attempts to make him reveal whom he suspected and what they had done was like tying down smoke. He could be so obstinate sometimes." She cleared her throat and wiped her eyes with the tissue. "He was a righteous soul, not an old sinner like me. Until he had proof, he said, he refused to engage in slander. He reminded me that *lashon ha-ra* is against everything Jewish."

"Not if it prevents a crime." Rachel was astonished that she could dredge up Jewish theology through the maze of Lydia's story. Involuntarily, her eyes sought the bearded portrait on the wall for approval.

"True, but he insisted that these acts had already taken place. His mission was to convince the perpetrators to turn themselves in and do justice to the victims." She cleared her throat. "It tortures me to think he died fearing that he hadn't accomplished that."

"Why didn't he report his suspicions to the police?" Though Rachel wanted to believe Lydia's story, her eyes narrowed with a skepticism she hoped was hidden by the dimness of the room.

Lydia shook her head and her earrings swayed. "That's what I said, to which he replied, 'The police use force but not moral force.' He wanted to educate criminals. Can you imagine?" Tears filled her eyes. "He was so naïve. A bit like you." Lydia's thumb grazed the C-shaped scar on Rachel's cheek. She flinched.

"That old scar. You always used to cover it. Now everyone can see. *Multo bene.* It means you are stronger inside."

Stronger? She remembered the panic attack that had seized her in Jerusalem. *Was it only yesterday?* She glanced at Malkie whose contours were low hillocks beneath the coarse woolen blanket; she longed to escape the funereal room and Lydia's meanderings.

"She'll be waking up soon."

Lydia ploughed on. "Elijah wanted to manipulate this person into coming to *him.* That's why he consulted me; to help him expose this person. And I, with my ego," she raised her fist to her heart, "invented a scheme that was so successful that it killed him."

"What scheme?"

Lydia clawed the tissue in her lap. "The *Shabbat haGadol* sermon. No one ever misses it. He crafted it in such a way that the criminal would think he'd been targeted and would seek Elijah out."

"I heard about the sermon."

"So you know how damning it was, especially for someone with a guilty conscience. He must have lured Elijah to the *shul* with precisely the kind of story Elijah wanted to hear— atonement and all the rest of that nonsense."

Malkie's breath quickened and she flung an arm over her

head.

"So Shmaya interpreted the Rebbe's sermon as an accusation against him?" Rachel whispered.

"Silly girl." Lydia hissed in exasperation. "You haven't been paying attention. Shmaya didn't kill Elijah."

The door creaked open. Silhouetted against the light from the hallway, dressed in black except for a bronze brooch that matched her cloud of hair, Alona appeared carrying a tray of tea and cake.

"Enough gossiping, ladies. Time to wake up Malkie. The baby's hungry and the kids are fidgety." She swished into the room, sat down beside Malkie and began rubbing her back. "We'll be having the *seder* here instead of at your parents' place."

"It's better for the kids; they'll need their familiar surroundings." Rachel glanced at Lydia, Sphinx-like in her wheelchair. The Passover seder had completely slipped her mind. With the whiff of normality Alona had infused, Rachel wondered if she'd imagined the whole conversation. Still, she feared for the old woman's sanity. If Lydia fell apart, it meant one more crack in the solid earth of Kerem El.

CHAPTER FIVE

LYDIA didn't leave her alone. The next morning, outside the synagogue after the Passover service, she lay in wait. Now that Rachel was going to "therapize us all," as she ironically put it, why couldn't she engage in some subtle sleuthing as well?

Lydia's eccentric demand continued to gnaw at her during the following days while unpacking her books and clothes in the chalet the Secretariat had provided at the Hotel Spa. Not only was Lydia's theory absurd, but the idea that Rachel could compromise her therapy by snooping around her patients' alibis was downright insulting. She'd distanced herself from Lydia, with the excuse that she had to get organized.

But there was no way her parents could be brushed off. Exulting in her return, Aviva and Nate plunked down a date and nut cake, took charge of her unpacking, carped about her clothes, and took their daily coffee afternoons for granted, "like in the old days." She knew they meant well, but they were like two spiders invading her territory, pinioning her in their tough web.

As for the chalet, located on the fringes of a spacious lawn, the comfort of her possessions did little to mitigate the Central European ambience, complete with rosewood furniture and heavy drapes, lace doilies and embroidered cushions, even a silver tea set. It reminded her of a nineteenth-century period room at a museum; all it lacked were velvet loops to keep the visitors out. The only space she'd made truly hers was the enclosed veranda at the back of the chalet, now revamped into a whittling room. She'd borrowed mats and Indian bedspreads from her parents' hippie living room. On a shelf, next to chunks of maple and beechwood, stood a slab of Dead Sea salt fashioned into a lamp. "For good vibes," her mother had said.

After she'd given the place a final scrub, she stepped into a shower the size of her bedroom in Jerusalem. As she lathered her hair and let her mind roam, it struck her that Aviva and Nate were weaving a fantasy: the wayward daughter returning home. Sooner or later, sooner most likely, they would flick their antennae in search for a suitable match, a *shidduch*.

Closing her eyes, she yielded to the darts of water that stung her aching back and shoulders, wondering whether the fantasy was theirs or hers. She was jolted by the potency of it. Would it be so terrible to wipe out Nahum and Jerusalem and the suicide bomber and come home for good? *Don't even dream of it.* She'd put on some clothes, have a quick lunch and plan a work schedule. Work was the best therapy, especially instead of what she called *Thinking and Sinking,* which sounded like the title of a bad pop song.

Shaking out her hair, she toweled and switched on the hair dryer. Beneath its drone, she sensed that something in the room had changed. She turned off the dryer. Watching from the door of her bedroom was Taleb Mahajna, his powerful body inking out the light.

Their eyes locked. Rachel grabbed the robe, knocking the hair-dryer on the floor. Taleb averted his gaze, but not before it had lingered a second too long on her nipples.

"*Slicha*," he murmured, bowing his head. He backed out and eased the door shut .

"It's okay," she sang out, hating the false shrillness in her voice. She'd forgotten Taleb's promise to hook up her PC to the kibbutz computer network. Her heart thudded as she flung open the clothes closet. *What do you wear after a man has seen you in the altogether?* The last man who'd seen her naked was Nahum; the only man, in fact. That was another thing on hold until she glued her life together: love, sex, commitment, what people called "a relationship." *You need a relationship,* Miri told her at least twice a week.

Not that Taleb was relationship material. Since his teens, he'd been the kibbutz handyman, chugging up the mountain from Jabal-e-Zeit in a rusty pick-up truck. From a gangly adolescent, he'd become husky and barrel-chested—and a bachelor, unusual in forty-something Muslim men.

Tossing on jeans and a sweater, she ran a brush through her tangled hair. A brief glance in the mirror revealed wide startled eyes, her scar white against burning cheeks. She managed to stroll nonchalantly into the sitting room where Taleb was crouched on the floor next to a toolbox assembling an electric drill. He rose to his feet and extended his hand. His fingers were square and short, she noticed, like stubs of wood.

His clothes reeked of cigarette smoke.

"*Shalom*, Rachel," he said, enveloping her hand in his. "*Baruch ha-ba'a*. Welcome home."

His grape-green eyes, the legacy of a Crusader forbear, appraised her with the usual friendliness. Nothing lingered. Paradoxically, she felt vaguely deflated. She disengaged her hand, resisting the temptation to wipe the moist touch of his palm on her jeans.

"I wish it had been a different kind of welcome," she said, parting the drapes. The weather was changing, clouds pushing in from the sea. "I saw you at the funeral. Why did Shmaya hate the Rebbe so much?" Unbidden, the image of the Rebbe's body rolling into the open grave flashed through her mind.

"Everything is from *Allah*." Taleb picked up the tool box and carried it into the bedroom. "It was his time. Shmaya was merely an instrument."

Rachel padded after him on the thick carpet, her hands stuffed in the pockets of her jeans. "Do you really believe that?"

His face was impassive. "Where do you want the computer?" With the drill, he gestured towards the narrow rosewood desk, which looked prissier than ever next to his bulk.

Rachel nodded, sidestepping him as he withdrew a pencil from the pocket of his work shirt and marked a small x on the wall.

"You Jews have the same belief as we do—that everything is God's will."

"Right. But *within* God's parameters there's free choice."

She'd been back less than a week and was already having a theological discussion with a Muslim. That was life on Kerem El.

"You've worked here your whole life," she persisted, "watching us from the sidelines. Do you really believe Shmaya could have done it?" Without conscious planning, she'd slipped into the detection role Lydia had plotted out for her.

His shoulder blades tensed. He drilled a precise hole and threaded a cable through it.

"Like I said, Shmaya was an instrument, like this drill." He turned around and arced it in the air.

"Still, he must've had a reason, at least in his own mind."

"You're the *psycholog*." Above the smile, a veil hooded the green eyes. "When someone has a bellyful of anger against another, he will strike." He fumbled in his trouser pocket for a cigarette, then seemed to think better of it. "Every man has a boiling point and Shmaya reached his." He shrugged. "He was married to the Rebbe's daughter. Who knows what happens in another man's household?"

"True." She remembered the bruise on Malkie's cheek and the card from *Herod's*.

"*Yallah.*" Taleb connected the cable. Now she was hooked up to the internal kibbutz network. Pull a plug, unhook a cable, and she'd be cut off. Then she recalled the tugs of war with her parents and the umbilical cord that bound the *kibbutzniks* to one another for better or for worse. She had forgotten the price such a bond could exact.

CHAPTER SIX

SUNLIGHT poured down on the square, gilding the facades of the old stone houses. The chill of spring was shot through with the tantalizing warmth of the summer yet to come. Despite the spate of drive-by shootings, the mild weather and the Passover holiday were luring people out into the mountains. They strolled through the village, jackets slung over their arms, browsing the display tables and chatting with the artists.

Boaz Kashtan stretched his arms above his head and grunted with contentment. So far, it'd been a productive day; his petition now had over five hundred signatures, almost a hundred from today's crowd. Even those who hadn't signed had shown interest in the flyers stacked on the table.

A fiftyish woman sauntered over. Boaz checked her out immediately—an artsy type with a flame-colored crewcut and ceramic earrings that dragged her earlobes down to her shoulders. Turquoise eye shadow caked wrinkled lids. He knew she was checking him out too. Women always did.

He looked up at her, blue eyes squinting in the sun. "*Shalom.*"

"*Shalom* to you too," she said, taking a flyer, but looking at him.

He grinned. "Having a good time?"

"Not until now." They both laughed.

"Make yourself comfortable." He gestured toward the stool opposite. "Would you like to see my wares?"

She chuckled. "I'd like nothing better." Her eyes flickered over his muscular shoulders, broad chest and blond pony tail.

No point encouraging the old girl. The last thing he needed was complications. He was up to his neck in them. Adopting a more earnest tone, but not breaking eye contact, he said.

"Have you heard of *The Olive Branch*?" He pushed the petition towards her, their fingers touching briefly.

The woman perused the letterhead, green on white, printed in Hebrew, Arabic and English.

"What is it? Some kind of peace thing?"

"*The* peace thing," he said, launching his spiel. "See this place?" He flung out his arm to encompass the square, the olive trees, the winding lanes and Arab houses. "Before the 1948 war..."

She narrowed her eyes as if to say, "This is not going to be fun." But he continued, passion fueling his voice.

"...Arabs lived peacefully in this place for hundreds of years. The houses, the fruit trees, the olive orchards... all belonged to the Arabs who were expelled from here."

The woman's jaw settled into a hostile lump. "So? They were taking potshots at the Jews, plotting to blow up innocent civilians. And they haven't changed one bit."

Boaz flashed his dimple. He'd underestimated her spunk.

"We're not having an argument, are we....what's your

name?"

"Leah."

"Leah. I'm simply explaining the aims of our group. Bear with me, please?" He placed his hand over hers. The blond hairs on the back of his hand glinted in the sun.

"Okay, okay." Leah insinuated her fingers through his. "But you're not going to turn me into one of those knee-jerk lefties who say we're always the bad guys and the Arabs are the good guys."

"All of us are the good guys," he said simply, gazing into her eyes, which softened a bit.

"The Mahajna tribe that was expelled from this village," he continued, "were driven into the mountains just south of here. After living in caves and shacks, they built a village of their own—Jabal-a-Zeit."

"The Mount of Olives," Leah translated. "like in Jerusalem."

"Though there's no connection. The Mahajnas are Muslims. They kept faith with their original village by preserving the 'olive tree' in the name. That's why our organization is called *The Olive Branch.*"

"Clever boy," Leah bantered. Boaz sensed she was hankering for the flirtatious atmosphere they'd enjoyed before, but he knew that his politically-fired enthusiasm usually proved to be a turn-on in itself.

"What we're after is justice, pure and simple. Why should the Mahajnas live without electricity or a normal access road when their original homes and lands are right here?"

Leah shifted uncomfortably on the stool. Her eye make-up

was smeared, he noticed.

"Time moves on, that's why," she said. "History moves on. You can't undo the past."

"No, but we can see to it that partial justice is done, at least."

"Well, pretty one," Leah said teasingly, "how do you propose to do that?"

He paused for effect. "By returning one third of Zeita's property to its rightful owners."

"That's ridiculous," she sputtered. "You'd give up this charming place, these quaint houses and throw the artists out of their homes, just so a bunch of Arabs can move in?"

Inwardly, he groaned. He'd heard this argument so often he could puke. But these racists had to be won over if he were to achieve his goals.

"First of all, no one is throwing anyone out. The artists would be given compensation to move elsewhere. You don't need an artists' colony to be an artist. All you need is a studio."

Leah swiveled around to survey the people crowding the square, buying handmade jewelry and watercolors of the village. The coffee house was packed with patrons enjoying the view of the mountains and sea.

"Why should anyone give up this jewel? Look at the view, the ambience. It's a terrific tourist place."

Boaz leaned forward. "Just imagine how many tourists would come to a joint Arab-Jewish village—The Village of Peace? Think of all the people from abroad who now avoid us like we're the leper colony of the Middle East. They'd come by the planeloads to see another side of Israel, the peace-loving side."

"I'd like to see the peace-loving side of those Arabs first," Leah mumbled, reaching for a pen. She looked up at him and grinned through orange-painted lips. "But you're such a sweetheart, I'll sign your petition and take your flyer." She filled out her name and address and jotted three exclamation marks next to her phone number.

He stood up, leaned across the table, giving her a faint kiss on the cheek. "You're a special woman, Leah."

"My phone number's right here if you want to find out just how special." She waved and melted into the crowd.

Boaz eyed her retreating backside and reached into the pocket of his tee shirt for a cigarette before thinking better of it. The public he needed to sway were into political correctness and smoking was a definite no-no. Yet, he itched for a smoke. It was already three o'clock and people weren't exactly inundating his table, so he ducked into a side alley for a few puffs.

Skirting the square, he was greeted on all sides by friends, neighbors, fellow artists and old lovers. Though he'd moved to Zeita only six years ago, he felt he could spend his life there in his rented hut, doing his art and pushing ahead with *The Olive Branch*.

For the first time that day the old bitterness rose up inside him like acid. He took a deep drag of his cigarette, feeling the nicotine kick in. He thought of the old man. What business did he have meddling in his past? As if it wasn't enough he'd destroyed his childhood. Like Leah had said, the past can't be undone. But Reb Elijah had threatened to destroy his future as well.

He crushed the cigarette butt beneath the heel of his boot and looked up at the cloudless blue sky. *And it won't happen,* he thought, *now that the Rebbe's dead.*

* * *

Dr. Reuven Ozeri waved the last patient of the day into his office. Her taut facial muscles and trembling hands reflected barely suppressed hysteria.

Hettie Trasker was one of the few guests, mostly elderly Holocaust survivors with nowhere else to go, who hadn't cancelled their Passover hotel reservations and lined up every day at the kibbutz clinic, begging him for medication that would stifle their nightmares. Reb Elijah's murder, the suicide bombings and drive-by shootings sparked horror-filled flashbacks of a Europe gone mad.

While deploring the violence, the doctor couldn't ignore the fact that the demand for tranquilizers and sleeping pills skyrocketed with every terrorist attack. Tonight he'd phone his supplier in Mumbai for an extra shipment of Lexium and Dormiton, the drugs that shrouded his patients in the stupor they desired. As usual, he wouldn't pester Dr. Singh with too many questions about expiration dates.

Seated opposite Hettie, the doctor calibrated his tone of voice to the highest rung on the empathy scale.

"I understand what you're going through. Insomnia is natural during periods of great anxiety." His dark, slim fingers reached into the pocket of his white coat, retrieving an oblong box.

"Will the medicine help me, doctor?"

They all asked the same questions, with the same tremor in the voice, the same plea in their eyes—half hopeful, half fearful.

"I promise." His hand closed hesitantly over the box. "There's one thing you should know, though. Since it's just come on the market, it isn't covered by the health funds." A faint grimace of regret. "I'm afraid it's rather expensive."

But *Giveret* Trasker was already fumbling with the *shekels* in her purse.

With a reassuring squeeze, he pressed the box into her palm. "Take a tablet half an hour before retiring, get into bed with a good book and you'll sleep like a baby."

"It's not dangerous, is it, doctor? The medicine my own doctor prescribes…"

In his heartiest voice he said, "Would I prescribe anything dangerous now, Hettie?"

The patient stood up, her wrinkled face beaming with gratitude and relief. "Thank you, Doctor. I don't know what I'd do without you. You've done a good deed, a real *mitzvah*."

Reuven Ozeri escorted her to the door, his hand on her elbow, ensuring her firm footing on the cobblestone path, then went inside again, locking the door behind him and closing the curtains against the mid-afternoon sun.

His eyes swept over the clinic; the iron-legged chairs and the floor tiles dating from the 'fifties. How he'd hated it after his return from Romania, where the private clinic in his luxurious Bucharest apartment financed a summer villa in the Carpathians. Orly and the kids could breathe crisp mountain air and boat on Lake Bucura.

Now, he knew he'd do anything—*had* done everything—to cling to even this shabby hut of a clinic.

He hung his white coat on a hook, slipped behind the desk and booted up the computer. How had Reb Elijah discovered that slip-up back in Bucharest? What an idiot he'd been, leaving a drunken intern in charge while he'd ducked out to visit a private patient. What had begun as a routine tonsil operation had ended in the death of a four-year-old boy. It had taken a hefty bribe for the hospital director to bury the results of the board of inquiry and write him a glowing recommendation.

He looked fondly at the photograph on his desk. He and Orly had six beautiful kids, but without the cradle-to-the-grave safety net the kibbutz provided, they'd be buried in some hick town where he'd be lucky enough to drive a garbage truck.

If Reb Elijah had lived to carry out his threat, his license would be revoked and irrevocable shame would stick to his wife and kids.

Thank God he could breathe easily now. The threat had evaporated.

* * *

At midday, the Paradise Restaurant on the Haifa promenade was packed with young couples, soldiers on leave, and multi-generational clans wolfing down pita bread dipped in hummus. Having paid homage to tradition by putting in a few days of gut-crunching *matza* consumption, enough was enough.

Absalom sat at a table adjoining the wall of windows through which the Mediterranean sunlight poured, stippling the sea with glitter.

He was in an expansive mood as he surveyed the breaded cauliflower, garlicked eggplant and *tabouli* that Francis, his favorite waiter, had spread out on the butcher-block table. Rarely did he have the luxury of savoring the holiday cheer of early spring, watching normal people going about their normal business. Three days had passed without a major terrorist attack. He made a comic face at a little girl kicking her feet on the rungs of her chair, her mouth smeared with ketchup. She giggled and stuck out her tongue.

Francis deftly swiveled his way through the diners and placed a steaming tray in front of him; *shashlik* and a heap of crisp fries.

"*Adoni, ha-detective.*" The waiter bowed, using the title he'd bestowed on Absalom who'd smashed a gang of Uzbekis gouging protection money from the Paradise. "It is good to see you so relaxed." His forehead wrinkled in sympathy. "And your father?"

"The same, Francis, the same." Touched at the man's concern, yet feeling a dip in his spirits, Absalom said, "Thanks for the interest."

Gathering up the small dishes of *mezze,* the waiter returned to the kitchen while Absalom sprinkled salt on his fries, recalling the visit to his father before the *seder.* The old man had been asleep in his wheelchair but sprang awake when Absalom kissed his cheek and placed the wrapped cake in his lap. The faded eyes registered his presence, but soon folded within their misty world.

Afterwards, he'd driven to his sister's, where the *seder* consisted of his nieces sulking, his brother-in-law snickering at *Lethal Weapon 2* on cable, and his sister crying as she swept up cracked sunflower seeds. Absalom did the dishes, hugged her and left.

He was relieved to get back to Haifa. To his shame, he'd clicked on the answering machine, hoping for a message from Christina, just Passover greetings, but there was nothing, not even messages from work. Even the criminals were celebrating the holiday.

Absalom wiped his plate with a wedge of pita, sopping up the lamb juices and the oil from the fries. As he sipped a Carlsberg, a couple walked in and sat down at a nearby table, a middle-aged man with a floral shirt stretched over a pot belly and a young girl in her late teens or early twenties in jeans and a leather jacket. Absalom's brain clicked; perhaps it was the bulk of the girl's jacket or the faint sheen of sweat on her upper lip. Perhaps it was the vacant look in her eyes. Francis was approaching them with his funny bow-legged walk, menus tucked under his arm. The little girl with the ketchup on her face was dozing in her stroller, clutching a toy rabbit.

Absalom leaped out of his chair toward the child. He yelled to Francis to get back but just then the blast hurled him against the window pane. Before blackness consumed him, his final sensation was that of his body smacking glass.

CHAPTER SEVEN

HADASSAH Levy paused to read the notice thumb-tacked to the bulletin board.

In light of the tragic events of the past week, the Secretariat has engaged the services of Rachel Shine for individual and group counseling. Rachel will be on call 24-hours a day. Phone 051-77629.

She caught her lip between her teeth. It never hurt to talk to somebody and Rachel was a serious girl. Maybe she could explain Hadassah's palpitations and her yen for chocolate, its bittersweet creaminess, and the hard snap as she popped a frozen square—or two, or three, or ten—into her mouth. There was no way Mordechai could avoid the scent of it on her breath, yet he'd never said a word, just like she'd never mentioned the odor that clung to his clothes, a sign he'd taken up smoking again.

Women with gray faces barely smiled in greeting; everyone was heartsick about the Paradise Restaurant bombing. Yet life must go on; tonight and tomorrow was the second *chag*, with its three festive meals. Shopping carts clogged the sloping concrete path. The fresh chickens had already been snapped up and the vegetable bins were rapidly emptying. Hadassah knew she'd better get a move on before there was nothing left—not that they were having guests; it'd just be the two of them, she and Mordechai, but she read the notice a couple of more times, trying to digest what it might mean for her.

In all her fifty-four years she'd never needed *therapia*, at least not on a regular basis. For women of her generation, it was enough to be devout and create a warm Jewish home. All this selfishness nowadays, the words young people threw around—personal fulfillment, *discovering* themselves (what was there to discover except God's miracles?)—were beyond her understanding. Yoel, her son, her treasure, hadn't gone the way of those hedonists, thank God.

She shifted her weight from one foot to the other and clutched her coat to her bulky figure. The weather had turned grim and cold like their lives together, hers and Mordechai's, since the murder.

Reb Elijah had been a foster father to Mordechai, showing how self-respect and love of the Lord go together. Thanks to him, Mordechai had become the *shul* sexton, not only a gardener. But still, that night in the Rebbe's study when he'd announced his *psak*—the rabbinical verdict that had sealed their son's fate—how the blood had rushed to Mordechai's face, how his fists tightened, and his voice broke and then threatened things so horrible she'd pushed them to the edge of memory.

She grabbed a cart and pulled open the door to the mini-market. A rush of hot air blasted from the air-conditioning unit, forcing her to remove her coat and drape it over the cart. These days she was either too cold or too hot. Maybe she should see Reuven Ozeri again for the pills that had helped her so much.

In the bakery section she scanned the rows of mass-produced Passover cakes. Should she take the easy way out or should she bake the anise-flavored biscuits Mordechai loved? On an impulse, she put a bag of *matza* flour into the cart. Yes, she'd pamper him a bit; he deserved it. They both did, after what they'd been through.

Suddenly, a blood surge pumped through her chest. *God in heaven*, she thought, leaning against the shelves, *what's happening to me?*

A couple of women standing in the aisle nodded at her and she nodded back, her head bobbing like a robot. How could they not see she was bursting apart inside?

After what seemed like forever, the palpitations wound down to a gentle patter, bearable enough for her to stand in the cashier's line and exchange somber words with the other women about how precarious life was, how we must have faith in the Lord, Blessed be His Name.

As she wheeled the cart outside, she fumbled in her coat pocket for some chocolate. She stared at Rachel's phone number trying to memorize it. Yes, she'd make an appointment. And she wouldn't tell Mordechai.

* * *

The turquoise and orange dinosaur gloated. Absalom tried to swat it when it swished its tail, but his arm was stuck in concrete. He giggled as the dinosaur floated away.

"He's awake."

"No he's not."

"It's the drugs. He's high."

Voices buzzed in and out of his head. He wanted to smash them like mosquitoes, but his arm…there was something wrong with his arm.

Fingers snapped above his nose. "*Yallah,* buddy, come out of it!"

He knew that voice. A wide face, red with a potato nose, glasses, loomed into his vision. A hand slapped his cheek. Absalom focused on the face, tried to say something but only a croak emerged.

A woman's voice whispered. "He looks terrible." Was she talking about him?

A third voice snapped gruffly. "At least he's alive."

Of course he was alive. Why shouldn't he be? If only he could lift his arm; it weighed a ton.

The voices moved away. Cool hands dabbed something on his face. It stung. He shook his head back and forth to escape those hands.

Another female voice. "Now, now, Chief-Inspector. Lie still. You want to get better, don't you?"

He blinked his eyes and the dinosaur sailed into his field of vision. Absalom smiled.

* * *

"Let it go, Lydia. I can't go through with it." Nausea eddied inside her like a swamp. Rachel felt like throwing up, right there on Lydia's Persian carpet. A mug of seaweedy liquid materialized under her nose.

Rachel shook her head, her curls damp with sweat. Behind shut lids, she tried to fight the panic. The frozen steppes of Lapland; reindeer, antlers, snow. But the vision melted in the heat of the wood fire and Lydia's voice. Flames rose and fell, casting shadows on the rich merlot and copper of the study.

"*Dio mio*, you are stubborn." Lydia unclenched Rachel's fingers and locked them around the mug one by one.

She shook her head.

"Swallow!"

Resisting Lydia was like banging a fist against rock, and since she felt bruised enough, Rachel downed the green gook, which surprised her with its mild herbal taste. The tide of nausea began to recede.

Lydia wheeled herself over to a low table on which a slim bottle of grappa rested on a silver tray. Her bracelets clanked as she poured the liquid into crystal glasses and handed one to Rachel. "Now, real medicine."

The grappa rolled through her like a slow-moving river and her muscles relaxed. "Maybe I should just become an alcoholic. This stuff is better than all my relaxation techniques."

Lydia's rough chuckle bounced off the book-lined walls. "*Bambina*, when you are able to poke fun, all is not lost."

Rachel closed her eyes, lulled by the warmth. "Isn't it? After what happened yesterday at the Paradise?"

Lydia placed her glass firmly on the mahogany desk. "One more link in the chain of man's passion for slaughter, all in the name of ideology."

Rachel gulped down the rest of her drink. "I could almost smell the blood on the T.V. screen." She put her head between her knees and took deep breaths. How childish she was, imagining she'd made strides, when the truth was she slipped into a vortex of panic whenever violent news coverage hit the screen. From the force of the bomb, the roof of the restaurant had collapsed on the diners, and body parts were strewn about in crimson pools.

She raised her head and stared out at the plunge of the mountainside into the ebony ravine below. It was easier speaking to the old woman's reflection in the glass, her earrings spots of glitter in the lamplight, her upswept hair, like an ancient goddess, mute and all-knowing.

" I remember a trip to the States we took when I was about eight and my brother was eleven, to one of those automatic carwash places. In those days there was nothing like it in Israel. My parents must've figured it'd be a treat if we sat in the car while it went through the machine."

She pleated the drapes with her fingers. "I was scared out of my mind and so was Michael, though he played the part of the big hero. My parents were thrilled; they thought it was Disneyland all over again." She leaned forward into the blackness. "Black and red brushes chewed up the car like gigantic caterpillars. That's just how I feel now. The monsters are rolling over me." She turned around, rubbing the scar on her cheek. "How do you expect me to carry out this crazy plan of yours when I can barely hold myself together?"

The silence that followed was broken only by the squeak of Lydia's wheelchair as she rolled across the room.

"Monsters."

"Yes, monsters. They're chewing me up from the inside."

Lydia barked out a laugh. "What about the monsters on two legs with cultured voices and crisp uniforms?" She touched her withered legs.

Rachel yearned to reel back her words. She sank down on the carpet and hugged Lydia's knees. "I'm sorry," she said. Tears stung her eyelids as Lydia stroked her hair. "When I panic, everyone else disappears."

"Listen to me," Lydia commanded. "The panic within you is your monster. It will devour your power if you let it. You must fight." She grasped Rachel's hair tightly and pulled her face upwards. Her eyes burned with a strange fire. "Like I did at Auschwitz."

"You're superhuman, Lydia, I'm not."

"*Patienza*. Next week you will hear how I triumphed over those Nazis. Everyone will. Ask your father. He's organizing the ceremony this year."

"My father?" Rachel sat back on her knees, stunned. The events of the past week had blunted her sense of time, as well as her memory. Nate had mentioned the Holocaust Ceremony this year, one in a chain of emotive memorial days that bridged spring and summer: Holocaust Day. Memorial Day. Independence Day.

Despite the fire's warmth, she shivered. "They've been begging you to tell your story for years. Why now?"

Lydia pinned up a lock of hair that had fallen loose. "Because I'm an old lady who's witnessed more than any human being should see in ten lifetimes." The firelight carved hollows in her cheekbones, deepening the death's head grin that spread across her face. "Let me have the satisfaction of sharing that pleasure with the younger generation."

* * *

It was close to midnight by the time Rachel trudged over to Reb Elijah's cottage. Her ankles were freezing in last summer's sandals and the shawl she'd borrowed from Lydia did little to dispel the chill. Aside from the distant lowing of the cows in the dairy, the only sound was the slap of her shoulder bag against her hip as she passed rows of silent cottages.

Exhaustion had replaced the courageous spurt that had galvanized her back at Lydia's. Over espresso and freshly-baked *biscotti*, the old woman had wheedled and hammered and commanded. Lydia was an arch-manipulator, all right. She'd even used the Holocaust as a weapon. But if her conviction held water, a more subtly dangerous murderer than Shmaya had killed Reb Elijah and may have left a fragment of his identity in the Rebbe's cottage.

The path curving down to the dead man's house was

hidden by trees, but as Rachel drew closer and caught a glimpse of the façade, grief sliced through her like a blade. It looked diminished, collapsed into the earth as though it too had shrunken and died. Ivy threads spidered the crumbly stucco, a counterpoint to the shreds of crime scene tape that fluttered in the wind.

Tying the edges of the shawl in a knot, she unlocked the front door. The fustiness of orphaned rooms enveloped her as she moved from the entrance hall into the living room with its faded corduroy sofa, dented cushions, and the worn carpet where she, Alona and Malkie had sprawled as kids, playing Chutes and Ladders.

She withdrew Lydia's flashlight from her bag and surveyed the room. The sideboard had been stripped of candelabras, *kiddush* cups and *hanukka* menorahs, probably by pragmatic Auntie Bracha, the dead *rebbetzin's* sister, who'd installed herself at Malkie's. Divested of curtains and pictures, the place had lost its uniqueness within the week, resembling a rundown version of Rachel's impersonal chalet. A thought struck her, unbidden, disloyal. Would another rabbi and his family inhabit this place as counselor, teacher and sage? Since the murder, the evening Torah lessons were divided up among the men, with an occasional boost from Haifa rabbis, but after the thirty-day mourning period serious headhunting would have to begin.

Thrusting such thoughts from her mind, she hurried down the corridor to the study at the rear of the house, the core of the Rebbe's life. Behind the oval worktable stacked with books and papers, wall-to-ceiling bookshelves loomed and a samovar rested on a stool. On the wall next to the window hung a print of Moses smashing the stone tablets.

Splayed on the table lay a volume of Talmud, open to the Bava Kamma tractate, dissecting the differences between what constituted a robber as opposed to a thief. Rachel had never warmed to the study of Talmud; its hairsplitting struck her as mercilessly analytical and lacking emotion. Not that her emotions had served her all that well, she thought. She leafed through the Bava Kamma and spot-checked the notes penciled in the old man's vigorous handwriting, then replaced them in their proper order, as if willing him to limp into the room, beetle his eyebrows and waggle a finger at her.

Unwinding the shawl and bunching it on the back of a chair, she chastised herself once again for being sucked in by Lydia's mission; she was violating a crime scene and the privacy of the dead to boot. Why? To find a tell-tale scrap, a letter, an incriminating photograph? Though the police had searched the house, she wouldn't bet on their thoroughness. As far as they were concerned, they had their man and their confession; case closed.

Itching for bed, she skimmed the flashlight across the library shelves, relieved to note that everything was exactly as she'd remembered: sets of Talmud and *mishna* sorted with appropriate commentaries, prayer books with gilt-etched spines arranged according to the festivals, tracts on *kabbalah*, Jewish philosophy, Jewish history. On the highest shelf the Passover *haggadas* were stored behind thick glass, to isolate them from the slightest trace of leavening.

Slogging through the canyons of books would take hours, but she'd have to make time tomorrow, between her first clients and the start of the two final days of Passover. She laid the flashlight on the table, but the heft of the woolen shawl sent it rolling to the floor.

With a groan, she knelt down to retrieve it. At first, she thought her eyes were playing tricks, but on the lowest shelf, illuminated by the needle of light, there it was; a 1695 edition of the Netherlands *haggadah*, an heirloom that had been in the Rebbe's family for generations. As a child, she'd gazed with fascination at the gilded calligraphy and the faded family tree that traced the Lachmann dynasty from Mainz to Lodz to eighteenth-century Palestine.

Her fingertips tingled. The volume was museum quality. Why wasn't it behind glass with the others? Stretching out on the cold tile floor, she scanned the length of the shelf.

It was practically bare except for a few editions of the Bible, among which she spotted the Rebbe's favorite, the volume that had always rested on the Shabbat table when he delivered his commentary on the weekly Torah portion. Within seconds, she grasped the paradox. Why was a priceless *haggadah* placed next to a book that regularly came in contact with crumbs from the Sabbath *challah*? It made no sense. Either someone else had moved the *haggadah* or the Rebbe had done it himself for some reason. Even if he'd been studying it for pre-Passover study classes, he could've used any one of the more mundane volumes locked behind glass.

She slipped the valuable tome from the shelf and held it close to her chest; sitting cross-legged on the floor, she opened its stiff pages. An envelope slid out. It was a manila envelope that could be purchased at the mini-market or in any stationery store. She hesitated. If anyone had the right to examine the contents, it was Malkie. Friendship between Lydia and the Rebbe notwithstanding, it didn't override his daughter's rights to his personal effects. And by the looks of it, the contents of the envelope would likely be very personal indeed.

At first her mind didn't register the creak of the front door, but her skin sensed the puff of air that cleared its way down the corridor to the study. Muted footsteps slid into the entrance hall. Stuffing the envelope into her bag, Rachel doused the flashlight and scrabbled under the table.

"You didn't lock the door the last time," a woman's voice murmured.

A man's low reply was followed by the woman's giggle. Rachel strained to identify the voices, but they were too indistinct.

"Shh!" The man. An intake of breath, and the slither of clothing as it fell. A soft moan, then footsteps again, towards the study, towards *her*. Panic iced her chest.

To her relief and horror, they sidestepped the study and entered the Rebbe's bedroom. The thump of shoes, the free-fall of limbs on the bed, the arching sighs and the woman's sharp cries left little to the imagination. The desire to rip into the bedroom and face them grappled with shame and curiosity. Who the hell *were* these people? Callous, spiteful, or knotted in a liaison so forbidden that they were forced to make love in the bedroom of a murdered Rebbe?

As she slunk further under the table, head in her hands, the appalling truth struck her that at age thirty-four, a therapist privy to the secrets of countless patients, she was witnessing passion that was volcanic and true. The dried-flowers-and-lace copulation with Nahum in their twin beds had been channeled toward procreation, not desire. Tears rose in her throat.

After what seemed like endless sighs and murmurs, they left. Unfolding her aching legs, Rachel stumbled to the bathroom window to catch a glimpse of them, but they were gone.

CHAPTER EIGHT

"IT'S a competency hearing." Rachel glanced sideways at Malkie, who was huddled in the passenger seat. "He won't go to jail."

"How can you be sure?"

From the back seat, Alona rapped her on the shoulder. "Because Shmaya isn't exactly what you'd call sane."

"So what'll happen to him?" Malkie twisted around, her hand draped across her throat.

Alona laughed. "Don't worry honey, the state will take good care of him."

"The state?" Her voice spiraled in panic as Alona sketched out Shmaya's psychiatric future.

The conversation pinged off Rachel like the rain that slashed against the windscreen. She punched in the *Kol Haifa* radio station. Eight-thirty, and the weatherman predicted more rain, which suited her mood. Misery had soaked her since yesterday, which had begun with the Paradise bombing and had ended with bitter ruminations about her ability to love. At the southern entrance to Haifa, the restaurant's twisted skeleton littered the beach where the sea roiled beneath slate-colored clouds. Next to a roadblock, a policewoman, runnels of water dripping from her raincoat, peered at them before waving them on.

From there, the Daihatsu segued into downtown traffic through streets too narrow for the glitzy new municipal office complex. One building resembled a glass fish standing on its tail; another was sleekly curved like a modern-day coliseum. Set low among them, stone houses from the British Mandate era skulked in the rain like orphans. The architectural jumble resembled her own life, Rachel thought; a mixture of chaotic styles that just wouldn't jell.

To her relief, Alona and Malkie had fallen silent, Malkie fidgeting with the pocket-size book of psalms in her lap, and Alona tapping her nails on Rachel's headrest in time to the music.

They filed into the visitors' section of Magistrate's Court, taking seats between a blond teenager in a red and white polo shirt and a bag lady who reeked of garlic. Either the weather had driven all the street people into the courtroom, or Shmaya's hearing had drawn a particularly large crowd, including a phalanx of young yeshiva students.

"Look at these kids," Alona hissed. "Aren't they supposed to be studying Torah or something?"

"I hope Shmaya isn't some kind of cult hero for them. Look at the crowd. And look at *him*." Rachel gestured toward a cameraman unpacking his gear. Nearby, a skull-capped forty-something in a tweed jacket perused his notes.

Rachel poked Malkie in the ribs. "That's the kibbutz lawyer?" Beneath her gray skirt with the ragged elastic band, Malkie kept crossing and uncrossing her legs like someone who'd bought an expensive seat in the theater and was impatient for the play to begin. If anyone looked like a street person, Rachel thought, it was her.

"Yes. Neumann." She sighed, "The Secretariat has such faith in him. I hope he'll be good for Shmaya."

"That depends on what you mean by 'good.'" Rachel tried her best to be diplomatic, aware that the denial of her husband's guilt was the glue that held Malkie together.

A side door opened and a low buzz filled the courtroom. Shmaya was ushered in, handcuffed and in ankle chains. The *haredi* looked melted down, his beefy shoulders and spongy midriff relegated to more robust days. Furrows lined his cheeks, and with his black suit and beard, he resembled an undertaker who'd laid out too many bodies. Rachel felt a twinge of pity and began to give reluctant credence to Lydia's theory. How could this *nebich* have committed such a crime?

"The bastard." Alona had pulled a small mirror out of her bag and was checking her eye make-up. "I'll never forgive him for how he treated Malkie."

"And the Rebbe's murder?" Rachel whispered. "Can you forgive him for that?"

She snapped the compact shut. "It's a matter of priorities, isn't it?"

"Priorities?" Rachel's retort was cut off by the judge's entrance and the noise of the crowd clattering to their feet. In her flowing robe, with a wispy chignon and weary eyes, she nodded for them to be seated, addressed the stenographer, and pulled the microphone towards her.

"This is a competency hearing, the purpose of which is to determine whether the defendant is mentally fit to stand trial. Detective?"

She nodded at a hefty cop with glasses and an oddly shaped head, who heaved himself out of a front row bench, tucked in his shirttails and proceeded to describe the murder scene; Shmaya kneeling next to the body, smeared with the victim's blood. Then, he detailed the forensic evidence, Shmaya's erratic behavior and subsequent confession.

Rachel's mind hummed the daisy petal game. "Did he do it? Didn't he do it? Did he...didn't he?" All the evidence pointed to Shmaya, and he had confessed, but still...

She tuned in again as the detective was quoting the pathologist's findings. "In addition to the wounds to the throat that directly caused the victim's death, the autopsy indicated cancerous nodules in both lungs."

A murmur rose from the crowd. Rachel's chest contracted and she heard Alona's indrawn breath. She grabbed Malkie's hand. "Did you know anything about this?" Malkie shook her head, tears streaming down her cheeks.

The judge cut in. "*Adon* Neumann, did your client know that his father-in-law was terminally ill?"

With an exasperated sigh, the lawyer said, "Your Honor, my client and I have not established any effective communication."

"Detective Gottwein?"

"Half the time he doesn't know what he's saying, Judge."

The judge swiveled her chair to face Shmaya, who was

breathing heavily and blinking his eyes.

"*Adon* Catz, do you comprehend these proceedings?"

Before the guards could intervene, the *haredi* sprang to his feet, an eerie sound emanating from his throat. "*HaShem,* God—forgive me!" With his free hand, he slashed a finger across his gullet.

"I'm filth, an abomination—*toeva.* Merciful God of Israel, kill me!"

Spitting into his palms, he smeared the wetness over his face and hair. Ragged groans poured out of him as he pounded his feet on the floor. The crowd went wild at the spectacle. A group of yeshiva boys began chanting, others booed. Someone shouted, *Dirty killer! Burn in hell!* The camera whirred into life.

"Shmayaleh!" Malkie shot out of her seat and raced over to the dock. The judge rapped out, "Guards!"

The crowd became a blur and howls of rage buffeted Rachel as she overtook Malkie and gripped her shoulder. "Let's get out of here. There's nothing you can do!"

"*No!*" She jerked away, stretching her hand toward her husband. He looked through her like glass, but swerved his eyes towards Rachel. For a split second, she was trapped by the stare of his fathomless black eyes. Afterwards, she could've sworn he'd wanted to communicate something to her, but the moment passed and he slumped into sightless catatonia. A policeman hustled him out, accompanied by the shouts and raised fists from the crowd that threatened to spill over into the dock. Outside, the wail of sirens could be heard. The judge disappeared into her chambers. Malkie and Alona were nowhere to be seen.

In a rising panic, Rachel ploughed through the mob, jostled on all sides by bodies and umbrellas. It was as though the slaughter of the holy man had popped open a cork of fury, at the snipers and the shooters and the suicide bombers, at the impotent justice system, at all the wars and all the blood. One of her mother's Brooklyn expressions rang through her head, *to scream bloody murder*. That's what she felt like doing, screaming bloody murder until she was hollow from her own screams.

A sharp crack and a groan diverted her from her race to the exit. Yelling and shouting, people ran from the courtroom, leaping over rows of seats, shoved into the lobby by police reinforcements. Rachel stood face-to-face with the detective. Beet-colored, glasses askew, he was breathing raggedly as he gripped the teenager with the red and white shirt in a stranglehold. The boy's face was turning purple.

"Let him go!" She'd seen enough police brutality on Jerusalem's streets, and the boy couldn't have been more than fifteen.

The detective looked up at her, the veins in his thick neck clotting with fury. "*Giveret*, butt out!"

"Show me your badge."

"Look, lady." The bullhorn voice petered out in a wheeze, as he scrutinized her. Slowly, he loosened his hold on the boy who shook himself off and scuttled out of the courtroom. The cop straightened up, as if in slow motion.

"Who are you?" he asked.

CHAPTER NINE

BUT Yossi didn't tell Absalom about the woman in the courtroom. Instead, he stared out at the fog. When it shredded, like cotton puffs, it revealed patches of sea and rain-soaked houses.

"Enjoy it," Absalom said, the first words he'd spoken in the forty minutes since Yossi had driven him home from the hospital. "There's no view like this where you come from." Easing himself down on the sofa, cradling his bandaged arm, he winced and shut his eyes.

Restaurants don't blow up where I come from either, Yossi wanted to point out, but didn't. Who in this crazy country was safe? Not even in Yokneam, his home town in Jezreel Valley nowhere.

Absalom was checking voice mail with his good hand. The explosion had scorched off all his hair, and pockmarked his face with metal pellets. His wounds would heal, the surgeon said; he was lucky he still had eyes. What the doctors didn't know, but what Yossi did, was that the eyes had changed since the bombing, still level and true, smoky olive in color. But they gazed out from a different place. Inside, he was different.

Feeling jittery, Yossi ducked into the lemony kitchen, which on sunny days was airy and optimistic. "Can I get you something?" he yelled, opening the refrigerator. He whistled, "Hey, your sister really went all out. Two roast chickens, schnitzel, salads…what's this? Cheesecake?" He resisted the urge to dig in a finger. Anything to make a dent.

Absalom didn't react, so he returned to the living room, springing on the balls of his feet; he needed bounce. His partner still sat on the couch, gazing out at the fog that curled against the window pane.

Yossi wandered restlessly around the room, touching things—CDs, candlesticks, notepads. He needed to feel objects beneath his fingers or else he'd drift into the cloud that was enveloping the house.

"So." He plopped down beside Absalom. "You shoulda seen that riot. The *haredi* goes nuts. Everyone starts screaming their heads off. All of a sudden, this kid runs over out of nowhere and kicks me in the shins. Never seen anything like it." He didn't bring up what he'd done to the kid after that; it might lead to the woman.

Yossi shifted uncomfortably on the sofa. Maybe he should speak to Ron Kozma or Human Resources about getting Absalom a psychologist. On second thought, better not say anything to the Superintendant. Something had happened between him and Absalom that had left bad blood.

"Hey, how's about I make us some coffee?" He needed to get away from the goddamn silence. Not that Absalom had ever been much of a talker. But he had what people called charisma, which pulled you in and made you say more than you'd ever intended to.

Poking around the kitchen cabinets, he found one of those yuppie filter things and coffee in a canister. He slammed the cupboard door viciously, hoping to provoke a friendly yell of protest, but the only sound was that of the water boiling in the kettle.

* * *

Rachel swept up the wood shavings on the veranda, the leavings of an angry teen-aged client who'd left a bit less angry, and glanced at her watch. If she didn't hustle over to the hotel soon, she would miss lunch. She pulled on her boots and reached into her bag for a lipstick, but her fingers closed around an envelope instead. Her heart quickened with the recollection of the envelope gliding out a moment before the front door creaked. She must have stuffed it in her bag, where it had remained throughout Shmaya's court appearance.

She sniffed it, trying to gauge a special Rebbe fragrance, maybe the cloves that he chewed or the eucalyptus oil he used. To clear his chest, he'd say wryly, aware of the deadly secret in his lungs.

Lunch could wait. She laid out the envelope's contents on her desk, trying to discern logic in what looked like a random collection. A faded photograph of a Jewish cemetery. A letter written in Dutch where the Rebbe had penciled *the Pregnant Virgin* in the margin. A death notice, announcing the *tragic deaths of Muna Rajoub and her baby*. And a scrap of paper with *Dima* written in Cyrillic-scripted Hebrew, followed by a phone number.

Once she would've been intrigued, like a child excited by a fistful of clues, *the* clue that pointed to an elusive mystery man. But in light of these disconnected remnants, Lydia's theory seemed increasingly pathetic, the wishful thinking of a sorrowful old lady.

The daisy game danced inside her head. Perhaps Shmaya had done it after all. He was violent, certainly volatile and eccentric, a religious fanatic. The judge hadn't needed much persuasion before sending him for a psychiatric evaluation.

Scooping up the documents, she returned them to the envelope. Except for the phone number.

* * *

Auschwitz was on his plate. Chicken vertebrae heaped like molars. In the camp, he'd extracted the gold teeth while the bodies were still warm. Even now, he scrutinized people's smiles to check if there was anything worth saving.

A young waitress was standing over him, holding a tray. "Fruit salad, apple strudel?"

He shook his head and cleared his throat. One day, phlegm or angst would choke him.

"Nothing, *maidele*, a glass of tea, maybe. And please…"

"Yes?"

"Take the plates away."

As she loaded them on the tray, the faint sunlight through the tinted windows washed her cheek in sepia, like an old photograph. She flashed him the automatic smile young people used when confronted by old age, particularly someone as decrepit as he was, stooped and bandy-legged, his feet barely touching the floor. White strings of hair meshed a pink scalp, which a skullcap partially concealed. One more *alte kacker* in a room filled with other *alte kackers*.

Glancing around the room at the other diners, he knew this would be their last year at the Kerem El Hotel Spa. The Pomorzany *Landsmanschaft* would vacation elsewhere for the High Holidays in the autumn. At least, those who were still alive by then. Despite its familiarity, Kerem El had become too frightening, the Rebbe's absence too painful. They had been shaped by losses, all of them. Enough, already.

A young woman was striding toward his table, dressed in the clothes they wore nowadays, a denim skirt with a black knitted sweater and high boots. He'd never seen her before, but then he made a point of staying safely in his room, so as not to see anyone. But his nerves were so raw that the tremor in his hands started, knocking his spoon to the floor.

"Oops," the girl said, bending down and picking it up. "I'll get you a clean one."

Then she walked off into the hotel kitchen, just like that, and brought a clean spoon for him and a plate of food for herself.

"Here we are," she said in the sharp *sabra* Hebrew they all used, as if spraying bullets. "I haven't eaten yet. Mind if I join you?" He nodded, staring at her plate, which was half-filled with green and red vegetables, a spoonful of tuna salad, a bit of hummus. Spare food for such a tall girl. Not at all what the *stetl* girls loved, like boiled *kartoffel* with sour cream, raspberry jam and thick slices of rye.

He willed his hands to stop shaking. He concentrated on her face, the kind which Papa had always called a *shiksa* face—eyes blue as a lake, but with a blot of brown in their centers, autumnal curls, but which the bony nose and full lips made a *stetl* face. She wore amber earrings. The girl met his gaze with sympathy. He wondered what was leaking out of him, like a bad smell. Cowardice? Old age?

"My name is Rachel," she said.

He peered at her more closely. She had a scar on her cheekbone. "Rachel," he said. It was his sister Raisl's Hebrew name, Raisl who was bone and ash in a Polish meadow.

"And you are…?"

He didn't want to burden her with names. "Just a tired old man drinking tea with a lovely lady."

She smiled. Her lips curved upwards at the corners. "Is this your first visit to the hotel?" she asked.

As if it made a difference, he thought wearily. But she wanted stories, he'd tell her stories. Anything to keep her with him a while longer, she was so young and pretty.

He explained about the *Landsmanschaft*, how important it was to keep the survivors together and preserve the memories of their old town. German reparations assured a fairly dignified old age, medicine, psychiatrists. As for treatments at the spa, a private fund paid for those, run by Polish *goyim* with guilty consciences.

"What about family?" she asked. She'd barely eaten, he noticed.

Before answering, he scanned the dining room. He knew he was taking a chance, but how long could he bury himself in his room, wrenched apart by regrets? The diners were emptying out. Soon it would be *schlafstunde,* naptime.

He faced her again, this Rachel. "My wife died sixteen years ago."

"A shame," she murmured.

"We have a son. Ari." The air vibrated with the name, infusing his son with movement and life beyond the respirator and the feeding tubes. After this nightmare was over, he'd ride out to the Jerusalem hills and visit him.

Rachel was talking softly to him now as she stirred her coffee, saying how difficult it must be, particularly at this time of year, with Holocaust Day coming up Sunday night. Was he planning to stay for the ceremony here at the hotel? It would be very moving this year. She was helping her father plan it.

"Holocaust." His rebirth as a monster. The word stuck to the roof of his mouth, dry as ash.

* * *

For the second time that day, Rachel drove into the city. The focus of her thoughts shifted from the old man in the dining room to this Dima who must have shoved his phone number into her bag where it had somehow got entangled in the Rebbe's envelope. Both exerted a morbid pull. Instead of her moving on to happier places, death stuck to her like a newspaper that hugs the ankles in a strong wind. Then, there was the strange policeman in the courtroom who had stared at her as if he'd seen a ghost.

She squeezed the Daihatsu into a parking space near Nordau Street, which skirted the seam between the largely Russian Hadar neighborhood and the *haredi* quarter, a grubby commercial section of town with broken sidewalks and crumbling concrete buildings. The Great Synagogue took up an entire block, its beige exterior covered with grime from years of accumulated traffic fumes.

As she walked the short distance from the car, sidestepping puddles from the recent rains, she speculated on the connection between the Rebbe's murder and Dima, but her imagination couldn't make the stretch. This neighborhood of inscrutable Cyrillic signs and pork delicatessens was poles apart from Kerem El.

Dressed in a brown suede jacket with a fleece lining, Dima lounged at the entrance to the synagogue's ritual bath, smoking. She recognized him as the boy who had nearly been strangled by the policeman. At her approach, he straightened up and ground the cigarette butt beneath the heel of his boot, his eyes upon her. They were luscious and oval, like pale blue fruit.

"*Toda raba, Giveret.* You will understand all when I give you something from Shmaya." He stripped her with a glance that was oddly asexual before nodding in apparent satisfaction. "*Da.* Shmaya said you are *sympati*. I saw it in court."

"*Shmaya* said….?" She and Shmaya were bound by mutual dislike. It had to be some sort of con.

She eyed the street, making sure that no hoods with leather jackets and gold teeth were lurking in the synagogue's many doorways. The Russian mafia was almost as deadly as the suicide bombers.

"Look, Dima," she said. "I phoned you, I came. I hope you're being straight with me."

His face radiated innocence, like a Renaissance painting. He pointed downtown. "Come with me, please. It is not far."

The slim figure wound his way through traffic-choked streets, down a steep alleyway leading to the *shuk*, and further down the slope toward the old Arab quarter of Wadi Salib. It was as though the rain had halted abruptly at this valley of neglect and ruin. The foliage was scorched, the sky a blinding azure. Sabra cactuses sprouted among the ribs of gutted houses. The area had been earmarked for development as an artists' quarter along the lines of Zeita, but aside from a few yuppie coffee houses and a renovated fringe theater, dingy wasteland reigned.

They picked their way down the cracked steps that led to the lower town where a ribbon of sea cut across the horizon. He led her to a building with a domed roof painted turquoise. At the entrance was a small sign with the same graceful calligraphy she'd seen on the card Alona had handed her— *Herod's*.

* * *

Dima steered her to a Formica table next to a kiosk that sold nuts and sunflower seeds. He handed her an envelope, the corner of which was ripped by the thick wad of paper it contained.

"This Shmaya wrote and told me to give you. I get coffee for us and you read."

She shook her head in disbelief. "If you're playing around with me…"

"*Nyet*," he replied. "Shmaya wrote from jail. He wanted that you should read. You are lady that understands people, he said."

Rachel shivered in the cold afternoon sun. The thin sheets of paper crinkled in the breeze that blew in from the sea. It was Shmaya's handwriting all right, letters leaping off the page, reeling with slants and squiggles. Dima brought two black coffees and smoked, gazing at her.

To Rachel,

I'm writing to you because you are a woman who knows the world. You will also know how to protect my wife and children. I may not approve of your way of life, but I trust your judgment in these matters.

You know all about the Evil Inclination, especially where it hides, at the gateways to our bodies, ready to tempt us. That is why the People of Israel allow only the purest sensations to enter these gateways. It is what separates us from the nations and from the animals, what prevents the coarsening of our senses and our thoughts, which must turn to God and the ways of

Torah at all times.

As you were taught, and as I hope you will discover again, the Holy Torah must be obeyed, including the strictures against forbidden bodily fluids. Even as a child, I felt a forbidden excitement when I would accidentally rub against another boy on the bench in the study hall. I felt it when I was eleven and looked at Yitzik Mandelbaum, with his soft blue eyes and blond curls. When he looked at me soulfully and held my gaze, I felt a yearning, a reaching out of the soul and the body.

But I could talk to no one. What I felt was beyond the realm of human relations; it was animal lust. As I reached adolescence, I experienced these urges more and more. Every once in a while, I felt a surge of feeling toward a particular boy, always the same type, blond, big blue eyes, a knowingness in the gaze.

I threw myself into Torah study. The more I immersed myself in my studies, the less dependent I was on physical hungers like food, drink, fresh air, and the less I could ignore or suppress that other hunger. The life of the flesh was like a door that had to be tightly shut. Opening it would let the demons in or let my demons out.

By the time I was eighteen I knew that a shidduch awaited me. I don't know what I dreaded more, meeting Malkie or meeting her father. He was legendary, a scholar and a firebrand. I was so worthless beside him. But meeting Malkie was a relief. She didn't repel me. In fact, she was the duplicate of what always attracted me—frail, blonde, wide blue eyes, soft. I am filled with shame as I write this, but when we were together as man and wife, I pretended she was a man. Until I could pretend no longer.

Rachel laid the pages in her lap. A ship hooted in the port, the sun had drifted lower in the sky. A breeze nipped sharply at her hair.

"Cigarette, Miss?" Dima held out a pack of Marlboros.

She shook her head. She felt sick.

After my marriage, the yeshiva in Haifa was a blessing and a curse. A blessing because in my battle against the Evil Inclination, Torah was my salvation. As it is said, "The Torah is a tree of life for those who grasp it."

Yet, it was a curse, located on the Hadar, with its filth and its Russians, many of them goyim. That's where I first laid eyes on Dima—a young boy, no more than sixteen, but with the same knowing look I'd seen in Yitzik Mandelbaum's eyes so long ago. He was standing near the Great Synagogue. Our eyes met, I quickly looked down and hurried away.

The next day he was there again. And again. Thoughts of him—vile thoughts—filled my days and nights. I would see his lips on every page of the gemara. I lusted for him whenever I had relations with my wife. The thoughts drove me mad. My children were like phantoms to me. And the guilt! What kind of person was I? What kind of husband and father?

Malkie began to ask questions and every once in a while I saw the Rebbe's gaze on me. But their pure hearts couldn't begin to plumb the depths of my depravity.

About half a year ago, I passed Dima near the Great Synagogue as usual. This time, we brushed up against one another, and liquid fire consumed me when his eyes held mine.

He reached out and put a gentle hand on my sleeve like a trusting child.

From then on, I was enslaved. I followed him to a bath house where we entered a private cubicle.

My mind fills with blackness as I recall those trembling moments of ecstasy. I cannot put them on paper. They are beyond thought. I knew then that I was in the grip of the Evil Inclination.

Months of torture began. My torment at discovering that I am an abomination, that my punishment is death, that I had betrayed my wife, my family, my people, God. My joy at having found love, at the exquisite uncovering and discovering.

I stopped having marital relations. I couldn't live a lie. It was being unfaithful twice over. Malkie pleaded with me to explain. I couldn't. I rushed out, avoided her, started spending every moment at the yeshiva. And with Dima.

Malkie assumed the blame and I let her. She's a devoted, pious wife. I am lower than filth. God help me, I even raised my hand to her in anger at myself.

The Rebbe had me followed to Herod's and then confronted me. I broke down and confessed, throwing myself on his mercy and his wisdom.

What a fool I was. I expected him to tell me to leave Dima, to try psychiatrists, to start anew. But he took the most rigid line of all. He ordered me to divorce his daughter. Otherwise, he'd expose my sin to my father and the rabbis in my yeshiva. Strangely, he didn't want to change me. He accepted my nature for what it was. He simply didn't want his daughter to live with a man who didn't love her the way a man should love a wife.

Divorce. What shame! What scandal! My family and the rabbis would inevitably find out why.

Reb Elijah had become dangerous. At the Shabbat HaGadol service, he hurled accusations. Everyone stared at me, everyone knew.

That night, I made a sacrifice to God and smeared my body with his blood. Now I am an abomination but I have offered an unblemished sacrifice to God. Perhaps now I will be cleansed.

Rachel refolded the document and stuffed it back into the envelope. It felt heavy as lead. Tears pricked her eyelids as she covered Dima's hand with her own.

CHAPTER TEN

"**I** CAN'T sleep nights."

Rachel focused on the heavyset woman seated across from her on the sofa, whom she'd last seen making *knaidlach* in Malkie's kitchen. With an apron over her imposing bosom, and a sequined scarf around her head, Hadassah Levy had radiated queenly grandeur despite the egg and *matza* meal crusting her palms. Now she looked flattened, as if dragged down by a ponderous weight.

"What do you think about when you can't sleep?"

"I cry," she said, "for Reb Elijah."

Over her third cup of coffee Rachel nodded sympathetically, stifling the impulse to rub the grittiness from her eyes. Last night she'd stayed up late emailing Miri about the meeting with Dima before sneaking half a sleeping pill.

"And I pray to Hashem to bless all the other poor souls... you know...the terror victims, like the ones this morning."

Rachel's lips tightened. "The woman and her kids."

Confirmed killing was the term the terrorists used. After targeting a vehicle with Israeli license plates, they'd fire through the windshield, approach the car and shoot the victim in the head for good measure.

The confirmed killings kept Aviva and Nate awake nights. Michael and his family drove along the settler highways on the West Bank, moving targets for Palestinian terrorists.

"Hunting grounds, those special roads," Aviva once admonished Michael and his wife. "Those maniacs smell blood when they see a Jew with a skullcap or a pregnant woman with covered hair."

Aviva's prediction had been grotesquely fulfilled. That morning's victim had been a woman in the eighth month of pregnancy and her three daughters; the dead fetus had been a boy.

"It *is* very frightening. No wonder you can't sleep."

Hadassah leaned forward. The tiny eyes that sloped down at the corners lent her face an expression of permanent misery.

"They're getting closer all the time. They want to kill us all," she whispered.

Hadassah had echoed Rachel's own thoughts. All her clients did. The walls of the ornate sitting room screamed nightmares.

"Why can't I simply count my blessings?" Hadassah fretted. "Especially now that God has been so good to us."

Rachel raised an eyebrow at the sudden switch.

A blush of pride tinged the doughy cheeks. "Our Yoel has a *shidduch*! He's going to be married!"

"*Mazal tov!* Who's the bride?"

Hadassah struggled to sit up straight, her fat thighs quivering beneath the long dress. "The granddaughter of Reb Horowitz, the head of the Berdichev yeshiva."

"Never heard of it," Rachel sighed. It hadn't escaped her notice that the kibbutzniks were becoming more stringently observant. Gone were the days when girls wore pants or attended after-school activities together with boys.

"It's not one of those showy yeshivas," Hadassah said indulgently. "It's very *frum* and very picky. They don't accept just anybody. And the girl's family comes from a long line of rabbis." She waved her hand in mock horror. "What a wedding, what a headache! Thousands, and I *do* mean thousands of *hassidim* plan to come, even a planeload from Boro Park."

"Yoel must be a fine scholar to have made such a match," Rachel said. She pictured an amiable, sturdy child with thatched hair and a placid expression. From a young age, he'd been targeted as an *ilui*, a Torah genius. She hoped his *shidduch* would be more successful than Malkie's had been. After reading Shmaya's letter, she realized just how doomed it had been from the start.

As Hadassah chatted on about her son's wedding plans, Rachel couldn't shake Shmaya's confession from her mind. The *halachic* trap into which his sexual identity had led him was merciless. There it was, in Leviticus, 20:13. *A man who lies with a man as one lies with a woman, they have both done an abomination; they shall be put to death, their blood is upon themselves.* In Shmaya's twisted mind, the only way out was to silence the Rebbe for good.

"Praise God," Hadassah was murmuring, eyes closed in thankful prayer. "Yoel is an ideal son. Mordechai is so proud of him."

"Yet you feel uncomfortable with the fact that you can't rejoice wholeheartedly."

Hadassah nodded. "It feels wrong, almost as if...."

"As if...?"

"There is something sinful in our *simcha*." Hadassah covered her mouth with her hand. Fear flickered in her eyes.

"Sinful? That's a very strong word."

A dull flush spread up the older woman's neck and onto her cheeks. "I don't mean *sinful* as in *sin*..."

Rachel leaned over and gave her arm a reassuring pat. "Of course not, but a joyful event can be very stressful, especially the marriage of an only child. And if everybody around you is in mourning, it's natural to feel a bit guilty for being happy."

Hadassah nodded and cast her eyes down, but Rachel had the feeling she wasn't really listening and that her thoughts were elsewhere.

"Yes," she sighed. "And then, there are the palpitations." She splayed her fingers over her heart. "They seem to come from nowhere."

"Have you seen the doctor?"

Hadassah frowned. "Yes, but the drug he gave me was so strong it made me dopey. I couldn't lift a finger around the house. And so expensive! I didn't dare tell Mordechai."

Rachel was puzzled. "But the kibbutz covers that through the health fund."

"Dr. Ozeri explained that the pill hasn't been approved yet."

Rachel had mixed feelings about Reuven Ozeri. He'd arrived at Kerem El after Rachel had married and moved to Jerusalem, so he wasn't part of her childhood matrix. During their meeting after the Rebbe's murder, she had sensed a pedantic artificiality in his manner that put her off. He seemed to be everything a doctor was supposed to be; too caring, too conscientious, just the correct amount of professional distance. As for his magical pills, she'd heard about them from other clients, but no one had mentioned that he was selling them privately.

She glanced at her watch. The session was drawing to a close.

"We'll talk again, Hadassah. Next week, same time?" She rose and helped the older woman on with her coat. It was heavy in her hands.

"That's fine with me. It helps to talk to you. Took me time to decide, but I'm glad I did."

Rachel escorted her to the door. The chilly noon sunlight poured in. "Good. Please send my regards to Mordechai and wish him *mazal tov* from me."

"Oh, I can't do that!" Her hand flew to her mouth.

"Why not?"

Hadassah shook her head back and forth. The fear had turned to terror.

"Because he must never know I came to see you," she whispered. "Never."

CHAPTER ELEVEN

NOTHING had helped; neither *shaharit* prayers nor the pre-dawn five-kilometer run to Jabal and back. Gideon Mann held his head in his hands, fingernails digging into his scalp; a dull ache radiated up from his neck and settled behind his eyes. The more he sensed events spiraling out of control, the more he felt clamped in this vise of pain. His harsh intake of breath startled his son who was assembling a sandwich at the kitchen counter.

"What's up?" Amir swerved around, cheese slicer still in hand.

Gideon tapped that morning's *Yediot Aharonot* with his pipe. "This."

Amir ambled over and laid his hand on his father's shoulder, peering at the feature on page three. "Not good." His reassuring squeeze made Gideon melt with warmth. He loved his son, not only because of his Nordic good looks—a carbon copy of Gideon at age twenty-four—but for his attentiveness, compassion and …well…goodness.

"Did I miss something?" Irene came up behind him and gave him a swift kiss on the cheek. The scent of the perfume she always used combined with the touch of Amir's hand and the cozy smell of filtered coffee calmed him a bit. *My family;*

the three of us against the world, he thought. No, he amended inwardly; it's only me against the world. They're managing fine.

"Look at the paper, *Ima*."

Irene pulled up a chair and slid the newspaper toward her. Her lips tautened and she tugged a lock of hair that curled around her right ear. At fifty-five, she was petite and compactly built, with the thick chestnut hair that was her reward, she claimed, for not wearing a head covering.

"Hmmm. Not good," she said, unconsciously echoing her son. She laced her fingers through her husband's. "Pick up the phone to Neumann. Maybe we should sue the paper."

Amir laughed grimly, plucking his jacket from the hook in the entrance hall and straightening his skullcap. "Take the newspaper to court? Get real. Besides, everything in the article is true." He stepped into the kitchen to retrieve the sandwich, which he stuffed in his backpack. "Don't let it get to you, *Abba*. I gotta go."

As the door slammed, Gideon sighed and lit his pipe. The pain had receded into a nagging ache. "Don't be late because of me," he told his wife.

"I'm the senior biologist in the lab. I can afford to have a second cup of coffee with my husband."

As she got up to pour the coffee, he felt a surge of pride. Irene was one of the few kibbutz members allowed to work 'on the outside,' in her case, at the Technion laboratory for genetic research. Salary, perks and pension went straight to the kibbutz.

"Thanks," Gideon said, as she placed the steaming cup at his elbow. As he pulled on his pipe, the tobacco aroma massaged his brain like balm.

Irene perused the article. "*Snakes in the Garden of Eden.* Where did they come up with this junk?"

"Remember the reporters stalking us the day of the murder? How they twisted around the most innocuous statements? As for the police, they're brilliant at leaks, when it suits them, that is."

"I thought that policeman was very nice: the quiet, handsome one who was on duty the day the Rebbe was killed."

Gideon rubbed the back of his neck. "I had more important things on my mind than his looks, believe me."

Irene reached for a defrosted croissant, grimaced, nibbled. "How much damage will this do?"

Gideon pushed back his chair and began pacing the length of the carpet. "A lot. Things are going from bad to worse. Shmaya confessing right there in the courtroom, starting a riot. The media are having a field day with their *haredi-*bashing. You'd think they had more important things to write about, like that poor dead woman and her kids."

Irene shuddered and sipped her coffee. "I hate to think that terrorist attacks are no longer news."

"It's guilt by association. In people's minds, we're no different from the fanatic religious fringe, the *Natorei Karta* or those other crackpots, the Modesty Patrols."

Irene eyed him. "You're worried about Kamienski, aren't you?"

Gideon nodded. The pain was returning. "Thaddeus is very concerned. I don't know what to tell him any more."

"Sit down, darling, you're making me dizzy." Irene got up and put the cups and plates into the sink.

He slumped down into a chair. "If so much weren't at stake…"

"You're taking too much on yourself as usual." Irene glanced at the wall clock. "It's not as if you're the CEO of a big corporation; we're a cooperative. Talk to Lydia and Reuven. Consult Nate." She grabbed her keys from the hall table. "Sorry, darling, but I really am late. We'll talk when I get home." She leaned down and put her arms around him. He nestled into the love that came so naturally from her. *I don't deserve this,* he thought.

When the door closed, the house seemed depleted. Gideon tried to take some comfort in Irene's vibrant decor—sienna and goldenrod, bowls of pine cones and sheaves of wheat—but in her absence, he felt the familiar erasure of warmth.

The minutiae of his job waited at the hotel in the form of faxes, emails, accounts. He'd have to placate Thaddeus in Warsaw again. Irene was right as usual; he *did* take everything on himself. Just like his father, whose Polish roots were intertwined with Teutonic thoroughness: perfection and precision, no sloppiness, no loose ends.

* * *

Lydia was making *pane del sabato*, the Sabbath bread of the Italian Jews. Wearing a chef's hat and apron, she crumbled a cube of yeast into a bowl of warm water, then dried her hands on a dishtowel.

"So he was gay," she murmured, smoothing out Shmaya's letter with the palm of her hand.

Rachel cranked the espresso machine. "And overwhelmed with guilt as a result. Because of the way he treated Malkie, I saw him as a sleazy tyrant instead of a tortured soul. Not that having sex with a street kid is a character reference." She carried the cups over to the table. "Don't think I didn't phone Haifa Social Services about Dima."

Lydia was absorbed in her own thoughts. "Why did Elijah keep it from me?"

Though it was as good a time as any to probe the nature of her friend's relationship with the Rebbe, Rachel let it go. Lydia had been hurt enough. "Maybe it was too shameful because of Malkie. Or else it just hurt him too much to share it with you."

She glanced around the spacious country kitchen the kibbutz had built for Lydia with the profits from her cookbooks. Hand-painted Tuscan tiles soaked up the morning sun and a huge Cucina oven crouched in the corner. Normally, she enjoyed watching Lydia work on the four-meter-square olive wood table carved by a Nazareth carpenter, but now an inner disquiet ruffled her usual calm.

She pulled Shmaya's letter away from the flour and eggs. "In the light of this confession, don't you have some rethinking to do?"

A smile curved Lydia's lips as she reached for the bowl of flour. "You are such a predictable one, *cara*. I was waiting for those very words."

"Shmaya's motive is right here." She tapped the letter with her finger.

Lydia cracked three eggs sharply against a bowl and added a pinch of salt. "So you think I'm mistaken."

"Let me do that." Rachel picked up a fork and started beating the eggs. "It's obvious that Shmaya killed Reb Elijah. When the Rebbe talked about evil, he meant Shmaya's betrayal of Malkie. As for immorality, the Torah stand against homosexuality is clear."

"Not so strong." Lydia grabbed the bowl and added the yeast mixture, sugar, oil and warm water.

Rachel pressed on. "You gave Reb Elijah advice about the sermon; Shmaya heard it and killed him. It certainly doesn't mean you failed him."

Lydia blinked back tears as she measured the flour. "I signed his death warrant."

"Did you know he was dying?"

For a brief moment, her face collapsed. "Yes, I did. He told me a month ago. He had to put his accounts in order, he said."

"And he wasn't referring to money."

"Obviously." Her jaw trembled. "I should have forced him to tell me what he meant."

Rachel laid her hand on Lydia's. The reptilian skin was cold to the touch. "Don't torture yourself. You were a loyal friend. You couldn't have helped him more than you did."

She pounded the dough with her fists. "I can help him now. You will be my eyes, ears and legs." She laughed bitterly. "I still have a brain, I hope."

"Let's go over your theory again." Rachel stood up and added more coffee to her cup. "The murderer, who just happened to be in *shul* that morning, heard the sermon, was convinced the Rebbe was on to him and lured him to his death."

Lydia concentrated fiercely on slamming the dough on the table. "*Si.*"

Rachel brought another round of coffee. She jabbed the letter with her finger.

"The murderer was Shmaya. It's here in black and white."

Lydia wiped her hands and leaned back in the wheelchair. "Life would be nice and uncomplicated if poor Shmaya had done it, eh?"

Rachel was losing patience. "He *did* do it."

"Which makes me a delusional old lady."

"I didn't say that," Rachel protested, but Lydia silenced her with a wave and gestured towards the letter. "Oh, Shmaya had his motive, and in his poor twisted mind, he *believes* he slaughtered Elijah. But there are other aspects of this crime that don't make sense. When did he purchase the murder weapon? Where? A *shochet's* knife is not an item one can purchase casually. And the rope that was so conveniently at hand? Would Shmaya be eloquent enough to persuade Elijah to leave the house on such a night instead of him going to his father-in-law's house? All of this suggests a degree of premeditation that is not evident in the writer of this letter."

"What are you driving at?" Rachel opened the refrigerator and took out a pitcher of cold water.

Lydia laughed. "Bring me the bottle of oil on the counter." She brushed oil on the ball of dough and covered it with a dish towel. "And you studied human nature! No, *cara*, this is a document of passion and the writer is incapable of logical thought. The ruthlessness of this killing is not in Shmaya's nature."

"But he was kneeling over the body with the knife in his hand. His prayer shawl had the Rebbe's bloodstains all over it." Rachel poured the water into glasses and handed one to Lydia.

"Hah!" Lydia snorted as she slipped her baubles onto her fingers. "Is it so difficult to discover where Shmaya keeps his *tallis*? The *shul* is never locked. Besides, anyone with eyes in his head can see that Shmaya has always been eccentric. Just as Elijah discovered the affair with Dima, someone else could have as well."

"Making Shmaya the patsy," Rachel murmured, cradling her coffee cup.

Lydia pulled off the chef's cap and the matted ebony hair tumbled around her shoulders like seaweed. "That's what I've been trying to drum into your head. The murderer knew Shmaya well enough to entrap him, which means only one thing—the murderer is one of us. Like I've been telling you all along."

* * *

That evening, at her parents' Shabbat table, Rachel listened with only half an ear to their small talk about the grandchildren. Her mind drifted back to the *khamsin* that had struck before the Rebbe's murder. It seemed to belong to a foreign climate, another lifetime; since then, events had stacked up like crockery. One more dish would topple the whole pile, smashing it to pieces.

She had argued with Lydia over Shmaya's letter for hours before saying gently, "It's clear to me, anyway, that there's no other killer. I'm taking the confession to the police. But I want you to have this." When she'd handed over the envelope from Reb Elijah's study, the old woman's eyes glassed with tears, her silence more piercing than curses.

Aviva passed the quinoa and grilled zucchini. "You're not eating. Don't think I haven't noticed how skinny you're getting."

"Go easy on the kid," her father said. "She has a lot on her shoulders."

If you only knew the half of it. She took a spoonful of quinoa. "Sorry I'm not sociable, but *Abba's* right. Most of what I know about people is confidential. Besides, there aren't many fun things to talk about nowadays, are there?"

Her parents exchanged looks and Nate topped up their wine glasses. He grimaced. "In that depressing mode, I thought I'd ask your help with these photos." He pointed to the sideboard where a pile of black and white photographs lay on a batik cloth. "I got them from the archives."

"Nate, you can't discuss this on Shabbat," Aviva admonished, pulling off a wedge of *challah*.

"I know, but the ceremony is on Sunday night and who knows when our daughter'll get a chance to help us."

Grateful for the diversion, Rachel pushed back her chair, stepped over to the sideboard and riffled through the photos. Her heart sank.

"Look at this." She pointed to a cluster of scrawny figures, no more than teenagers, with haunted skittish expressions and rifles cradled in their arms. "They made it out of Europe by the skin of their teeth only to start fighting here in '48," she murmured.

Nate nodded and sipped his wine. " I wanted to show heroism instead of concentration camp photos, the way these camp survivors fought for the country's independence."

"Some of the old-timers from Kerem El fought off Arab snipers from Zeita," Aviva said, "like David Cherniak."

By then, Rachel had stopped listening. She was studying a photograph of a man and a woman dressed in shorts and white shirts lying on the sand with barbed wire in the background. What radiated from the picture was the vital beauty of the woman whose hair was upswept in a thick dark braid.

A jolt riveted her spine. It was Lydia. And her bandy-legged partner with the naughty sparkle in his eye was the old man she'd eaten lunch with in the hotel dining room.

CHAPTER TWELVE

LOCATED on the road connecting two Druze villages, squeezed between a grocery and a pita bakery, the Carmel Ridge Precinct was a neat white structure with iron grilles on the windows and the blue Israel Police logo above the entrance.

After parking opposite the building, Rachel crossed the road, Shmaya's letter at the bottom of her bag. The police would ask routine questions, yawn politely, file the confession away and then move on to the latest wave of terror attacks.

She shoved the door open and walked down a musty corridor to the squad room, a less dilapidated version of its Jerusalem counterpart. Directives plastered the walls: photographs of explosives, missing persons, wanted suspects. Even the racket was the same: the hum of printers and photocopiers, the clacking of keyboards, the drone of the radio, and above it all, the shouts. The squad room was a kingdom where cops decompressed after coping with their unsavory clientele.

On the whole, Rachel didn't trust cops, despite the few committed do-gooders, like Miri's boyfriend. In the course of her work for the city's social services, she'd come across the whole range of police officers, those that slept with whores, those that took bribes, the brutal ones and the indifferent ones.

She drummed her heels impatiently on the floor next to the reception counter. A policewoman talking on the telephone caught sight of her, stopped in mid-sentence and elbow-poked a colleague at the next desk. Silence rippled the room as people stared.

* * *

Absalom attempted to focus. The butchered corpse of a Filipina caretaker had been fished out of a garbage can near the Turkish market and the suspect was the woman's lover, an illegal Chinese worker named Liu, whose photograph would be broadcast on the nine o'clock news, if Absalom could summon up the energy to pick up the phone to the studio.

Outside the office, footsteps clomped down the corridor, followed by Yossi's enraged bellow.

"*Giveret,* you can't just barge in!"

The door flung open and Absalom felt air whoosh through his chest. The floor dropped away. Lumbering up to him, Yossi leaned his palms on the desk and muttered, "Couldn't stop her, ran right past me. I don't know who the hell she is or what she wants, but just say the word and she'll be out on her ass."

Absalom lifted his good hand. "I'll be okay. Just…leave us alone for a second."

"You sure?" Yossi's glasses steamed and he breathed heavily through flaring nostrils. Absalom nodded. Yossi glared at

Rachel, hitched up his pants and slammed the door so hard that the windows rattled.

Absalom cleared his throat. *Calm down,* he told himself. *So she resembles Christina, so what?* When she looked at him, her eyes widened: they were blue, he noticed, and her hair fell about her face like tangled autumn leaves. Her nose was a bit off-center. His gaze moved to the hollow at the base of her throat, to the swell of the collarbone beneath the open-necked sweater.

"What happened to *you*?" Her voice was less languid than Christina's, crisper. The tension in his diaphragm loosened, and his feet touched earth again. For a moment, he'd forgotten that his face was as perforated as a pumice stone.

"It's nothing. Just something that happened."

"Because if I've come at the wrong time…"

"No, just stay." His voice was brusquer than he'd intended. "How can I help you?"

She rummaged in her shoulder bag and withdrew an envelope which she placed on his desk. Her fingers were tapered and cross-hatched with nicks and scratches.

"Here, take this. Maybe *you'll* appreciate good citizenship when you see it." She tossed her head in the direction of the door. "Unlike your sergeant out there."

She settled herself on the chair opposite, crossed her long legs and explained how she'd acquired the *haredi's* letter. As he read about Shmaya Catz' sexual proclivities, he felt a stir of interest. It was as good a motive for murder as any he'd come across. It also explained the strange combination of guilt and absolution that shone from Shmaya's face; now that he'd sacrificed the rabbi to God, his soul was free. Absalom shook his head as he read. What a nut. He raised his eyes and studied Rachel. Was she also religious? Through a confused haze, he hadn't concentrated on what she'd been saying.

"Does his wife know about this?"

The woman's eyes clouded over. "Of course not. She has enough to deal with. Besides, it's something she'll never understand."

He'd run out of words, but he had to see her again.

She gave a little sigh and stood up, holding out her hand. "Well, glad I could help put an end to this thing, even a little." Pointing to the cast on his left arm, she said, "Take care of yourself, okay?" She peered at his name tag. "Chief-Inspector Brill."

* * *

Mordechai Levy scraped his boots on the mat before changing into the house slippers that rested next to the telephone table. Except for his ongoing argument with Zvi the electrician, about how the cypresses near the petting zoo were threatening to topple the high-tension wires, it'd been a good day. He grunted with satisfaction as he caught a glimpse of his face in the hall mirror. Now that he was on top of things, the stress ridges on his forehead were fading. He was sleeping better and smoking less. The worst was over. *HaShem* was on his side.

"You're home early." Hadassah stepped out of the kitchen

wiping her hands on a towel. "What happened?"

"What's with you, woman?" He gave her a mock scowl and grabbed the towel, aware of the spark of fear ignited by the closeness of his body. *The demon*, he called it, the brief thrill of power that surged through him, though he'd never laid a hand on her. Still, he felt uncomfortable, as if he'd filched coins from a charity box. "Since when can't a man come home whenever he wants?"

The smell of chocolate floated in the air as he followed his wife into the kitchen where beef and chickpeas were bubbling on the stove. When was she going to take herself in hand with this chocolate business? The secrecy of her addiction bothered him, as though she had a separate life away from him. Maybe after Yoel's wedding in late July, after Tisha b'Av. He'd give her till then before demanding she act like a wife again.

"How was Yoel's Shabbat? You talk to him today?" Mordechai's pride was strong and swelling, nearly bursting through the muscles in his chest. What a son! A true *talmid chacham*; almost saintly, so modest despite his great Torah knowledge.

Hadassah sliced black bread, and placed it on the table next to the tangy pickled vegetables he liked so much. After making the blessing, he bit into a piece of vinegary cauliflower, yellow with turmeric.

"No," Hadassah answered with the aggrieved sigh he hated so much. She arranged her bulky body on the chair across from him. "But how can I complain when he spent Shabbat at the great rabbi's table?" Ladling stew over mounds of rice, she laughed self-consciously.

"Sometimes I'm afraid the boy will forget who his parents are."

Has she gone mad, this big-mouthed woman? Mordechai glowered at her across the table.

"What are you prattling about now? You have a loose tongue," he growled, stabbing the air with his fork.

She squirmed, her face reddening under the headscarf, eyes darting back and forth like small insects. "It's just a way of speaking that's all; I didn't mean anything by it."

"Good," he said, chewing on a chunk of beef. "Now that *that's* put to rest I want no more careless jabber, even if it's just beneath our own roof."

Hadassah slid her hand into her apron pocket, as if even the touch of chocolate would comfort her. Mordechai pretended not to notice.

As he tore off a piece of bread and mopped up the gravy, the demon pricked him again. "How's Rachel Shine keeping?"

Hadassah's knife clattered onto her plate, chipping the china rim. "Oy, what a *klutz*!" After scraping her food to a clean dish, she flipped open the garbage can and tossed in the broken plate. A full minute passed, during which she wiped sinks and countertops before she replied, her wide back turned to him.

" Aviva says she's fine."

"She planning to stay here long?" Mordechai pushed his empty dish away. He was dying for a cigarette. "Has a job in Jerusalem to get back to, doesn't she?"

Hadassah paused, washcloth in hand. Her shoulders sagged. "Maybe. I hope she can stay longer."

"Sit down and finish your meal." He wanted to get a look at her face. She was keeping something from him. "The food's getting cold." He waved in the direction of the countertop.

Obediently, Hadassah drew up a chair, set her plate down, and began furrowing the rice with her fork. Her eyes were filmy with tears.

"*Nu*? What's the matter now?" he asked. "What did I say?"

She sniffed and wiped her eyes with a napkin. "Nothing."

He rolled his eyes. "It was something about Rachel, wasn't it?"

Hadassah pressed the napkin to her mouth. "No, no, I swear. I was just thinking of Aviva and Nate, how sad it is for them to have their daughter up in Jerusalem so far away, just like Yoel."

Suddenly, it struck him. "Do you talk to her about our son?" At the menace in his tone, she shrank against the back of the chair.

"Only what everyone knows about—the *simha*."

"So you *do* talk to her."

"Everybody talks to her. I've known her since she was a child." Hadassah's face pouched in bewilderment. "Why are you asking me these things?"

He scowled and pushed back his chair with a loud scrape. "She's a bad influence, that's why. Divorced a perfectly decent guy, wears pants, a woman alone. It'll come to no good, her meddling in our lives. Next time you talk to her, tell her she's got no place here anymore. Tell her she should go back to Jerusalem where she belongs."

CHAPTER THIRTEEN

BY the time Mordechai slipped into the third row, the fifth memorial candle was being lit.

"In memory of the Jews from Czechoslovakia and Hungary..."

His heart was pounding and he stank of sweat. Sinking down into the seat next to Hadassah, he felt her recoil at the accidental touch of his knee against hers. She didn't even glance at him; she was wiping her eyes with a tissue. At the end of the ceremony, she'd be so eager to rush home to watch the Holocaust broadcasts on Channel One, she wouldn't even bother to ask why he'd arrived late, which was fine by him.

"In memory of the Jews from Poland and Russia..."

The sixth candle.

As always, the crowd that filled Pinetree Hall was caught up in a collective hypnosis, riveted to the front of the room as photographs of murdered relatives flashed in succession onto the projector screen. Apart from the Yiddish songs—*Mein Yiddische Mama, Der Stetl Brennt*—that accompanied the slides, only the occasional sob, quickly stifled, punctuated the utter silence.

Holocaust Day was getting to him. Last year, he'd wept along with the others, mourning the tragedy that had struck his people. Those tears had stemmed from his desire to be one of *them*. Now, it was different. He felt a rush of acid to his gut and he locked his arms rigidly against his chest. For the first time, he felt like a bitter outsider, *was* an outsider, as Reb Elijah had cruelly reminded him a little over a month ago.

In the dark, he spread his calloused hands in front of him. Broad gardener's hands; the hands of the boy the Rebbe had plucked from the Jaffa slums. What a fool he'd been all these years, thinking there could be a link between him, the Holocaust and those pale European faces.

He glanced sideways at Hadassah. She belonged, all right, Kerem El born and bred, with roots in Budapest and Vienna. As for Yoel, their son…his son…he suppressed a groan and his heart contracted with love and fear.

* * *

Though it pained him to think about it, Dr. Reuven Ozeri had no choice but to lie to his daughter about watching her performance at the ceremony.

Sarit had been chosen among the fourth grade girls to assist six elderly survivors in kindling the six memorial candles. For weeks, she'd practiced solemn faces in the mirror and had driven Orly crazy about her outfit, in the end selecting a black velvet dress with white stockings and a black ribbon to set off her blond ponytail.

However, he'd missed his daughter's big moment, sidling into Pinetree Hall in the middle of a video clip about the youth delegation to Poland. No one noticed him, and even if they did, they wouldn't think twice if a doctor arrived late.

He readjusted the bobby pin that battened his skullcap onto his hair, swirled into a wiry bush by the *khamsin* raging outside. The gusts that hammered the building seemed to reverberate inside his head.

Briefly, he glanced at the images flickering across the screen. Youngsters wrapped in blue and white flags laid wreaths inside the crematoria ovens, then lit candles and recited *kaddish*, the mourner's prayer. In a few years, his oldest son would also take part in what Ozeri privately called "the concentration camp circuit." The whole thing had become commercialized, totally disconnected from the pitiful shards of humanity he treated in the clinic this time of year.

A disembodied sensation enveloped him, in which his thoughts seemed to float in comic-strip balloons above his head. Orly always griped about his hyper-rationality, what she liked to call his lack of *passion*, as if he suffered from a chronic vitamin deficiency. True, he distanced himself from people and situations; it had been essential to his medical training, but it also enabled him to zoom in on his goals, to assess pluses and minuses. To survive.

Like this evening. What he'd done had been unconscionable, against the Almighty, a mockery of his faith as well as the Hippocratic Oath. Was he any different from the German soldier that aimed a rifle at children and old women huddling together in the snow? He tore his gaze away from the screen and scanned the audience, searching for his family. They were his anchor and his religion; they were all he cared about.

* * *

Shaking dust out of his hair, Boaz Kashtan sprinted up the carpeted staircase to the second floor. The lobby was deserted; even the security guard was attending the ceremony. Power crackled through his veins, as though the hotel were his private mansion; he could slash the upholstery, scratch "fuck you" along the length of the front desk and still remain invisible.

He strode toward Pinetree Hall, chuckling at the irony of the situation. He'd just committed an atrocity of sorts and a Holocaust Ceremony would be his alibi. He was bound to be noticed; tall, red tee shirt, shoulder-length blond hair. One of those bohemians from the village, people would say. But when this whole thing was over they'd remember him, all right. Just like he'd never forgotten them.

* * *

The microphone squawked as Rachel adjusted the sound, inwardly cursing Taleb's absence, though he was well aware how much they counted on him. At the last minute, Rachel, Nate and the culture committee had lined up the chairs, connected the cables, the computer and the sound system. The heavy *khamsin* that blanketed the mountain meant revving up the air-conditioning and lugging cold drinks up from the hotel kitchen.

However, once the ceremony got under way, Rachel immersed herself in the atmosphere. Her father had struck the right balance between prayers, music and visuals, and the audience was deeply moved. Her thoughts strayed to the ceremonies of years past and sorrow seeped into her. The Rebbe's empty chair in the front row was another mute reminder of the losses surrounding them on all sides.

As she surveyed the elderly survivors, she tried to pinpoint the old man from the dining room. More importantly, where was Lydia? She wondered about the two of them. Did the old man come to Kerem El twice a year to see her? Was he even aware she lived here? So much about Lydia was a conundrum.

A tingle of anxiety rippled through her. She'd been so preoccupied that she hadn't spoken to Lydia since Friday, let alone asked how she planned to get to the ceremony. She just assumed that someone would drive her, but felt guilty that she hadn't even inquired, especially since deep down, she had the uncomfortable sensation that the "someone" should've been her.

Peering at his watch, Nate whispered, "In a few minutes, Lydia does her thing. Does she know her cue?"

"I don't see her."

He frowned. The children's choir was singing its final song. "What's the back-up?"

"We don't have one. We'll wind up the ceremony in the usual way. *El Maleh Rahamim* and *HaTikva*."

Rachel's tension rose. "Do you think she's all right?"

Nate was concentrating on adjusting the sound. "Sure, kiddo," he murmured, though she realized he was not really listening.

She gave him a peck on the forehead. "You did a terrific job. Finish up here. I'll see what's happened."

Skimming down the stairs to the lobby, she felt the walls tremble from the force of the wind. Outside, a maelstrom nearly lifted her off the ground. Slitting her eyelids against the sand that frosted her eyes and mouth, she groped her way down the hotel steps. The street lamps were covered with fuzzy swirls and she could barely make out her car in the parking lot. Curving into the wind, she fastened onto the hope that Lydia had decided to stay put.

The road was shrouded in orange mist and the mountains were invisible, as though the kibbutz were an island lashed by pounding surf.

The ravages of the weather had also wracked Lydia's cottage. Rattan chairs scudded across the veranda and chimes slapped crazily against a flower box. Earth from overturned plants spilled out on the floor tiles.

She knocked, then opened the front door, releasing waves of trapped heat. Her throat constricted with fear and she called out Lydia's name, but her voice echoed through emptiness.

She raced to the bedroom and switched on the light. The room had been ransacked as if by a frenzied hand; drawers yanked out, garments and papers scattered. The bed had been overturned and the mattress slashed, spilling out gobs of yellow sponge. Rachel zeroed in on the nightstand, grabbed the envelope from the Rebbe's study and shoved it into her skirt pocket.

In the living room, the couch and chairs had been ripped apart. Books had been hurled to the floor, pages torn from their spines. The elegant bottle of grappa had been smashed, and the sticky liquid oozed down over the rich mahogany.

Her knees shook, but she propelled herself toward the kitchen. At least Lydia's sanctum had been spared. On the stove stood a pot of water and eggplant slices drained in a colander, their juices forming brown rivulets into the sink. Chopped basil and tomatoes stood on a cutting board.

She shouted out Lydia's name again, but the wind howled a mocking echo. Running outside, she circled the grounds, leaves swirling up around her face. A branch from an oak tree had cracked and fallen on the path. Returning to the house, she leaned her back against the door, forcing her pounding heart into submission. If she reported back to the hotel, mass hysteria would result; besides, Lydia might return.

Drawing a shaky breath, she picked up the phone.

∗ ∗ ∗

I'll be right there; the words wove through her like a mantra. His voice had been cool and authoritative; she'd begun trembling the moment she hung up.

The defilement in the house drove her outside. Smoke wafted on the wind, and in the distance she heard the drone of cars returning from the ceremony. Her parents would be wondering where she'd gone. She prayed they wouldn't come looking.

After what could've been ten minutes or half an hour, a police Toyota pulled up, the pugnacious Yossi Gottwein at the wheel, while Absalom was talking into a cell phone. Electronic voices crackled from the police radio on the dashboard.

As Rachel ran to the car and Absalom's eyes met hers, she could see his gaze alter, like sand shifting at the bottom of a lake.

"Backup and forensics are on the way," he said.

She led the way across the veranda and into the cottage, while Yossi remained outside yelling instructions. The wind sucked the door shut behind them. Absalom's scalp shone beneath the hall light; it was punctured with scars and his facial bruises had turned black and yellow.

Rachel noted that he was only slightly taller than she was, yet compactly built. He was impeccably turned out in jeans with knife-sharp creases and a white shirt. His shoes were polished. Next to him, she felt gangly and loose-jointed. He stood motionless in the doorway as though absorbing the atmosphere of the place. After a full minute, his body relaxed and he drew latex gloves out of the pocket of his jeans.

"Touch anything?" His glance took in the ransacked living room.

"Only the phone."

"Where's the bedroom?"

She tipped her chin to the left, unable to stomach another glimpse of the old woman's underpants and brassieres tossed on the floor like rags.

"Who could've done this?"

Absalom paused. "I was hoping you could tell me."

She shook her head. "Come into the kitchen." Her

voice emerged cracked and unsteady as she gestured at the vegetables wilting on the counter.

She pointed toward a bookshelf. "Lydia was a world authority on Italian cuisine. For her, cooking was art, science and culture combined. She never would've left the kitchen like this, except in an emergency."

With his good hand, he removed a small notepad from his pocket. "I'll need some background. What was your relationship with the missing woman?"

Irritation mixed with panic welled up inside her. "Can't that wait?" she flared. "Lydia didn't stroll out of here by herself. She's an invalid in a wheelchair."

Absalom's jaw tightened. "We'll get to that after you answer my question. And we might as well sit down."

"I don't want to sit down." *Is he stupid or just bull-headed like most cops?* Raking her hand through her hair, she paced the room and tried to steady her voice. "You're wasting precious time. I should've known better than to call in a two-bit police force."

He shrank into a silence so profound that she suddenly became aware of the muted shouts and thumps of what she realized was the arrival of the forensic team. He briefly passed his hand over his eyes, then seemed to zoom back in. He thrust his pitted face so close to hers that he blotted out everything else from her vision.

"I've been here twice and each time you were involved in a questionable event; Shmaya Catz' confession and now this." Every word was a whiplash. "As you say, we're wasting precious time."

She became aware of his scent—like dried crysanthemums—and felt suffused with shame. Lydia's safety, maybe her life, was at stake and here she was sparring with this cop.

She motioned for him to sit down, a stranger in Lydia's kitchen. She pulled out a chair for herself. "I've known Lydia my whole life, yet I've never really known much about her, if that makes sense."

The policeman nodded.

"Our relationship is special, maybe because both of us are outside the box. My parents are American ex-hippies and Lydia's roots are Italian." She smiled wryly. "Not exactly typical kibbutzniks."

"Family?" Absalom scribbled some notes.

Rachel shrugged. "She's never mentioned any. And with Lydia, believe me," she laughed, "you can't ask. When it comes to personal things, she puts on a veneer no one can crack."

"So she's a woman without a past?"

How dimwitted he is! "Of course not." Rachel said testily. "Everyone has a past. She was a Holocaust survivor. In fact, she was supposed to be the key speaker at the ceremony tonight but never showed up. That's why I came down here."

Absalom's gaze sharpened. "What time frame are we talking about?"

"The ceremony started at eight-thirty and she was scheduled to speak a little over an hour later."

He was scribbling furiously. "She starts preparing a meal

and disappears."

Rachel pressed on. "And the vandalism?"

"We don't know enough yet," he answered. "The forensics team will give us more to go on."

Despite the heat in the room, Rachel felt cold. Forensics didn't only mean fingerprints. It also meant bloodstains.

* * *

They smelled the smoke as soon as they left the cottage. Absalom's cell phone bleeped.

"Fire," he snapped. "Below the hotel."

Rachel caught her breath. In the dry wind, one spark from a cigarette was enough to ignite a conflagration that would spread through the parched *wadi*.

"I'm coming with you." She clambered into the back seat of the Toyota. Yossi gunned the engine as a caravan of kibbutz vehicles streamed past them, vanishing in fogs of dust.

From the road to the hotel, they saw pillars of smoke staining the sky. The slope beneath the road was aflame. Rachel jumped out of the car and pushed her way through the heaving crowd, making out her mother's pale face and Malkie with her herd of children. The flames arched and danced among the dry undergrowth, which crumbled in crackling sputters. Combusting from the heat, pinecones became spools of fire hurtling into the dense woodland. Rachel squinted through the acrid smoke. The mountain was being devoured before her eyes.

In the haze, firefighters, kibbutzniks, villagers from Zeita and Jabal-a-Zeit hauled hoses from fire trucks and beat the flames with hoes and shovels. Police cruisers pulled up, their red and blue flashing lights creating a grotesque disco atmosphere against the backdrop of the orange flames.

Rachel broke through the crowd to the edge of the ravine, the intense heat scorching her skin. Her mind exploded with the events of the past few hours like the flames that were leaping higher and higher in a manic dance, demolishing all that was alive and green below. The solid earth that had nourished her was proving to be a volcano: Reb Elijah's murder, rampant terror, Lydia's suspicions and her disappearance, the trashed cottage.

Suddenly, she spotted a movement further down the slope, at the edge of the fire, where flames licked the rocks. A tortoise, squat and helpless, unable to flee. In seconds, the fire would engulf its shell, roasting the creature to death. Adrenalin pulsed through her limbs. Ripping a swathe of material from her skirt and tying it around her nose and mouth, she slithered down the slope, clutching at rocks and clumps of foliage. Thorns gashed her palms and flames seared her hair and clothes. On the ridge above someone yelled her name, but she centered in on the hapless animal only a few feet away. Coughing now, choking on the smoke billowed by the wind, she knew in a serene core of her being that it didn't matter what became of her. In the chaos that enveloped her, she would make a difference. She had to save that small shred of life.

The stony ground bruised her spine and brambles scratched her calves. She was almost there at the rock, stretching out her arms for the tortoise, buried in its shell. There, she grasped it, feeling its compact armor in her ripped hands. The fire was only a few feet away. She started the upward climb, clutching the creature, keeping it alive. Amid the shouts, someone was trying to reach her. She looked up as Gideon Mann slid down the slope, holding out his arms. His face was lit up by the fire, his white shirt, usually so immaculate, blackened and torn.

"Give me your hand." Holding the tortoise against her body, she reached out and felt the strong grip of his hand around her wrist.

CHAPTER FOURTEEN

As dawn layered the mountain range, Absalom slumped in the seat of the car sipping cold coffee, fatigue bleeding into his bones. His eyes scoured the mountainside where Yossi and the firefighters poked through the charred rubble, exhausted and smeared with grime. The mountain looked as though armies had battled and died there, twisted cedars and pines stretching black arms to the sky.

They had worked throughout the night. Lydia di Rossi was still missing despite an all-points bulletin and an announcement on Israel Radio. As usual, the crank calls hadn't been long in coming: a terrorist group holding her for ransom, a truck driver swearing that an old woman in a wheelchair was chugging along the Tel Aviv-Haifa highway. All the leads had been followed up, though Absalom knew that within a few hours manpower would be directed to safeguarding the roads against terrorist shootings.

The day would be spent sketching in the details about Lydia's friends and enemies. The ransacking of the cottage was more than a run-of-the-mill burglary. It stank of malice.

The *khamsin* had petered out and the sun was climbing, hinting at a warm day with a hard blue sky above the smoky ruins. As Yossi trudged up the slope, Absalom poured coffee from the thermos and handed it to him. He gave a grunt of thanks.

Absalom waited until he'd downed half the cup before asking, "Any sign of arson?"

Yossi leaned against the side of the Toyota. "So far, there's none of the usual signs. Probably some prick with a cigarette."

"A hiker after dark? On Holocaust Eve?" His tiredness must be acting up if he was playing devil's advocate. With all the other work on their plate they could do without an arson investigation.

Yossi gave a weary shrug. "Why not, with all the freaks around?"

Absalom rubbed his bad arm. "Let's leave it. When will they be finished down there?"

"I don't know. But maybe we can get a couple of hours sleep."

Absalom's eyes burned from smoke and fatigue. He was tempted to go home, take a shower and lie down for two hours: even one hour would do.

At the bottom of the *wadi* the team yelled. "We've found something."

The urgency in their voices caught his attention. His instincts warned that he wouldn't have that shower and nap. He eased himself out of the car and joined Yossi at the edge of the slope.

"What is it?"

Beneath the black sheen on their faces, Absalom could

make out spasms of distaste and something else. Shock.

"Get forensics back here. We've found a body."

* * *

Absalom climbed up the scorched hillside, leaving the forensics team to their grisly task. After exchanging a few words with the driver of the pathology van, he trudged over to the chalets where flapping doors and sooty towels testified to mass abandonment; the guests had been evacuated to a Haifa hotel during the night. Surveying the ash that blanketed the great lawn, he wondered whether the kibbutz economy would survive another suspicious death; then discovered he was too weary to care.

The bristles on his chin itched and his arm ached. He was running on empty, his well of sympathy dry, yet when Rachel opened the door in cut-off jeans and a wrinkled sweatshirt, he experienced the same loss of altitude that had knocked him off balance the first time. She was the first woman he'd been attracted to since Christina left. True, there was a resemblance, like a pair of blurred artist's sketches; long legs, honeyed coloring. Paradoxically, Rachel's grave vulnerability, the lack of which he'd relished in Christina, drew him to her.

He tried not to stare at her blackened curls and bandaged legs, but it occurred to him that, with his pockmarked face and frozen arm, they were mirror-images. They both looked like alley cats that had survived too many fights.

Her hand flew to her cheek. "Tell me."

"It's not good news, I'm afraid. A body has been found." Though he'd uttered these words countless times, he wished he were less clumsy with her. "We're waiting for confirmation from Abu Kabir, but it's clear enough. Lydia died in the fire." He winced at the memory of metal fused into the charred skeleton.

She swayed slightly, but motioned him through the sitting room where ash covered the furniture like charcoal upholstery. In a corner near the window, a tortoise in a cardboard box munched on lettuce leaves.

On the kitchen table, he glimpsed a knife and a chunk of wood, the source of the shavings that clung to his shoes along with layers of soot.

Picking up the knife, she gestured for him to sit down. "I've been doing this all night." She shrugged apologetically as though caught engaging in a secret vice. "I lose myself until reality knocks on my door." Red-rimmed from smoke, her eyes flashed with accusation.

Rotating her wrist, she sheared the wood with strong downward motions, gouging out chips with a violence that unnerved him. "How did she die?"

Absalom tore his gaze from the hypnotic motion of her hand and reached for his notebook. "After the autopsy, we'll know more. We don't even know how she reached the cliff, let alone how she fell to the bottom of the *wadi*. Any idea what she was doing there?"

Tears streamed down her face as she peeled off layers of wood. "No. She couldn't have gotten there on her own in that *khamsin.*"

"Who might've accompanied her?" He realized the question was absurd. It encompassed kibbutz members, hotel guests and anyone who'd been lurking in the Carmel forest area.

She wiped her nose on her shoulder, then continued whittling in silence. Absalom waited, letting the rhythmic movements accomplish their almost meditative task.

Throwing the knife on the floor, she padded through the wood shavings, took a dishtowel from a cupboard, and wiped two cups. Then, she poured water and coffee grinds into the percolator, her shoulders relaxing as if the ritual steadied her.

"Milk? Sugar?"

"Black, please."

"Sorry there's nothing to go with it. There was no room service this morning." Her lips curved in a quirky smile.

Absalom was tempted to chuck the case aside and ask the questions a man asks a woman when they drink their first cup of coffee together. Why she was so obviously single, a religious woman, who wore jeans. But he shoved the thoughts away.

She straightened her shoulders and placed the coffee things on a tray. "If I tell you what I know, you'll throw me in the loony bin with Shmaya."

"No chance of that." He tried not to smile at the image of her and the *haredi* teaching Torah to the other inmates.

As she poured the thick black stream into the china cups, her voice assumed a metallic drone, as if to distance herself from what she was saying. He listened impassively to the spiral of events the dead woman had revealed.

"So Reb Lachmann didn't name any names."

Rachel shook her head and sipped the coffee. "Lydia was definite about that."

"Why did he go to Lydia and not straight to the police?"

"They had a very close and long-standing friendship and Lydia was a very wise woman."

"Lydia never hinted at the person who might be behind this?" He tried to sound non-committal, soft-pedaling his incredulity.

She put down the cup. "Not a word." She paused. "That was *my* job, you see."

"I don't see."

Rachel's eyes panned his face, as if searching for a grain of trustworthiness she could grab onto. "She wanted me to use my therapeutic work as a cover."

"I don't understand."

She wiped her forehead with the back of her hand. "If only I'd known the danger she was really in. She talked me into doing some amateur detecting, though I doubted her story. So do you; I can see it in your face."

"They pay me to have doubts."

"It's not the same thing. She's *Lydia*, and when Lydia believes something's true, it is!" Her voice broke, but she steadied it with a gulp of coffee. "And I thought she was getting old and a bit.."

"Senile?"

"That's too strong a word; not senile, but remorseful about

what she saw as her part in his murder. I thought she'd created a minor fantasy, which happens sometimes when someone feels guilty. But now I know she was right and I was wrong. There's a murderer out there who killed both of them."

He took a deep breath, treading softly now. "Maybe her guilt became too much for her."

"Suicide? Lydia?" To his relief, she chuckled. So she can laugh after all, he thought. "No way."

"Remember Shmaya's letter?" She bent down and retrieved the knife. "I thought that'd clinched it, you know, that he'd done it." She attacked the piece of wood.

Absalom shuddered, hoping he would never be at the receiving end of such fury. "He did, and the forensic evidence backs up his confession. Thanks to that letter, we have a motive."

She threw up her hands. "So who trashed Lydia's cottage and set the fire? Shmaya?"

He sipped his coffee. "We don't know if it was arson. As for the break-in, there've always been drug-related thefts in the area." The artists were notorious for their drug use. "It was no secret that everyone would be at the ceremony."

"You can do better than that, Chief-Inspector Brill!" she flared.

"Absalom."

"Absalom." A faint blush tinged her cheek. "Did this so-called drug addict steal Lydia's silver or jewelry?"

"My men are going over the house now." He sounded lame and defensive. "Lydia's family will have to give us an inventory of her things."

"I already told you, she had no family." Rachel's mouth tightened into a firm line. "That's just the point. *We* were her family and we failed her." She shot up from the chair and limped across the floor. "We killed her just like she thought she'd killed the Rebbe!" She fingered the gauze on her temple. "I can't believe this is happening. I can't believe she's dead."

Absalom longed to put his hand on her shoulder, but said nothing. He knew she had to ride out the waves of shock.

"This person has destroyed two people I loved and he's destroying everything dear to me—my home, my parents, my friends, my community. Even," she gulped down tears, "my memories. I won't let this go. I won't let *him* go."

"You're tired and upset." He hated his verbal awkwardness, especially when he saw the animosity in her glance. "Feelings of revenge are natural. But promise me one thing."

"What?" She nearly spat out the word.

"Leave this to us. People will need you even more when they find out that Lydia is dead."

She stared out at the ruined lawn. "I've heard that so many times before. Be patient, bide your time, wait on the sidelines and let the men, time, God, whoever, do their work. Be there to listen and comfort."

Her voice cracked. Absalom had the feeling that it wasn't him she was addressing at all.

CHAPTER FIFTEEN

AFTER the official confirmation of Lydia's death, the nightmare burgeoned; communal weeping, prayer and preparations for the funeral. Clusters of people huddled in the lanes trying to make sense of the latest tragedy, the whispered verdict being that Lydia had killed herself, the Rebbe's murder and her Holocaust memories having literally sent her over the edge.

Rachel plunged into isolation. No one knew what she knew; that both the Rebbe and Lydia had been murdered by an unknown killer. She couldn't burden her parents, confiding in Malkie was out of the question, and Alona was too volatile. Besides, if Absalom Brill hadn't believed her, no one else would. Even Miri in Jerusalem, though appalled, doubted Lydia's story.

The moon was high by the time Rachel walked back to the chalet from Malkie's. The sour smell of burning pervaded the room. She collapsed into bed. Snapshot memories of Lydia clicked through her brain: chunky rings dusted with flour as she rolled out linguini, the crisp square of lace on her hair in the synagogue where she'd stubbornly sat in the men's section. The memories sifted into half-dreams, half-fantasies. Lydia's face hovered in the air, an icy, black presence, before morphing into a hand that pressed down on Rachel's face.

She struggled to breathe as she shook herself into full consciousness. The bed was drenched in moonlight and she drew the blanket more closely around her, the coldness of that hand still chilling the edges of her awareness.

She broke out into a cold sweat. *Take deep breaths. Visualize snow, sifted, pure.* Behind her lids, the snow became a shower of ash, drifting like obscene snowflakes to the earth. She threw off the blanket. A message was flashing on her computer. Miri, responding to Rachel's account of Absalom Brill's interrogation session.

Why didn't you show him the Rebbe's envelope?

Rachel's fingers skimmed over the keyboard. *Not sure it's relevant. Besides, he's a strange character; hard to read, bit of a cold fish. I don't know if I can trust him. He must think I'm a wacko. More tomorrow..*

By that time she had been shaken into wakefulness. She pulled on jeans and sneakers and slipped outside. The dark bulk of the hotel sliced the sky and the stretch of lawn opened up before her like a silver lake. The chalets stood like ghosts with shuttered eyes.

She was the only person left in the hotel complex. It would be days before a full clean-up and the guests' return. *If they return*, she thought grimly. Customer loyalty only stretched so far, even if Kerem El was still the most secure religious hotel in the area. Until now, the deadly drive-by shootings hadn't encroached on the Carmel forest. *We have our own private murderer.*

She needed to move, to feel the sting of fabric against the welts on her legs, the pain fueling her anger and sorrow. Her eyes smarted with the smell that hovered in the air as she limped past the hotel and back down the road to the kibbutz houses. It was eerie, making her way in the soft wind, moonlight streaming through the cypresses that lined the road like sentinels. White luminescence stained the mountains. The acrid smell became stronger. She quickened her pace, then halted. Directly below her, at the foot of the cliff, Lydia had been pushed to her death. Instinctively, she murmured a prayer. "*Baruch ata Adonay, Dayan emet. Blessed be God, the true Judge.*"

On the path to Lydia's cottage, she acknowledged her need to reenact the gnawing ritual of visiting the houses of her dead. She ripped open the crime scene tape and groped for the spare key Lydia kept hidden beneath a broken step.

As she entered the front hall, her throat swelled with tears. Facing her was the ravaged living room, blanched by moonlight. In the kitchen, the eggplant and tomatoes still bled on the counter in a grotesque still life. She tossed the food into the garbage and scoured the sinks. Tears stung her eyelids at the thought that Lydia's legacy would be a stinking kitchen. Unscrewing the lids off the spice canisters, she inhaled Lydia scents; basil, oregano, marjoram, dried thyme.

Suddenly, she heard a thud. Dousing the light, she grabbed a kitchen knife. An agile figure was picking his way through the living room towards Lydia's desk. Rachel flicked on the light switch and thrust the knife out in front of her. Her legs were rubbery, but this time she wouldn't cower like she had at the Rebbe's cottage.

"I can use this you know," she said in a low voice. The intruder raised his hands above his head. Dressed in black sweats, he was tall with the long legs of a runner. Blond hair tumbled around muscular shoulders.

His eyes narrowed as he stared at her, then a throaty chuckle rose from his throat.

"Rachel?" he said, walking towards her.

"Stay right there."

He lowered his arms. "Little Rachel. You haven't changed one bit; well, a bit. Still got that birthmark on the back of your knee? The left one, if my memory serves me."

She raked his face with her eyes, taking in the cleft in his chin, the cornflower blue eyes, the Aryan look.

"I'm calling the police," she said.

"Come on, Rachel, we're not kids anymore. "

She slid into folds of memory. She'd been nine and he'd been ten when his family had moved to Kerem El from Tel Aviv. Impish and handsome he'd been, tanned brown by the sun, hair bleached even blonder. She'd been pale and scrawny, and had envied his beach boy looks. But every once in a while she'd catch him cowering in their tree house, nursing bruises and burn marks on his arms and legs. Then, compassion turned to terror.

"Boaz Kashtan." Her stomach roiled. She struggled to regain control of her voice. "What are you doing here?"

He reddened and shrugged, his confident features slipping.

"Looks like somebody trashed Lydia's place. She promised to return something of mine. Now I've come to get it."

How many other facets of Lydia's life remained unknown? Rachel never realized she and Boaz had kept up a connection. Her gaze flickered toward the debris on the dead woman's desk. "What was it?"

"Something too embarrassing for your delicate ears, Little Rachel."

"As you said, we're not kids. Tell me why I shouldn't call the police."

His eyes danced, but she could tell he was appraising the seriousness of her threat. "It wasn't *me* who broke through the crime scene tape. And put the knife away—for old times' sake." He steepled his fingers in supplication.

"Old times' sake? You always did have a twisted sense of humor." The heft of the knife melted her fear.

As usual, he wasn't tuned into her. "I'm in need of a smoke. Do I have to beg, Sergeant?"

Boaz hadn't changed one bit; he could still snare her with his narcissistic charm. She led him outside to the back yard where scents of mint and wild thyme emanated from the garden, overlaid by the sultry jasmine Lydia had loved so much. It overlooked a pine-carpeted chasm beyond which the lights of Zeita twinkled. As they sat down on a bench, and he lit a cigarette, a sense of unreality gripped her. How was Boaz Kashtan connected to this loop of death? And if so, why should she be surprised?

He exhaled a stream of smoke and moved closer until

their shoulders almost touched. "Last I heard you were the kibbutz rebel. Enlisted in the army instead of doing National Service like the good girls."

"That was a long time ago. What about you?"

In the flare of the cigarette, his face slackened into bleak folds. "The usual routine—army service, then a trek around the Far East. I really got my act together when I studied painting." He brightened. "Bet you don't know we're neighbors." He pointed to the lights of the artists' village below.

"Now I know. So what?"

"You've never noticed my kitschy crap in the hotel dining room?"

"How come I haven't seen you up there?"

He glanced around at the hedges, cardboard silhouettes in the moonlight. Aside from the crickets, they were surrounded by silence. Wisps of smoke floated down from the hotel ridge.

He heeled his cigarette. "I keep a low profile. Aside from popping in to see good old Lydia once in a blue moon, I need to keep my memories of this place on a firm leash. Who knows where they might drag me."

Rachel felt her insides turn sour. "I know where they drag me." She slid further away from him. She knew she should just leave and wipe him out of her life once more, but curiosity, and yes, she admitted, the pull of the past, kept her glued to the bench. Her hand tightened on the knife handle.

"Tell me something."

"Anything, Little Rachel."

"Why did you do it? Then. To me."

149

His face emptied out like when he was a child. The eyes grew stark, like black holes.

"I wish I could tell you, but I can't. I erase those things from my mind. I guess I never had a chance to apologize, did I? Well, I'm apologizing now." He held out his hand, but she ignored it and wrapped her arms around her body.

"Fine. I deserve that." He fished another cigarette out of his sweatshirt pocket. "You're some kind of shrink, aren't you? Well, you should be able to figure out why I behaved the way I did. It's a cliché. The battered child, and all that. And your parents were so perfect, so loving…"

"They were crazy about you. So was Lydia."

He sighed and took a deep drag of the cigarette. "Yes, they were good to me." He stood up and began pacing, staring at the pinpricks of light from the village. "Lydia, with her Italian ices and Aviva and Nate with real American M&Ms your Aunt Claire shipped over. How is she, by the way?"

"Loud and bitchy as usual. She's still sending over those M&Ms to my nieces and nephews."

"How's Michael?"

"Studying Torah and raising goats on a hilltop in the West Bank." As if he really cares, she thought, the egocentric bastard.

He ignored her. "Do you know what it's like keeping a secret from you spoiled kibbutz kids? The beatings, the scorched iron on my ass? I was the outsider, the misfit. What had I done, I thought, to deserve such abuse? Maybe I really was bad."

"Maybe your parents were bad."

"I suppose." He paused. "You all meant well, I guess." He bent down and savagely ripped a weed from the soil. "One day Lydia saw my bruises. Practically made me undress, right there in that house." He gestured towards the cottage. "Swore up and down in Italian, then wheeled herself over to Reb Elijah's house."

"She told him about the abuse."

Boaz snorted. "What do you think? They were thick as thieves. Never found out what there was between them, probably never will. Anyway, he confronted my parents. You can imagine what they did to me then." He slumped down again.

She remained silent, attempting to pry out some pity through the layers of her old fear of him.

He breathed deeply and shut his eyes. "But it was nothing compared to what came afterwards."

"What came afterwards was what you did to me."

"Yeah, yeah, well…I told you I'm sorry about that. I must've been a crazy little kid."

Rachel sensed that he was acting out the role of the contrite adult looking back on his childhood peccadilloes. But it was all lip service. He immediately went back to the groove of his own hurts.

"Should I tell you the rest?" His voice was mocking now. "Mustn't speak ill of the dead and all that?"

She nodded.

"In his wisdom, Reb Elijah decided that our family didn't

fit into Kerem El Happy Families. We were sociopaths, dysfunctional…forgot exactly what he said. The bottom line was we had to get out." He flicked ash onto the ground. "So much for Jewish compassion."

Rachel shivered in the night air, reminded of what Shmaya had written in his confession, how the Rebbe had demanded he divorce Malkie: a clean excision, a lopping off with no compromises.

Boaz sighed. "I saw him, you know, Reb Elijah."

"When?"

"At the Shabbat HaGadol sermon. Couldn't resist. He was at his prime, all fire and brimstone. Wanted to change the world and nail the bad guys. Only sometimes…". His voice dropped to a murmur. "He nailed us good guys instead."

"What happened to you after you left the kibbutz?"

" Foster homes, some better, some worse."

"And your parents?"

"Dead. No love lost there." His jaw tightened and his eyes narrowed to slits. Then he turned to her. "But let bygones be bygones. I've found a way to reclaim my life, to heal instead of hurt. Come down to Zeita and I'll tell you about my organization." He chuckled. "Maybe even rope you in as a member."

"What organization?"

"*The Olive Branch*," he said, "for Arab-Jewish co-existence. It's right up your alley."

"Why do you say that?" she asked warily.

He smiled, his teeth gleaming in the moonlight. "Justice,

fairness, helping the underdog. That's always been your thing, hasn't it? After all, you adopted me, didn't you?"

He touched the scar on her cheek. "Hey," he said teasingly. "You look like you've been through the wars."

She slapped his hand away. "You're despicable."

"Come on, you've always taken things too seriously."

"It's a serious world we live in. Maybe you should wake up to that fact."

"What do you mean?"

She leaned over and cut off a sprig of mint with the kitchen knife. "I can't help wondering about you," she said. "Reb Elijah destroyed whatever happiness you had in this place. And Lydia, your great friend? She didn't help you. Couldn't influence the Rebbe's decision to expel your family. Brought it on, actually, by her interference."

"What are you implying, Little Rachel?" he asked softly.

She took a deep breath. "I'm not implying anything; I'm saying it straight out. The two people who ruined your life are both dead."

CHAPTER SIXTEEN

As though caught in a fog that steals in from the sea, blurring the contours of the landscape, Rachel tried to find a footing. The soul-numbing events of the past few days had driven more distraught clients to her sitting room, and she had doubts about the solace she provided. However, there was one promise she intended to keep; driving Malkie to visit Shmaya.

A blazing sun anchored her to earth. No fog there. She squinted through the glare at the Tirat HaCarmel mental hospital, a white cube of a structure that shimmered in the heat. Thrust up against the mountain, it seemed to shrink away from the rest of the town like a pariah.

Malkie reached into the back seat for a freshly-laundered prayer shawl.

"Sure you feel up to it?" Rachel asked.

"That's the third time you've asked." Malkie linked an arm through hers as they ploughed through waves of heat. "Shmaya's still my husband."

"For now."

Malkie reached up and adjusted Rachel's bandage with cool fingers. "Not again, please. Let me get through this day in one piece." Her voice was crisper and more authoritative, as if layers of tragedy had fused into hard sediment.

"You could file for divorce. He's in no mental state to grant you one." They both knew that Jewish law gave the husband the power to grant or withhold a divorce, but that in the case of mental or coma-ridden patients, this power was invalidated.

Malkie stiffened. Sweat was beading around her black headscarf. "This isn't the time to discuss it. I'm going to visit my husband now."

Rachel raised her hands in the air. "Okay, truce. I promise."

They stepped into an air-conditioned lobby painted in ice-cream hues of strawberry and lime. Children's drawings hung on the walls and rattan chairs were grouped around coffee tables. A thick-waisted woman with *Iris* embroidered on the pocket of her yellow smock, leaned against the counter of the nurse's station, tapping a pen against her teeth and leafing through a magazine.

"*Shalom*," Rachel said, "We're here to see a patient— Shmaya Catz."

The nurse straightened up and blinked a few times, appraising Malkie who was swathed in black like a Greek widow. Compassion vied with curiosity in her glance.

"Yeah, well, I'll tell them you're here." She buzzed the intercom.

An orderly led them down a glass-walled hallway through which ranks of banana groves could be seen marching towards a slash of sea. As one corridor led to the next, the pastels faded to institutional gray, as though the inmates in the maximum security wing were already bleached of color. Outside a steel door, the orderly nodded to a guard with a walkie-talkie and a pistol in his belt. Rachel realized that her visits to mental hospitals had never included the murderers' wing.

Unlocking the door, the guard turned to Rachel. "Only one visitor. The wife."

"Look officer," she said. She'd nourished a wild idea—to accompany Malkie, concoct an excuse to be alone with Shmaya and angle in on his so-called confession. "*Giveret* Catz is very tense about this visit and I'm her therapist." Having told this white lie, she might as well slather it in black. "She's so distraught I don't know what she might do in there."

The guard sneered indulgently, as if her lie were amateurish compared to what he usually heard. "This place is filled with therapists, *Giveret*. She don't need another one. She goes in alone, or she don't go in at all."

Exasperated, she turned to Malkie. "Sure you want to go through with this?" Ignoring her, her friend stared at a door at the end of yet another corridor, as though studying a dead-end future.

"I'll go back to reception then," Rachel said to no one in particular. Retracing her steps, she returned to the colorful walls of the living. Iris was pouring a cup of coffee from a machine on the counter.

"Want some?"

"That would be great."

Iris stared at her, finger poised on the button of the machine. She wore chunky rings that reminded Rachel of Lydia. "What happened to you?"

Rachel's hand flew to her charred hair. "This? Just an accident." She decided that a gawk at the murderer's wife would have to satisfy Iris' curiosity for the moment.

"Accident? I'll bet." Like an expert barmaid, Iris whisked a cup of cappuccino across the counter.

"That kibbutz of yours." Her voice dropped to a whisper as she jerked her chin in the direction of the corridor. "Shame. Her own husband murders her father!" As she shook her head, dark hair streaked with blonde shifted in scallops around her cheeks.

"You know what they say?"

"Who's 'they'?"

Iris steamed ahead. "That he's a homo and the rabbi nixed him for good."

Rachel nearly choked on her drink. "Where did you hear that?"

Iris chuckled. "Believe me, sweetie, there are no secrets in *this* place."

Rachel could believe it if Iris exemplified patient confidentiality. She wondered how far the news had spread and whether she could keep it from reaching Malkie.

But Iris had moved on. "What's with your kibbutz, anyway? Some kind of curse or something?" She grinned and slapped her hand on the counter. "Hey, I know someone from there."

Rachel tried to smile back, but the watery coffee combined with Iris' garrulousness made her stomach churn. "Really?"

Iris snuggled down in her swivel chair.

"Must've been…what…twenty years ago. I was a student

nurse, and she was a patient. We got real friendly."

"What was wrong with her?"

Iris lowered her voice. "Depression. Couldn't get pregnant. Had treatment after treatment, but nothing worked." Her eyes scrunched at the memory. "The reason we got friendly was I was in the same fix. I knew what it was like."

The coffee stuck in Rachel's throat like tar as she remembered month after month of clockwork periods, her parents' tactful questions, Nahum's accusations. The child that never came.

She forced her thoughts back to Iris. "Who was it, you said?"

"I didn't say." She laughed at her own joke. "Name's Hadassah. Big woman." The nurse sketched balloons in the air in front of her own ample chest.

Twenty years ago. Yoel, Hadassah and Mordechai's only son.

"But that was a long time ago," Rachel said. "Her son's going to be married."

Iris waved her hand dismissively. "Oh, I know all that. She told me when she checked in here about six weeks ago." She made it sound as if Hadassah had casually checked into a motel for the night.

"She was here?"

Why hadn't Hadassah mentioned it? Maybe it paled in the aftermath of the Rebbe's murder, when she was clearly more terrified than depressed.

Iris nodded, eyes gleaming. "Yep. Depression again. Showed up in the middle of my shift. We hugged and kissed plenty, I can tell you. Poured out our hearts to each other like sisters. She sat just where you're sitting now. Couldn't cry a tear, she said. 'All my tears are dried up, Iris,' she told me."

"Why was that?"

The nurse's eyes darted around the waiting room.

"That rabbi of yours that was murdered…you know, by *him*." She yanked her head in the direction of the security wing, "gave a ruling about her son that made her and her husband crazy. He nixed the boy's marriage with the religious rigmarole these rabbis do. Not that I'm against religion, God forbid, I light candles every Friday night, I swear." Iris' mascaraed eyes widened in alarm.

"Don't worry. I'm not going to turn you in to the Inquisition," Rachel snapped. "What do you mean, the Rebbe 'nixed' her son's marriage?"

Iris looked wary. "I have a big mouth. I shouldn't be telling you these things."

"Come on, Iris." Rachel flashed a confiding smile. "I'm a therapist myself. People are always telling me things."

Iris laughed. "Oh well…I suppose it's okay then." She leaned her elbows on the counter and cleared her throat.

"I don't know the ins and outs but it has something to do with the boy's birth. Something not kosher there. Hadassah is shy talking about this stuff, like all the religious gals." She eyed Rachel's jeans and sandals critically. "Well, not you, I guess."

Rachel needed to think. According to Iris, Reb Elijah had been an impediment to Yoel's dream *shidduch*. Yet Hadassah had seemed so animated when talking about the upcoming marriage. Was it because the impediment no longer existed?

"Have you spoken to her since?"

Iris shrugged. "You know how it is. Ships crossing in the night and all that. She had a few sessions with a shrink, got medication and left. But we'll always have that special bond."

Rachel knew she had no chance of gaining access to the files of the Tira shrink. "And what about you?" she asked. "Did your problem ever work out?"

An impish smile lit up the sallow face. "It sure did. I got a sperm donation. And you know what? Our daughter is the spittin' image of my husband! Isn't that something?"

* * *

After dropping Malkie off at the kindergarten, Rachel stepped through the empty waiting room into Ozeri's office. The curtains were drawn against the sun and the doctor was scowling at the computer screen, legs crossed on his desk while an ancient air-conditioner roared out blasts of frozen air.

"Why didn't you tell me Hadassah Levy was hospitalized for depression six weeks ago?"

"Rachel!" His legs flew down from the desk. He smoothed his wiry hair and folded his hands, as if reassembling the professional parts of himself. "Please sit down." He gestured to the water cooler in the corner. "What about a cold drink? I'll never get used to these erratic spring days."

She shook her head, aware of what she must look like,

sweaty and disheveled, in the skimpy jeans and tee shirt she'd worn to the hospital, while Ozeri had an ironed, seamless look that projected total control of his environment.

"You promised to pass on all the information about my clients. Now it turns out that Hadassah Levy suffered from fertility problems."

"Fertility problems?" He looked genuinely puzzled. "I don't know anything about that. It must've been before my time."

"And her depression? That's not before your time."

The doctor relaxed, clearly on his own turf, his lips tilting upwards in a sculpted smile. This was a man, Rachel realized, who didn't welcome surprises.

"After the Rebbe's funeral, we feared a collapse on all fronts. I apologize if I didn't dot every *i* or cross every *t*, but since then, I've been buried in work, as you can imagine. By the way" he continued, "Hadassah is very pleased with you. She's told me so on a number of occasions."

Once again, she experienced a swell of dislike for the man's facile smarminess.

"I understand you prescribed a tranquilizer. Which one? Lorivan? Valium?"

His gaze flickered momentarily towards the computer screen. "You may not be familiar with it. Lexium, a new generation SSRI, perfectly suited to dysthymia patients."

"Except that Hadassah reacted badly to it and you didn't prescribe an alternative drug. And you're right," Rachel said. "I've never heard of it." Like most of the medications her clients had mentioned. Based on what they told her, Ozeri could be orbiting in pharmaceutal outer space.

Ozeri's voice turned velvet. "As a medical man, it's my responsibility to be up on the latest drugs."

"Especially if they're unlicensed in this country."

His features locked into a frown. "You've lost me. I don't know what you're talking about."

She sat down on the white-painted chair opposite him, too angry to pick and choose her words. "It took me a while to figure out you've been taking advantage of people's distress by peddling illegal tranquilizers."

Teeth gleamed against dusky skin as he gave a soft chuckle. "Where did you hear that nonsense?"

"My clients usually tell me the truth."

"Ah," he said, "client-therapist privilege. That puts me at a disadvantage, doesn't it?"

"Does it matter how I found out?"

"There's nothing to find out." His face smoothed into a teak mask. "Since we're being frank, you continue to arouse my concern; the after-effects of your nervous breakdown, for instance."

The air-conditioner roared inside her head. She stabbed her nails into her palm.

"I thought you took that into account when the Secretariat asked me to come here."

He waggled a pedagogical finger in the air. "Perhaps we overestimated the extent of your recovery. Your traumatic experiences have clearly proven too much for you."

She wanted to smear away his placid face, but she kept her voice steady.

"I think we both have a lot to learn about each other's backgrounds."

It was a shot in the dark, but it hit home. At her words, a shade descended over his eyes. "Are you threatening me?"

She stood up. "What kind of threat can an unbalanced woman like me pose to an upstanding doctor like you?"

Ozeri rose, circled his desk and opened the door. For the first time she noticed how lean and supple he was, how light on his feet.

"Please leave my office."

"I'd like nothing more." As she walked into the waiting room, she turned to face him. "Let me make myself clear, Reuven. If there's anything about you that turns out to be… let's say…unprofessional, I'll make sure the kibbutz finds out. And the police, as well."

* * *

The stones of the old quarry lay pearly in the moonlight. Winding the blanket around their bodies, he nuzzled Alona's hair, which always smelled of faraway countries, spicy as seawater. No matter how hard he scrubbed, he could never get rid of the undertow of sweat that lived beneath his skin. She loved it, though, could lick his skin for hours.

" *Ya habibti,*" he whispered in her ear, "Wake up. Time to go."

She snuggled closer to him, and insinuated her hand between his legs. Flames seared his balls.

"Not yet," she whispered, "It's so cozy here. Like Adam and Eve."

Sighing, he removed her hand, lifted it to his mouth and kissed her fingers before reaching for a pack of cigarettes. As his lighter flared, he sensed her retreat, as if her pores were closing up like flowers.

"Alona." He reached for her, but she'd turned her back. "Alona, don't do this." *Don't make me beg,* he wanted to say. No woman had ever made him beg, and neither would she.

Her curls stirred in the night breeze and she shivered beneath the blanket. "I can't do this anymore, all this sneaking around. Everyone thinks I'm such a hard-hearted bitch."

She turned around to face him, clutching the blanket around her shoulders. "I've gone through hell since Lydia died, and Reb Elijah…despite the way he treated us…I see Malkie's suffering." Her eyes reflected pools of moonlight as she stared at the distant mountains. "It was a terrible thing we did, Taleb."

He grabbed her shoulder and twisted her around so sharply she let out a cry of pain. "We did nothing. Get that through your head once and for all."

"Let me go." Her voice was an animal growl; it could've been a night creature rustling through the undergrowth. "See what's happening to us? We're poisoning each other. Look," she said, stroking his face, "I thought we'd build a life away from this hole. I've been ready for years. You're the one who can't leave the village, your family, your mother. I don't know how much longer I'm willing to put up with it."

Taleb heard the ragged note of despair in her tone. He kissed her and stroked her hair. "It won't be long now, *ya'ayouni*. I'm onto something that will make me a lot of money. It won't be long now, I promise. Then we can get on a plane to Europe, America, wherever you want."

"But I have enough for us to go *now*," Alona pleaded, "What's mine is yours, you know that."

"And *you* know I won't live off a woman."

"My macho man," she chuckled, running her hands over his body. He felt the shift in his loins again and ducked beneath the blanket. As he drew her to him, tasted her salt with his tongue and heard her indrawn breath, he knew that he was trapped in a circle of fire that threatened to engulf them both.

CHAPTER SEVENTEEN

RON Kozma called Absalom into his office, the first time they'd met face to face since Lydia's death. The Superintendant had been holed up at Police Headquarters in Jerusalem in the wake of the spiraling terror war.

Tension lines scored his razor-smooth cheeks as he clicked a monogrammed pen on his desk.

"How're you doing?" He gestured for Absalom to take a seat, then scratched his forehead and opened a folder on his desk.

"I've been studying the Lydia di Rossi file. All in all, I'd say there's a pretty convincing case for suicide."

Absalom was ready. "Aren't you jumping to conclusions?"

Ron's eyes were red with fatigue. " That was one depressed lady, God bless her soul. A cripple, her oldest friend murdered by that Shmaya character." His voice rose and the muscles in his neck tightened. "But she doesn't accept that, does she? She's convinced there's a mysterious killer that did the rabbi in. She gets the guilts because she gave him bad advice. Even her friend, what's her name?" He rummaged through the papers in the folder.

"Rachel Shine."

"Yeah. Even she thought di Rossi was losing it." He paused

to take a deep breath. "Then, there's the Holocaust angle. Wasn't she supposed to speak at the ceremony?"

"Yes."

Ron beamed. "That clinches it then. Everyone's forgotten her, no one even bothers to pick her up for the ceremony. She wheels herself up to the hotel…"

"In a *khamsin* with zero visibility." Absalom said dryly.

Ron waved him away. "According to this," he said stabbing the folder with the pen, "she was a very determined woman. All of a sudden, the loneliness hits her, the rabbi's dead because of her, those Holocaust flashbacks—God know what she went through—come over her. Life isn't worth living. Bingo." He snapped his fingers. "She throws herself over the cliff."

"When a fire just happens to break out." Absalom closed his eyes briefly; it wasn't easy to wipe out the sight of the charred twisted body or the rings that had survived the fire, blackened gold on matchstick fingers.

Ron leaned forward across the desk. "Fires start all the time in a *khamsin*. Don't you remember a couple of years ago….?"

"I know…an electric spark from a car nearly burnt us down."

"So you agree with me." A triumphant grin spread along Ron's face.

Absalom shook his head. When Ron was on a roll, there was very little he could do to stop him. "That's not what I said."

"Find me an alternative. An accident?"

Absalom smiled. "Wishful thinking."

Ron clicked the pen furiously. "I know what you're driving at but I don't buy it. Who the hell wanted her dead? Why shove her off a cliff? An old lady like that, in a wheelchair; anyone could get rid of her in a hundred simpler ways."

"Just listen for a second." Absalom almost believed that they were partners again, bouncing ideas off each other before the rift that had torn them apart. "You're saying that the break-in, the fire and the victim's death were coincidental?"

"Each of these incidents has a logical explanation."

"Logical." He knew how Ron clung to logic like a cloak. The problem was that he often twisted the facts to suit his needs.

"Take the break-in." Ron rapped his pen on the table. "Every junkie in the area knows the *kibbutzniks* never lock their doors and that they'd be up at the ceremony."

"There were valuables that weren't even touched."

Ron gave a thumbs-down gesture. "These guys are junkies, not antique dealers."

"What about the vandalism?"

Ron snorted. "They don't find cash, they get mad and rip up the place."

Absalom didn't answer for a long time. Noises from the operations room filtered in; phones ringing, photocopiers, shouts and bursts of laughter, and in the background, as always, the drone of the radio.

Ron finally broke. "What do we know about the handyman?"

"Name's Taleb Mahajna from Jabal. Been working there

since he was a teenager."

"Anyone check out why he never showed?"

"Food poisoning."

"Maybe he was busy killing the old lady."

Absalom sighed. Whenever Ron was pushed to the wall, he jumped into "the Arab did it" mode.

"So all of a sudden she *was* killed?"

Ron raised his hands in a gesture of defeat. "Okay, okay, Ab. What do *you* think happened?"

He took a deep breath. It was a victory of sorts, but he didn't know how long it would last. "I'd like to look more closely into the old lady's theory about the rabbi's killer."

Ron's eyebrows nearly hit the ceiling. "For Pete's sake, Ab, you investigated that murder. Shmaya Catz confessed. He's sitting in the loony bin crocheting *yarmulkes* as we speak."

"It's only a small detour, Ron."

"During a terrorist epidemic?" He slammed his palms on the table. "We have a civil rebellion on our hands. Our good citizens are burning tires and blocking intersections in protest—not against those fucking terrorists, against *us*. We don't protect them enough. Isn't that a laugh?"

Though Ron usually contained his passion, he was blowing like a geyser.

"I can't turn my back on a shaky case…"

"That's just it. It's not a shaky case. There's no evidence whatsoever that this woman was murdered. Get it out of your head."

Absalom felt his pulse surge. "So you're going to put me at

an intersection with a water cannon?"

Ron shouted. "I'm going to put you wherever I need to put you. We're on red alert here, Ab."

"That's nothing new," he said bitterly. "It's never stopped us from catching criminals. We even did it together sometimes."

Ron sighed. "Come on, Ab. You've always been a team player, a good guy, the best."

It was true. That's why he'd acquiesced in Ron's corruption or when Christina returned to Denmark. Team player. Nice guy. It made him sick.

"The Commissioner is leaning on me," Ron complained. "Starting tomorrow, all leaves are cancelled. We'll be working twelve-hour shifts."

Absalom moved to the door. "I'll work your twelve-hour shifts. But I'll be adding two on my own time. I'm not giving this one up, Ron."

He slammed the door as he left.

* * *

Rachel strode down the mountain. She had to get her limbs moving and her thoughts clear. Kerem El was sucking her in just when she should be leaving. Still, how could she abandon clients whose scars were constantly being ripped open by drive-by shootings and so-called martyrs blowing themselves up in shopping malls? She above all, should know how deep these scars were. Then, there was Lydia. She had deserted her old friend just when she was needed most. If she'd believed

Lydia's theory of an alternative killer, Lydia might still be alive.

Lost in thought, she found herself at the wrought iron gate that led to the artists' village. The lane beyond was lined with whimsical trees and flowers forged in metal, contrasting with the riotous bougainvillea that hugged the stone walls. In the main square, the French restaurant that had stood on the ruins of an old mosque had metamorphosed into an Argentinian steakhouse. A group of German tourists stood respectfully as their guide gestured towards the cobbled lanes and stone steps winding down to the maze of old Arab houses.

Rachel hadn't visited Zeita in years. More and more houses were being snapped up by celebrities whose connection to art was tenuous at most; T.V. personalities, rock stars, even a prominent banker. Ambling through the village made her uneasy. Though it had lain in ruins for decades after the War of Independence and the artists who'd come to settle there weren't responsible for the expulsion of the Mahajna clan, Rachel still felt the presence of the original inhabitants float beside her in a whiff of za'atar and the ghost of a *muezzin's* wail.

She'd stumbled on Boaz Kashtan's studio before she was even aware of it. His name was carved on a plywood sign leading to a scraggly eucalyptus grove at the end of a dirt track. Sheds dotted the back yard, while a rusty kiln and twisted canvases littered the approach to the house. She hesitated. The house was isolated, and it was midday, the siesta time. Trying to shuffle off her fear, she convinced herself that Boaz could no longer hurt her. Why would he? Like so much else, her apprehension was a holdover from the past. As long as she was here, guided by her unconscious mind no doubt, she would try and press him more about Lydia. She ducked into the shade of the porch and riffled her fingers through the chimes that swung from the doorpost. Down in the village, a dog barked.

Boaz looked startled to see her. Sleep had matted his long hair and the reek of cigarette smoke spilled out into the drowsy noon air. He coughed into a rag which he then thrust into the side pocket of his sweats, blinked in the bright sunlight and stared. "God, you *are* beautiful. That light on your hair." He raised his hand to touch her, but she sidestepped him and scooted inside.

"Oh, shut up."

He grinned. "Excuse the mess. Let me just…"

He stumbled across the room, picking up newspapers and mugs of dried coffee, while Rachel sat down on a futon and gazed at the walls on which Boaz's paintings hung in splashy display; huge canvases splattered with crimson and black, like a slaughterhouse from hell.

"This stuff is not like the paintings you sell to the hotel."

He grabbed a cigarette from a pack on the floor. "Gideon wants that shit—soothing and uncontroversial. It's no crime signing my name to pictures other people like."

"And it's good money."

He laughed coarsely. "Yeah. That's no crime either." He flashed a conspiratorial grin as if they'd just stolen the toilet paper from the bathroom underneath the *shul,* one of their childhood escapades.

"An idealist like you," she said, shaking her finger. "Naughty, naughty." If only she could attribute his filthy surroundings to the fact that he was an artist and idealist, but she realized that he was simply a slob.

He snapped his fingers and pointed at her. "I've always loved that about you, Rachel! Quick on the uptake! Hey! Where are my manners? How about some coffee?" He heaved himself out of the beanbag that served as a chair. "You still keep kosher?"

She made a see-saw gesture with her hand. "So-so." She knew full well that 'so-so' kosher is like being a little bit pregnant. Either you are or you aren't.

"I'll take my chances with your coffee."

Barefoot, he shuffled into the kitchen where she heard him fumbling through cupboards followed by swishes of water from a tap.

She got up, crossed the room and flung open a window to let in some air. The shed directly in her line of vision was plastered with stickers like football streamers in a teen's bedroom. Slogans in jagged letters of red and black—Boaz's favorite colors by the look of things: *Remember 1948* and *The Olive Branch*. Curlicues of green Arabic letters underlined the slogans in an upward swirl.

"You're serious about this organization of yours." She turned as he handed her a mug of black, thick coffee.

Boaz settled his muscular body on the beanbag, tossed his hair and lit up another cigarette. He beamed, sparking the dimple in his handsome face. "You remember, I see. The one I told you about during our rendezvous at Lydia's."

"So now it was a rendezvous, was it?"

He ignored her, his eyes fixed in the gleam of a fanatic homing in on his obsession.

"*The Olive Branch* is pragmatic, not some airy-fairy scheme; to restore the land rights of the Jabal-a-Zeit Arabs, allowing them to return to their homes here in Zeita."

At her snicker, his eyebrows bunched in annoyance. "That's a typical reaction, though I didn't expect it from you." He hauled himself up and fished among a stash of papers in a bowl. "Maybe you'll take me more seriously if you look at some of these names." He thrust a handful at her.

Under *The Olive Branch* letterhead and a brief description of the organization's goals, about fifty signatures were affixed to every page. Out of curiosity, she scanned the names as Boaz's bare heels paced the floor at the perimeter of her vision.

Though most of the signatories were Jewish intellectuals, a few of whose names she recognized, there was a sprinkling of Arab names as well. One in particular snagged her attention.

"Who's this Rajoub person?" She pointed to the name and his pacing slowed. He turned around and sank down next to her on the futon. As he leaned over her shoulder to get a better look, she could smell anxiety beneath the sweat and cigarette smoke.

"Rajoub?" He shrugged. "Never heard of him."

She peered closely at the signature. "Or her. The first name's pretty illegible. I've come across that name, though."

Her mind roved back to the envelope in her desk drawer. *Muna Rajoub and her dead baby.*

"I don't know what you're talking about," he mumbled, his irritation evident in the flick of his hair.

"Why are you so annoyed? I thought you wanted to impress me with these names."

"I'm not annoyed," he said, with a hostile stare. "Stop pinning me down like a damn butterfly in a glass case."

Rachel whipped out her therapist arsenal. "Now you're hostile. I only asked a question."

He grabbed the papers and stood up. The hunch of his shoulders and the slicing motion of his arm aroused images of Boaz as a child, erupting like fireworks, instantaneous and spectacular, scattering sparks in every direction.

"Did you come here to torment me? I bet somebody sent you." He fumbled through the petitions and shook one in front of her face. "Why didn't you ask about *him*?" He shouted out the name of a famous left-wing author.

The swift escalation of anger frightened her. "I think you should calm down." She placed her coffee cup on the floor and stood up to face him. A small muscle twitched his upper lip. She reached for her bag. "Thanks for the hospitality."

He seized her shoulder, but she shook him off and strode to the door. "Rachel," he said, with a pleading note in his voice. He was as predictable, as boring as an Israeli summer.

She whirled around. "You don't understand what came over you, you're sorry you hurt me. See? I know the script backwards, forwards and sideways."

He hung his head and picked through his pockets for a cigarette. "And I thought we were getting along so well the other night at Lydia's," he said in a choked voice. "I thought that maybe we'd even…"

"What? Take up where we left off when we were ten years old?"

"Something like that," he mumbled.

She opened the door and the chimes burst into song. "See you around, Boaz. Maybe one day I'll even sign one of your petitions."

* * *

Dusk was falling by the time she'd made the rounds of the dairy, the chicken runs, the synagogue plaza and finally, the trek up to the hotel. She let her lungs and muscles take over in an attempt to burn away the memory of Boaz' unpredictable behavior.

It dragged her back to that steamy summer when they were playing hide and seek in the cowsheds. Suddenly, he had raced up from behind and shoved her into a heap of mud, held her down and tied her arms behind her back, oblivious to her shrieks, which were soon stifled by the muck in her mouth and nostrils and the lowing of the cows. When he turned her over roughly and straddled her, she spied the jagged shard in his upswept fist. Through a pitch of terror, her gaze fastened onto the glint of sunlight on that scythe of glass, how alive it was, while Boaz' eyes were lifeless.

Somehow, the sliced flesh of her cheek, the streams of blood mingling with cow dung were less powerful than her sense of abandonment and shame. No wonder she had repressed his family's banishment from the kibbutz. In her child's mind, it was all her fault.

She swallowed deep breaths of the night smells, lilac and jasmine lulling her back to equilibrium as she stepped onto the veranda of the chalet. Unlocking the door, she switched on the lights, and saw the familiar tapestried leisure, cleansed of fire damage, the bowl of fruit and silver-wrapped chocolate on the coffee table.

It was only when she turned on the bedside lamp that she spotted the doll. It lay on the pillow, tucked under the neat fold of top sheet and blanket, as if a loving parent had sung it to sleep; a Hassidic doll with wispy sidelocks and silken skullcap, the kind sold in every tourist and hotel shop. Gingerly, she picked up the figure in its black frock coat and trousers, white stockings and black plastic shoes covering pigeon-toed feet. Its head lolled like a broken sparrow.

She gasped and dropped it on the floor. Prickles layered her scalp and her knees buckled. While her gaze jerked away from the obscenity on the floor, in her mind, the severed head of the suicide bomber coalesced with visions of the Rebbe's corpse .

It was a crude, tasteless prank, the kind one of her teenage clients might pull to test her boundaries. Yet, it took a shrewd sadist to break the neck of a *haredi* doll, so reminiscent of that severed head. No teenager she knew was capable of doing that.

CHAPTER EIGHTEEN

HE sank down on the sitting room sofa, struck by her isolation, the stiff unwelcoming brocade and the velvet silence of the night. Like with Boaz in the cowshed, the killer could attack her the way he'd broken the doll's neck. He'd already killed twice. Lydia's phantom murderer was sprouting skin and sinews.

She sprang up and checked the door. The fact that it was locked gave her cold comfort: the intruder had a key and could come and go at will, someone who was aware of her Jerusalem trauma, which meant just about everyone. But who besides Absalom Brill and Miri knew she was pursuing a murderer?

Is that what I'm doing? As she moved towards the coffee-maker, she realized with a jolt that she had shouldered Lydia's mission. Her analyst's mind tried to disentangle her motives. Was it a way of clinging to Lydia, guilt at having abandoned her? Or was it an excuse to linger on at Kerem El and slink back into her childhood?

She carried the coffee cup onto the veranda, covered the floor with newspapers, then reached for a chunk of oak and studied its thickness and grain. In the silence of the night, she whittled and peeled as her mind settled into its unconscious ebb and flow.

Once again, Boaz Kashtan hove into her thoughts, his features twisted with hatred for the Rebbe and for Lydia, the Rebbe's accomplice in his expulsion from Eden. The claim he was searching for something in Lydia's cottage was clearly a lie; he was more than capable of trashing her house in a fit of rage. As for Rachel herself, despite his so-called affection, he had hated her when they were children and he hated her now. He'd gone ballistic at the mention of the name Rajoub.

She laid her tools on the table and returned to the bedroom, swerving her glance away from the doll. She retrieved the Rebbe's envelope.

There it was; the obituary for Muna Rajoub and her baby from Jebalya. Googling *Muna Rajoub, Jebalya*, she was astonished by the slew of newspaper accounts that flashed on the screen—*AP, the New York Times, The Guardian*. A major story. She scrolled down to the local dailies first.

The story from *Haaretz* was filed in Gaza City on July 8, 1992. Rachel did the math. Twelve years ago, at the height of the first intifada, the Palestinian uprising, stones that had led to bullets and trails of bodies.

Gaza City, July 8, 1992—In a raid on a house in the Jebalya refugee camp yesterday, a 24-year-old pregnant woman, Muna Rajoub, died after suffering a miscarriage. In the same operation, the woman's 81-year-old grandfather, died of alleged heart failure. The soldiers who carried out the raid are suspected of causing the deaths through neglect and possible abuse.

The soldiers broke into the Rajoub house searching for suspected terrorists. An investigation is underway regarding allegations that the soldiers refused to evacuate her to a hospital, causing her to bleed to death and lose her unborn child.

World leaders, including the Israeli government, mourned the loss of innocent lives and the brutality of the occupation. Rachel felt nauseated.

Scrolling down further, she browsed the entries for the Rajoubs, an extensive Palestinian clan. One name caught her eye. Professor Amal Rajoub from Haifa University had conducted research on gender in Islamic society. A Muslim female professor was unusual, to say the least. Perhaps she was the Rajoub signatory on Boaz' petition, the one which had agitated him so much. She noted the professor's details for future use; she might be able to enlighten her.

First things first; the doll. Wrapping her hand in plastic, she plucked the thing from the floor and inserted it into a garbage bag, together with the pillowcase she stripped from her bed, sealing it with duct tape. Now, Absalom Brill might start taking her seriously. With a sigh of relief, she imprisoned it in a bureau drawer out of sight. Then, she shoved a heavy armchair against the front door and collapsed shivering on the bed.

CHAPTER NINETEEN

s Rachel returned to the chalet after lunch the next day, a woman was waiting for her on the veranda, smoking a cigarette and jiggling a veiny mini-skirted leg. A barrette swept ash blonde hair away from a triangular face. Black eyes bled azure eye-liner.

"You're Rachel," she said, jutting out a hand. "Emanuela, Lydia di Rossi's niece. They told me at the office you'd agree to clean out my aunt's cottage and get rid of books and her other junk." She pulled a face. "I have a key."

Rachel's head reeled. *A niece? The office? Who was this woman?*

"This is the first I've heard of a niece." She scoured the woman's face for a resemblance. Perhaps something about the cast of the chin, the smoldering eyes.

Emanuela coughed and waved away a cloud of cigarette smoke. "You were friends with my aunt, right? You know she didn't talk about anything personal. Let's just say that I was one of her big secrets. The Germans got rid of the good di Rossis, but let the lousy branch of the family live." She brushed off an imaginary insect from her tight spandex skirt.

Rachel felt a pang as she pictured Lydia. Perhaps Emanuela might illuminate more about her friend's life story. "You look like you could use something to drink."

Emanuela tossed the cigarette stub on the grass. "Not really. I'd like to get this out of the way." She wriggled her skirt a bit and brushed it off again. Some kind of tic, Rachel thought, as she pointed to her car. Emanuela stared straight ahead, clopping along on her wooden heels.

"How did you find me?"

"A woman in the office gave me the key to my aunt's house right away. She was middle-aged, with a kind of," she patted the top of her head, "rag up here." *Just about anybody.*

She locked smudgy eyes on Rachel's face. "*Nonna* Lydia talked about you all the time. It was always Rachel this and Rachel that. I know she'd want you to be the one to clean out her stuff."

They were silent during the drive down to Lydia's. Emanuela smoked and didn't ask a single question about her aunt or the funeral or the kibbutz, made no comments on the colors that burst forth from every vine and tree, or the sea sparkling in the sun like a sequined turquoise scarf.

In the cottage, Lydia's presence still lingered—the cactuses, the top-heavy book shelves, piles of old bills and receipts— even after Rachel had tried to straighten up the worst of the mess, folding Lydia's clothes and underwear modestly into drawers and cupboards. The slashed mattress had been removed and taken to the junkyard. The herbs on the window ledge in the kitchen had shriveled in their terracotta pots. She wondered about asking Emanuela if she could have them as a keepsake, but the brisk sound of drawers slamming in the living room made her think better of it. Emanuela was evidently not the sentimental type.

She'd already dumped out the contents of the living room drawers and was stuffing papers and photo albums into black garbage bags she'd brought for that purpose. A cigarette was clamped between her teeth like a lollipop.

"Do me a favor," she said, gesturing at the canyons of books. "Pack these in cartons—the office said they'd send some over—and mail them to me. I've left my address…"

"In the office."

Emanuela threw her a suspicious glare. "Yeah. This stuff," she pointed at the garbage bags, "I'll take with me."

It had all gone so quickly, like a tornado scything through her afternoon. Before she could question her further, Emanuela had checked her wristwatch, switched on her mobile and called a taxi. "Look, I gotta run," she said. "Could you help me with these?"

They knotted the bags and dragged them up the footpath to the road. Emanuela lit another cigarette.

"What about Lydia's clothing, furniture, jewelry?" Rachel asked.

She flicked ash onto the lawn as the rumble of the taxi was heard. "I took the jewelry. I'll be in touch with the office for the rest. You can take whatever trinkets you want."

The taxi driver nodded a greeting and loaded the bags into the trunk. Emanuela climbed into the back seat, flashing cellulite thighs, and slammed the door.

"Don't forget to send those books!" she called out as the cab drove away.

CHAPTER TWENTY

THE dining room had been transformed into a palace straight out of the History Channel—the Winter Palace, Versailles—opulence from a bygone era. Perfumed candles floated on lily pads, a string quartet played Albinoni and silver trays gleamed in the soft light as waiters ladled out roast lamb with honey glaze on wild rice. *Cordon bleu Glatt,* Rachel murmured to herself as chuckles rose in her throat like the sizzly liquid Thaddeus Kamienski was pouring into her glass.

She was grateful for the champagne haze that blurred the edges of her consciousness. True, the thirty-day mourning period was over and the kibbutz members had approved the gala by a substantial majority, but Rachel knew it was tantamount to waltzing on the graves of the dead.

Across the table, flanked by a glamorous Irene, Gideon nodded his approval. Alona raised her glass and smiled. Ozeri darted icicles at her, but she didn't care. For the first time in ages, her goblins were banished to their murky glen. It wasn't every day she could wear the burgundy silk blouse that showed just a hint of cleavage, and the diamond stud earrings Aunt Claire had bought her after the divorce. The admiration in Kamienski's periwinkle blue eyes lifted her into a world that was elegant and humane, eons away from murder and garrotted dolls.

He was impressive, she noted, with the good looks that marked international tycoons of a certain age, silver hair swept back from a high forehead, dark-blue suit, stylishly cut. Only the bullish face and the thick fingers resting casually on his mistress' knee hinted at Polish peasant stock. Anya was at least thirty years his junior, a redhead with a model's cheekbone looks, but when she smiled, crooked teeth stained with nicotine indicated that perhaps Kamienski didn't consider her enough of a long-term investment to correct this unfortunate flaw.

Rachel had spent most of the morning with Thaddeus, as he insisted she call him, reassuring him that the mettle of the hotel staff was as flinty as the Carmel cliffs. He dragged her to the death scenes. The jaw muscles in his thick neck strained with anger as she pointed out where Lydia's body had been found. Silently begging Lydia's forgiveness, she repeated the mantra that the old woman's death had been an accident, sparked by confusion and grief.

In the *shul*, Kamienski had wept as he knelt by the *bima;* he'd known the Rebbe well, and his grief seemed genuine. Yet, beneath the skullcap perched on his pile of hair, Rachel could sense his shrewd mind whirring. Should he keep pouring his largesse into this deathtrap? Perhaps he could benefit "his" Jews more by subsidizing their vacations in a less violent setting?

The fabric of wishful thinking and half-truths Rachel wove

was deliberate; yes, the kibbutz was ruptured by the discovery of a murderer in its midst, a schizophrenic who was safely behind lock and key. Yes, the mourning process was taking its toll, but the *kibbutzniks* were God-fearing pragmatists—Thaddeus nodded vigorously at this—and would take up their lives again. She knew that he'd spent the previous afternoon talking to the guests at the hotel and seemed satisfied that the hotel was attentive to their every need.

In the late afternoon, she'd sketched out her treatment strategy over coffee and cake on the hotel veranda. Luckily, a spectacular sunset lit the horizon, shafts of golden light emanating from purple clouds, melting over the green mountains. Thaddeus was smitten. At that moment, Rachel felt guiltless about her whitewash of the facts. Everyone that mattered to her depended on the Hotel Spa. She wouldn't jeopardize their future by confiding to Thaddeus that the tragic deaths were anything other than coincidental.

She emerged from her reverie to the slur of Thaddeus' vodka-soaked Polish consonants as he addressed the diners.

"My dear friends," he said. "How honored I am by your hospitality and warm friendship."

Gideon clinked his glass with a spoon. A chorus of agreement rippled around the table. Even Ozeri's rigid features mellowed. Rachel took another sip of champagne, the buzz in her brain intensifying. Out of the corner of her eye, she glimpsed a blur of people clustered across the room.

"…will consult with the board members and give them my heartfelt recommendation…"

Gideon had begun to fidget and Irene laid a placating hand on his wrist. Alona's gaze was riveted to the doorway of the dining room, where an altercation between the security guard and a group of elderly guests threatened to spiral into a shoving match. At the center of the crowd, a skullcapped old man was trying to break into the dining room.

"Excuse me." Gideon rose, his lean body skimming towards the fracas. By now, all necks were craned in the direction of the melee.

"What's going on?" someone shouted.

The crowd parted and Rachel glimpsed Gideon's vain attempts to pacify the intruder. Throwing off Gideon's arm, the man stumbled towards Rachel's table. As their eyes met, her mind flashed back to that day, over a month ago, when she'd joined him for lunch.

The old man lurched forward, his face mottled with purplish pink stains, raving in Yiddish, "Raisl, Raisl!" he shouted hoarsely, pawing at Rachel's arm. She hugged his heaving shoulders. He reeked of alcohol. "Come sit down over here, by me," she soothed.

His body heaved with coughing. Ozeri propped him up on the other side and together they led him to the table and sat him down. Rachel caught Thaddeus' open-mouthed stare.

Gideon stood on a chair, overlooking the sea of alarmed, upturned faces. He wiped his face with a handkerchief. "Everything is under control, *haverim*. Dr. Ozeri is attending to our guest."

The old man was gasping into Rachel's ear, a mixture

of stinking breath and broken Yiddish she could barely understand. In the babble, she picked up Lydia's name.

"Lydia," she said urgently, "What about Lydia?"

Ozeri had loosened the man's collar and was feeling his pulse. The eyes rolled upwards and drool gathered in the corner of his mouth.

"Call an ambulance," Rachel snapped. The doctor shot her a venomous look, but punched in the number on his cell phone.

Suddenly, the man clutched his chest, his mouth opened in a small round "o" of surprise and crumpled to the floor.

Later, Rachel would recall shoving Ozeri aside and kneeling beside the limp form. As she lifted his chin and placed her mouth over his, nauseated by the alcohol fumes and sputum, all thoughts evaporated as she worked like an automaton, trying to pass the flame of life into him, straining to wipe out every futile death she'd ever mourned—the Rebbe, Lydia, even the suicide bomber who'd blown away bits of her own life.

"Enough, it's enough now." Ozeri grasped her shoulder with surprising tenderness. Thaddeus Kamienski helped her to her feet. Her legs trembled.

Ozeri had resumed his former stance, fingers on the old man's wrist. Before he even spoke the words, Rachel knew the old man was dead.

CHAPTER TWENTY-ONE

A KALEIDOSCOPE of crimson whirled behind her eyes; burgundy silk, a smear of lip gloss, the old man's scarlet cheeks, a wine-stained tablecloth. A gentle hand pushed her head between her knees and whispered. The whispering billowed and flowed into roars and echoes. Strong arms scooped her up and laid her gently on a hard surface. Covered her with something light and cool. Cold, like the corpse. Maybe it was she that was dead.

* * *

At the opposite end of the dining room, Yossi Gottwein jotted down the names and phone numbers of the guests and staff, while the rattle of dishes and the hum of dishwashers from the kitchen provided an air of bizarre domesticity.

"I'll repeat my question. Does anyone here know his name?" Despite his attempts at civility, Absalom was ragged with anger as he struggled to wipe out the memory of Rachel, ashen and shaking.

He rubbed the scars on his face, giving him time to collect himself and to survey the disheveled group slumped at the banquet table. They resembled survivors of the Titanic, marooned on expensive-looking chairs, faces pasty beneath glaring overhead lights. Beneath *No Smoking* signs, Gideon was lighting a pipe and Alona Golan sucked on what seemed like her umpteenth cigarette. Judging from the bottles scattered on the floor, they'd had a go at the champagne as well. A half-empty liter of vodka stood in the center of the table.

A florid-faced man murmured something to Gideon. Clearing his throat, he addressed the policeman in accented English. "His name was Jacob Lifschitz."

"Who might you be, sir?"

Gideon frowned. "Must you trouble our guest, Chief-Inspector? He's been through enough this evening; we all have."

"It is not necessary to protect me, Gideon." Rising to his feet, he extended a fleshy hand to Absalom. "Thaddeus Kamienski at your service." *Polish? Ukrainian?* Absalom wondered. He gestured for Kamienski to resume his seat. "What can you tell us about Mr. Jacob Lifschitz, then?"

From across the table, Alona giggled, drunk, hysterical or both. Frizzy hair tumbled to her shoulders and her cheeks were smeared with mascara. "He's dead. That's all *I* know."

"Shut up," Gideon snapped, and Alona dissolved into her chair, shaking her head and chuckling to herself like a demented geriatric case.

"Go on." He nodded to Kamienski, who had been joined by an anorexic redhead with frightened eyes.

Her hand was swallowed up in Kamienski's paw. "I knew

Jacob for many years; he came from Pomorzany, my town in southern Poland, one of our few Jews that survived the Nazis. He went through the Auschwitz hell together with others. In time, he became the president of the Pomorzany *Landsmanschaft*, the survivors' organization."

"What's his connection to the hotel?"

Kamienski wiped his flushed face with a napkin. "When I established the Trust, the first person I consulted was Jacob. He comprehended the need to compensate our Jews for the calamities my people…yes, the Polish people, had brought down on the Jews."

"Compensate?" Absalom asked.

"Of course that is the wrong word," Kamienski hurried on. "There can be no such thing. But at least a bit of serenity, a dignified old age and suitable medical treatment. Jacob and I decided that the Kerem El Hotel Spa was ideal for our project. And so it has been." He voice faltered as he glanced at the spot where the corpse had lain.

"Any family?"

"A son, who suffers from a rare nerve disease," he said mournfully, as he poured a shot of vodka.

Absalom's distaste for the kibbutz and its members rippled through him. Despite their so-called religiosity—though the way they were carrying on tonight made him wonder—not a *tut-tut* of compassion was heard. Except for the Pole, Absalom thought, none of them had shown any sign of pity for the dead man or his son.

Kamienski bolted the drink and dragged his shirt cuff

across his lips. "Ari was all Jacob had left. His biggest worry was what would happen to the boy after his death."

"Where is the boy?" Absalom turned a page in his notebook.

"In an institution in Jerusalem, I believe," Gideon commented. He'd removed his tie and there was a stain on his jacket. The fingers that stroked his pipe trembled slightly.

"You wouldn't happen to know which one." Absalom asked.

Ozeri smacked his palm on the table. The bottle of vodka jumped and cutlery clattered. "Enough is enough, Chief-Inspector. For the life of me, I can't understand why an unfortunate heart attack justifies this interrogation. It's outrageous."

An ugly flush stained his mahogany complexion. He struck Absalom as the kind of doctor whose diagnoses were seldom questioned. Or perhaps questioned all too often.

"What is he saying?" Kamienski asked, bewildered by the rapid-fire Hebrew.

Absalom switched to English, aware of his hackneyed reply. "There's nothing to be worried about if you have nothing to hide."

Alona swayed to her feet and spat out a bitter laugh. Her eyes were glassy. "Hide? Name me one person here that doesn't have something to hide."

"Alona," Gideon's voice steeled over. "Thaddeus isn't interested."

"Maybe it's time he was."

She screamed. The tension in the room cracked open. Chairs toppled backwards onto the floor, the kitchen staff ran outside, Yossi Gottwein lumbered over. Ozeri grabbed her wrists but she kept shaking her head, shrieking like a slaughtered animal. Absalom whipped out his cell phone to summon an ambulance, but Ozeri seized a fistful of Alona's hair and slapped her on each cheek. The silence echoed as loudly as the screaming had, until she collapsed at the table, laid her head on her arms and began to sob.

"What am I not understanding?" Kamienski asked, his sweaty face puckered like a confused child.

Absalom exchanged glances with Yossi Gottwein. "The same things I'm not, Mr. Kamienski."

CHAPTER TWENTY-TWO

THE next morning, Rachel pushed open the door of Jacob Lifschitz's hotel room. Though she hadn't slept all night—a combination of the panic attack and a colossal hangover—images raced through her head; the old man clawing at his chest, his pitiful cry, *Raisl, Raisl,* and her mouth on his clammy lips in her attempt to breathe life into him. What had he wanted to communicate about Lydia in his last moments?

She was determined to fight for him and see that justice was done for the Holocaust survivor with the hopelessly ill son, orphaned now. She wanted to decipher the significance of his appearance at the hotel before the police sealed off the room and the technicians invaded. Even if Absalom Brill was emotionally impaired, he wasn't stupid enough not to grasp the suspicious nature of this third death. The remoteness in those olive green eyes, the understated flat tone of voice, reminded her of PTSD victims. Reminded her of what she'd become.

Sealing off her thoughts, she surveyed the room. In the early morning light, it glowed with the splendor of a European drawing room; carved mahogany furniture, thick apricot carpeting over parquet floors, gilt mirrors, and Swiss chocolates in a crystal dish. In the bathroom, acres of veined green marble gleamed.

A cardboard suitcase lay open on the floor. Vintage 1950 transit camp, caramel-colored with ancient splotches and a filthy rope lying next to it, as if Jacob had dragged it on his life's journey from Poland to Israel. Common sense told her not to handle the items within, sparse as they were. With a tissue from the night table, she went through the leavings of a sad life: two shirts with frayed collars, two sets of underwear, denture paste and a toothbrush, cracked leather phylacteries and a prayer shawl folded in a velvet bag.

Lifschitz had flitted through like a moth, leaving little imprint. The Holocaust survivor, the anguished father, the man smiling in the photograph with Lydia —those identities were erased.

Suddenly, the door opened and Alona walked in. Her milkmaid skin was sallow, and dark circles ringed her eyes. In a calf-length skirt and long sleeves, her provocative femininity had been wiped out as neatly as the old man's presence had been.

"Lifschitz's key is missing." Her voice was ragged. "What are you doing here, anyway? You should be at your parents' place waited on by the good housewives of Kerem El." Her feeble attempt to flounce past Rachel was hampered by the narrow skirt.

Ignoring the self-pitying whine, Rachel peeked into the garbage bin. "Has this room been cleaned since Mr. Lifschitz died?" Saying his name aloud brought a lump to her throat.

Alona wrinkled her nose. "The things you think about. What difference does it make?"

"It makes a big difference if Lifschitz didn't die a natural death." Rachel wondered whether it was wise to share her suspicions, but Alona might have tracked the dead man's movements from her post at the reception desk. Meanwhile, she'd stretched out on the bed, her head propped up on her hand, curls springing out between her fingers.

"Murder? But that's impossible. Crazy."

"Crazy, yes. Impossible, no. Doesn't it strike you as strange, three old people dead on the kibbutz in five weeks?" She opened the bureau drawers. Wiped clean.

"They *were* old," she said, as if old age were a disease. "At least we know who killed the Rebbe. As for poor Lydia…"

"Did he ever have visitors? People he spoke to in the lobby?" She opened the closets where empty hangers clanged within.

"What is this, the third-degree?" Alona pleated the bedspread with manicured fingers. "Sure you're not getting into…you know…one of your obsessions?"

Rachel tried to stifle her temper as she went through the hotel brochures on the desk. Anything that didn't directly concern her friend's moods, love life or looks, was attributed to a quirk in the interlocutor's personality, especially if he or she had suffered a nervous breakdown.

"I'm the shrink, not you. Could you answer my question?"

"Okay, okay." Alona rolled her eyes. "I hardly saw him. He never came into the lobby or the dining room. The day you ate lunch with him? It must've been a fluke. And no, no one ever asked for him, not while I was on duty, anyway. Happy now?"

Rachel looked out the French windows at the sky, which was brushed with dark clouds. She frowned. For someone who was the head of the *Landsmanschaft*, Jacob Lifschitz had not mixed and mingled. During lunch, he'd seemed haunted, depressed, twisting his head around to the entrance as if looking for someone. At the time she'd attributed his mood to the memories Holocaust Day had evoked. Now, she wondered if it had been fear.

Alona sat up against the headboard, coughed and fumbled in the pocket of her skirt, pulling out a pack of *Marlboro Lights*. Lines creased the corners of her mouth.

"I didn't know you'd started smoking." Rachel slid open the door that led to the balcony. The spicy smell of thyme and rosemary flooded the room along with the early morning chill.

"How could you know? You make yourself pretty scarce." They moved outside and sat down on rattan chairs upholstered in a fuchsia and green flowered print. The cascade of mountains shrank darkly beneath the gathering clouds. Streaks of pale yellow stabbed the horizon.

Alona took a puff and shook out her hair. "Besides, you're not the only one who's stressed around here. Seems I made a spectacle of myself the other night. Bet the gossips couldn't wait to fill you in."

"What happened? I must've fainted." Rachel felt ashamed, her fragility exposed for all to see, especially Ozeri.

Alona's features relaxed, as if finally releasing toxins from her system. "It was the best thing that could've happened to you. Things got horrible—I lost it. It hit me what the whole spectacle was all about. Here we were, living it up, slobbering all over Thaddeus like he was the Golden Calf, while the Rebbe and Lydia rot in their graves." She flicked an ash over the balcony and murmured, "Not that I have any great pity for Reb Elijah at this point."

"That's a strange thing to say."

Splatters of rain pinged off the balcony railing. They moved their chairs beneath the teak pergola. Alona's eyes roamed sightlessly over the landscape.

"Don't jump all over me."

"I'm not jumping. I'm surprised, that's all. We were like his daughters."

Alona gave a brittle smile. "Up to a point. Until his rigidity about religion kicked in. Sometimes our laws and rules were not made with mere humans in mind."

"Where are you going with this?" Rachel's mind felt so overloaded, she felt it would snap in a theological argument.

Alona shifted in her chair. "Let's say, for instance, that two people fall in love and want to get married."

Rachel's therapist's ear prickled. "Let's say."

"But one of them isn't Jewish." Alona drew her lip between her teeth. "They go to a sympathetic rabbi to talk about conversion classes for the non-Jewish partner, okay?"

Rachel nodded. *Oh, Alona, who is it now?*

"The man even agrees to study with this rabbi and

learn about Judaism, but in the end," she broke off, her jaw hardening, her eyes filling with angry tears. "In the end, the rabbi isn't as sympathetic as they'd figured. He tells the couple no, he won't accept the man for conversion after all."

"Why not?"

"Because the man's motives aren't 'pure,' that's why. He doesn't really want to hook up with the Jewish people, but only wants a 'ticket'—that's the word the rabbi used—to marry a Jewess. The rabbi said he couldn't be party to a fraud."

Thunder growled in the west. Alona stood up and began pacing, heedless of the raindrops that sprinkled her hair.

"Hours of begging and pleading didn't move him one whit." She whirled around and faced Rachel. "The fact that one stubborn old man can ruin people's lives…"

Rachel tried to keep her voice gentle. "Can I assume that the stubborn old rabbi you're referring to is dead?"

Alona's eyes blazed. "Yes, and I'm glad. Does that make me wicked or does it make me human?"

The thought flashed unbidden into Rachel's mind. *It makes you human, all right, but maybe it also makes one of you a murderer.*

* * *

At lunchtime, Absalom found Ron Kozma in the canteen eating his usual turkey schnitzel and mashed potatoes. On the chair next to him lay the preliminary forensics report on the dead man.

"Cyanide." Ron's lips puckered distastefully, as he poured out mineral water. "All those people doing CPR, and not one of them smelled almonds on his breath?"

"It's more common in books," Absalom replied, sliding into a chair. "Not everyone can pick up the smell. It was the pink flush that made the medic suspicious."

Ron wolfed down a chunk of schnitzel. "The old man sure liked his whiskey. His stomach was full of it, along with poppy seed cake and tea with plenty of sugar."

"Probably so drunk he didn't notice the cake tasted funny."

Ron laid down his fork and focused his gaze on Absalom.

"Okay. You've got your murder." Leaning back in his chair, he raised his hands defensively. "But it doesn't mean you were right about the others. That moron is still in Tira, and the old lady's death is inconclusive. Suspicious—I'll grant you that—but still inconclusive."

That was Ron and his need to be right, but Absalom didn't care. Now he had a free hand and the manpower to officially investigate the Lifschitz murder, which meant he could check out the other deaths too. Plus, he would be in Rachel's orbit.

He got to his feet. "I'll take Yossi and the team."

"Right." Ron fiddled awkwardly with the table napkin. "Uh, how's your dad doing?"

Absalom's stomach tightened. Though he still made the weekly trip to Pardess Hannah, winter rains had given way to May foliage, sweet yet stifling, like the smell in his father's room. The old man was shrinking in on himself with every visit, cocooned in some blocked-off corridor of the mind.

"No change." He hoped Ron wouldn't ask him about Christina next.

* * *

Rachel hefted the chunky globe in her palm, reddening as she traced its origins from her subconscious through her fingers to the sweeps of the whittling knife. More apple-shaped than round, its core was deeply cleft. *Sexy.*

Heat rose to her cheeks. The story of Alona and Taleb's love affair had shaken her in a way that was more profound than the complications of a Jewish-Muslim marriage. It was Alona's radiance when she spoke about her lover.

"One thing the rabbis taught us is true—we all have our *beshert,* our soul-mate." Alona had practically sung out the words to the falling rain. "What Taleb and I have together is magic. Much more than sex."

With defiance, she'd confessed that they'd made love on the dead Rebbe's bed. "Wipe the shock off your face, Rachel, and try to understand. We were so furious; we had to stick it to him somehow."

Peeling off her sweaty clothes, Rachel made for the shower, stopping to gaze at her reflection in the mirror. Her eyes blazed in gaunt sockets. Her mother was right. She *had* gotten thinner; her chin had sharpened and unattractive valleys dipped around her collarbone. The combination of fire-scorched hair and scarred hands made her look like a weather-beaten pioneer, sapped of vitality. *Love-starved.*

Sniffing back incipient tears, she let the soothing needles of water massage her skin until her thoughts tunneled towards the task at hand. *Back to work.*

She threw on some clothes, brewed coffee, and punched in the number of Professor Amal Rajoub.

CHAPTER TWENTY-THREE

PROFESSOR Rajoub's office was located on the twenty-first floor of Eshkol Tower, a rectangle of glass and steel that capped Mount Carmel's highest promontory. Its wafer-thin silhouette could be seen from as far north as Lebanon and, on a clear day, as far east as the Jordan rift.

The vitality in the hand that grasped hers caught Rachel off-guard. Though draped in a long *abaya,* her head covered in *hijab,* the professor projected more femininity than her more scantily-dressed secular counterparts. Her creamy complexion was highlighted with make-up, and the *hijab* was tastefully threaded with sequins. Almond-shaped eyes beneath gold-rimmed spectacles sparkled with irony.

"Thanks for seeing me at such short notice," Rachel said, taking a seat opposite the professor and surveying the room, where books in numerous languages lined the walls, and what looked like a text from the Koran hung in a silver frame. The desk was almost Spartan in its neatness. Aside from a computer and appointment diary, a basket of multi-colored marbles and a bowl of frangipanis were the only ornaments. The white blooms filled the room with exotic sweetness.

The professor nodded. "I'm going to a conference in Milan next week but when you said you wanted to discuss Muna, I did everything I could to squeeze you into my schedule."

"I appreciate it." Rachel pulled a pad out of her shoulder bag. "Do you mind if I take notes?"

"Not at all," Rajoub said dryly. "There's nothing that Amnesty International and other human rights organizations haven't publicized."

Rachel took a deep breath. *Amnesty International. This sounds bad, very bad.* "Muna was your sister-in-law?"

Rajoub folded her hands on the desk in front of her. "Yes, my brother Ahmed's wife. She was about to give birth to their first child. At the risk of sounding sexist, the family was thrilled when we heard it was to be a boy."

"How long had they been living in Jabalya?"

The professor shed a kindly, almost pitiful glance at Rachel. "The Gaza branch of our family had the dubious honor of refugee status bestowed upon it in 1948. Before that, they lived in Ramle—for generations, I might add."

Rachel winced at the subtle mention of the *Naqba*, the Catastrophe, suffered by the Palestinian Arabs as a result of the Israel War of Independence when family tragedies intertwined with national upheavals.

"Who else lived in the family compound?"

Rajoub gave a bitter laugh. "You make it sound like a villa, when it's a collection of tiny rooms with dirt floors. Muna's mother and grandfather lived with them." She lowered her head. "This is going to be more difficult for me than I'd imagined. Somehow I thought I'd be," her eyes moistened, "hardened by now. I guess I was wrong."

"Would it be easier to send me a written account?"

Rajoub sniffed and waved her hand. "No. You're already here. I'll be all right."

"What exactly happened that night?"

"It was summer: July 7, 1992, to be exact. Jebalya was boiling." She scooped up a handful of marbles from the bowl and began rolling them in her palm. "Have you ever been to a refugee camp?"

"No."

"You're extremely fortunate. It's not a pleasant experience. Almost two million Gazans exist like rodents in concrete cages with sewage flowing through the streets. Water and electricity depend on whatever some Israeli general deems necessary. There are curfews, searches and seizures, families awakened at all hours of the night. For some reason, Israeli soldiers prefer kicking in doors to knocking on them."

Rachel was silent, not keen to tread on the mine-field known as *ha-matzav*, the Situation. Yet, her thoughts flashed onto the blood spilt by the suicide bombers the Gaza Strip had spewed out for over fifty years.

Amal Rajoub cleared her throat. "Luckily, Muna's mother had gone to visit relatives in Khan Yunis. My brother had driven her and decided to stay over. He's never forgiven himself for that. Excuse me." She reached into a fold of the *abaya*, drew out a handkerchief and wiped her eyes.

"Muna was in her ninth month when soldiers raided the house. They claimed a terrorist cell was using it as their headquarters. It was three o'clock in the morning when they rammed down the door and ransacked the place, breaking mirrors and throwing ornaments against the wall. Then the commander started on Muna's grandfather. They tortured an eighty-year-old man in front of his pregnant granddaughter until his heart gave out." Her eyes turned stony. "Would you like to hear the details?"

Rachel shook her head. She was nauseous and fascinated at the same time. She was aware of abuses during these raids, but what Israeli commander would commit such atrocities?

"Muna went into labor and the baby was coming fast. Despite the pleas from his own soldiers, the commander refused to allow her to be taken to hospital. She gave birth on the dirt floor. The baby died and Muna bled to death right there, in front of all of them."

Except for the click of the marbles, the silence in the room amplified the sounds from the corridor—the whoosh of elevator doors, voices talking on the phone. When Rachel found words, she wasn't sure whether she was murmuring to herself or addressing the professor. "I wonder if that's why Reb Lachmann kept Muna's obituary. As a reminder of what human beings are capable of."

Light from the window glinted off Rajoub's glasses, rendering her expression inscrutable. "Perhaps. In my opinion, it was connected with that commander."

"What do you mean?"

The professor's finely wrought eyebrows arched. "He's someone your rabbi may have come across. Today he's some kind of peace activist. Can you imagine? Before I realized who he was, I actually signed one of his petitions."

* * *

Rage pulsated through her as the Daihatsu hurtled down the mountain curves. As the sea opened up at the rim of the *wadi*, the setting sun blotted out her vision, causing drivers in the opposite lane to honk as she swerved dangerously over the white line.

The skewed, battered little boy had turned into a sadistic murderer. Reb Elijah had saved Muna's obituary, not as a reminder of human cruelty, but as proof of what Boaz Kashtan really was. And who was to say that after a confrontation, the murderer-turned-peacenik hadn't slaughtered him as well?

Past the Fureidis junction on the way to Zichron Yaakov; a diner on the right-hand side of the road, Absalom had said. *Hovav's*, it was called. They serve great fries.

There it was, in a grove of trees. As she eased into the parking lot, she wondered what had made her phone Absalom Brill. In her rage, she had fantasized that as a policeman, he'd put Boaz Kashtan through the wringer for the murders of Reb Elijah and Lydia.

On the phone, he had hesitated. He was driving back from Pardess Hanna; perhaps they could meet midway for a meal. Thus, the fries, his favorite dish. It was the only personal detail she knew about him.

Hovav's was homey and unpretentious, sporting a framed *kashrut* certificate on pine-paneled walls and an enormous grill opposite the counter, on which spiced onion and chicken cubes sizzled. A skinny teenager in a red tee shirt was tending the grill, the spatula bopping in time with the bouzouki music playing on the radio. It was hard to ignore the odor of smoking fat; she hadn't touched meat since the suicide bombing.

He sat at a corner table, flirting with the waitress. Rachel blinked and shrank into the doorway. Was this the Absalom Brill she knew, animated, smiling, dimple flashing? His hands gesticulated and the waitress, a lithe, big-bosomed girl in her twenties with a ring in her eyebrow, threw her head back and laughed, as if pearls and diamonds were flowing from his lips. Rachel felt an upsurge of resentment. How come she'd never discovered this playful streak of his; maybe the waitress was the reason he'd suggested this remote place.

When he spotted her in the doorway, he shot up from his seat, nearly toppling the chair behind him, making straight for her, somber-eyed. Why did she have a dulling effect on him, like curtains drawn shut?

"*Shalom,*" he said, guiding her towards the table, where the waitress stared at her before vanishing into the kitchen. "Thanks for coming all the way out here. It's a ritual for me."

"Ritual?" Despite herself, she was intrigued as she sat down across from him. It was a word she never would've associated with him; it suggested a depth she didn't think was in him.

"My father is hospitalized down the road in Pardess Hana; not hospitalized exactly, but in an old age home." He stared down at his fingers, which were drumming the table top. "The weekly visits aren't easy, and this is one place I can wind down in before heading home."

As though catching himself in an illicit act, he thrust his hands under the table.

"What about those famous fries?" Rachel infused lightness into her voice, to lift the heavy atmosphere.

"Exactly.Vered!" He called to the waitress. "What's happening back there?"

He was smiling again, almost impishly, Rachel thought.

"*Rega, rega*," the waitress barked from the kitchen. She appeared holding a tray of salads, a heap of French fries and fragrant grilled chunks of lamb. She set down the tray and cutlery, and then, with a proprietary hand on his shoulder, cocked her head to one side and peered at Rachel.

"Amazing resemblance."

Absalom cut her off. "Leave it for now."

"If you say so." She gave him a meaningful look and flounced off, waving as she left. "Tell me when you're ready for coffee."

In the silence that followed, Rachel noticed that despite his previous lightheartedness, he looked tired, crows' feet filigreeing the corners of his eyes. His wounds had faded to punctuation marks dotting the tanned face and scalp, where his hair had begun to grow in.

She shoved the thoughts from her mind. After all, she'd phoned him for a purpose. As she drew the Rebbe's envelope from her bag, anger against Boaz Kashtan stirred once again. She slapped the envelope on the table, while he frowned in concentration, reaching for a French fry.

"May I open this?" He wiped his hands on a napkin and removed the contents of the manila envelope.

"Too many things are happening too fast, so I've decided to tell you everything. Maybe you can make some sense out of it. I found this in the Rebbe's study after his death." She dished out the salads and reached for the fries. They were crisp and light.

Pointing to the contents of the envelope, she launched into a recital of the events that had tumbled out of control, leaving out nothing except for the Alona-Taleb episode in Reb Elijah's bedroom: her discovery of the envelope, lunch with Jacob Lifschitz and the discovery of the old photograph of him and Lydia, Emanuela the niece.

When she described the Rebbe doll with the twisted neck, he thumped the table so hard that the skinny cook winced and glanced their way.

"And you didn't call me? This is a direct threat."

An icy calm encased him and he reverted to the focused robot she knew. He probed and analyzed and interrogated until she gasped for coffee. By the time it arrived, she'd told him about Hadassah Levy, Mordechai's violent background and the nurse at Tira Hospital.

Absalom ordered another stack of fries. Their golden crispness seemed to fuel him; he chewed thoughtfully, licked his fingers, bent them and caressed them, as he dunked her into what seemed like vats of boiling oil with his interrogation.

Over a third cup of coffee, she pointed to Muna Rajoub's obituary and summarized her meeting with the professor.

Reluctantly, she got around to Boaz Kashtan and his sadistic background.

"That's when I phoned you," she said. "I was afraid of what I might do. Storm down to Zeita maybe, and strangle him with my own two hands." She swirled her finger in the oil on the empty plate. "On top of that, there's poor Jacob Lifschitz. I swear he knew something about Lydia's death. I think he was murdered."

"I know he was murdered," Absalom said quietly. "His body was full of cyanide."

Rachel felt the tears well up, but she turned her face away, surprised to see that darkness had fallen. The traffic on Route Four hummed beneath the crackling of the grill and the restaurant had filled up with youngsters wrapping spiced chicken in Iraqi pitas. The normality of their laughter jolted her back to a world where people took pleasure in good food and companionship and weren't steeped in violent death.

"Where were you just now, Rachel?"

She shook her head, stretched and glanced at her watch. "We've been sitting here for over two hours."

He smiled wearily, but his eyes almost danced. "I'm glad you called me."

She took another sip of coffee. "So am I. Tell me something. Is this a date, or what?"

CHAPTER TWENTY-FOUR

"**B**y looking at his bank account, you'd never think Jacob Lifschitz was rich."

Absalom dropped into his customary chair, unfazed by the wisps of wood shavings littering the table. He zeroed in on the bags of potato chips —plain, ruffled, onion, garlic— Rachel had set out.

"You're a potato freak," she'd said when he'd first appeared at the chalet for coffee during the Lifschitz investigation, displaying the bags of chips he'd bought at the mini-market. Though they were fumbling their way to a friendship of sorts, Rachel still found it disconcerting to sit opposite him at the table.

"How do you know he was rich, then?" She shoveled a heap of potato chips into a bowl and set out paper napkins.

Absalom snagged a handful. "The hospital that treats his son charges thirty-thousand shekels a month for round-the-clock care. The director doesn't know how they can keep Ari on now that his father is dead."

"Poor Ari. I wonder if he realizes his father won't be coming to see him anymore." Rachel shook her head, contemplating yet another Lifschitz tragedy. She poured coffee. "Where would Jacob get that kind of money?"

"That's what we're trying to find out. He had no investments or safe deposit box. It's clearly undeclared income."

"As a survivor, he'd get reparations from Germany, wouldn't he?" Rachel took out two bottles of mineral water from the refrigerator.

He twisted off the plastic caps. "Sure, but no one becomes a millionaire on German reparations. We even looked into the Pomorzany *Landsmanschaft*. He headed it, but it's a voluntary position."

"Thaddeus would know."

Absalom smiled. "I felt sorry for Kamienski when he gave his deposition. He couldn't keep his hands off the vodka. He had nothing to add except old Holocaust stories." He grimaced. "Told me that the poor guy extracted gold teeth from the victims after they were gassed."

"What a horrible life!" Rachel suddenly felt suffocated, rose and opened the window. The evening air smelled of roses. "Maybe someone from his past wanted to kill him?"

"It's a cold, cold trail."

Rachel rubbed a salty potato chip between her fingers. "Remember the photograph I found of him and Lydia. It's disappeared."

"What do you mean?"

"The day after the fire, when you came to tell me about Lydia, I was a wreck. Before I knew it, I found myself in Pinetree Hall where the ceremony had taken place. Nothing had been touched except for one thing. The picture was gone."

"Why didn't you tell me about this before?"

Rachel raked her fingers through her hair. "I have no idea. I'd forgotten about it until now. Someone didn't want that photo displayed."

Absalom wiped his fingers on a napkin and punched a number on his cell. "Yossi." A smile creased his face. "No, it's none of your business where I am. Get me a list of everyone who was at the Holocaust Ceremony." At the torrent of shouts on the other end of the line, Absalom's dimple flickered. "I know it was a month ago, and yes, I know I'm a pain in the ass. Just do it."

Rachel munched on a potato chip, then swigged down some water. "I can help you with that. I have to warn you that it's a very long list. What else did you find out about Jacob?"

"He kept pretty much to himself, except to visit Ari. The hospital was his whole life. He lived in a hole-in-the-wall in Makor Baruch, one of those black-hat neighborhoods in Jerusalem where kids set fire to dumpsters because a woman walks by in pants."

"Don't be nasty." While conceding his point, Rachel refused to encourage what she considered his ignorant *haredi*-bashing. "Besides," she murmured, crushing a potato chip on the table, "my ex-husband lives in Makor Baruch. Not that that's any kind of recommendation."

"So you're divorced." He folded his hands in his lap, stating the fact without the dismay, shock or pity she was used to.

"My ex-husband grew up National Religious, like me. That's how Kerem El was then. All the boys served in the army and we had activities together with secular kids. You can see for yourself how things have changed."

He nodded. "Shmaya Catz and his ilk."

"That's taking things a bit far. Most of the *haverim* are really good people. When Nahum and I met when we were fourteen we weren't closed off from the world; we wanted to change the world. We even opened our own soup kitchen, stealing food from our parents' refrigerators and hitching rides to Tira to dole it out." She laughed at the memory.

"Did they ever suspect anything?"

Rachel shoved her hair back from her face. "Probably, but never said a thing, a hold-over from their sixties craze in the States, I suppose."

"After we married and moved to Jerusalem, I studied for my degree and Nahum just," her eyes clouded at the memory, "felt the pull of those *haredi* yeshivas. There's something so comforting about absolutes with authority figures spelling out proper attitudes and behavior. Nahum was sucked in more and more. And then…there were things in our married life that were difficult to take."

Again, the monk-like silence. *He'd make a good therapist.*

She took a deep breath, like a diver ready to jump. "We couldn't have children and Nahum refused to go for fertility tests."

"That must have been very hard on you. And very cruel of him."

"That's why I can't get Hadassah Levy out of my mind, and why I've got to check out this *Pregnant Virgin* thing."

* * *

Eight men and three women looked up from their volumes of *gemara* and stared at her.

The *beit midrash*, the study hall, nestled in the *shul* basement as an intimate venue for lectures and study sessions. Paneled in walnut, boasting a library of thousands of holy books, its windows faced the gently rolling hills. Rachel pictured Reb Elijah against the backdrop of those hills, conducting the children's Shabbat services, hypnotic and commanding. Now, his chair at the head of the long rectangular table remained achingly empty, and the windows were squares of black against the night.

"Sorry to interrupt. I thought the study session ended at nine."

"We're winding things up," her father said. "We'll be done in a couple of minutes."

Moving over to a corner of the room where the women were exiled, she nodded in response to hand squeezes and murmurs about how well her injuries had healed. One or two glanced at her skirt which had ridden up to mid-knee. She surreptitiously tugged it down.

The scrape of chairs on the tiled floor signaling the end of the session, was her cue. She took a seat between her father and eighty-two-year-old David Cherniak, one of the kibbutz elders, who was snoozing, veined hands clutched around his walking stick.

"There's this Talmudic reference I came across." Rachel

looked around the table. Gideon Mann raised an eyebrow and fingered the bulge in his shirt pocket. *His pipe. He's itching for a smoke.* A bleary-eyed Mordechai Levy sat in a surly slump.

She plunged right in. "Anyone ever hear the term *the Pregnant Virgin*?"

Silence.

Good God. Now I've offended them.

She continued nervously, "I mean…it sounds paradoxical, doesn't it?"

Gideon broke the tension. "Why not ask the doctor?" The men chuckled, the women tittered.

"Going through Reb Elijah's papers, I saw the reference. It looked like it might be a Talmudic question. I remembered the study group meets tonight, so I popped in."

The atmosphere contracted into an airless chill. Someone coughed.

"And why were you going through the Rebbe's papers?" Her father looked wary.

"Lydia asked me to." At the mention of Lydia, the faces around the table grew somber. "She wanted me to get something she'd left in his study and didn't have the heart to do it herself."

"And did you," her father asked, "retrieve them, I mean?" The heartiness had disappeared from his voice, hurt she had kept this from him.

"No." At least this part was true.

"Babylonian Talmud, *Hagigah, yod dalet, bet-tet/vav.*" With a snort, David Cherniak shook his white feathery hair.

They jumped as he banged his stick on the floor.

Rachel turned towards him. "What?"

The old man looked at her with sharp eyes. "You asked a question, you got an answer. Write it down, girlie."

"Could you repeat that?" He quoted the Talmudic source once more.

"I didn't know you were an authority on pregnant virgins, Dovidl." Her father smiled behind his beard.

"*She'll* tell you," the old man said, pointing a finger at Rachel. "Look it up, girlie, in the Babylonian Talmud."

After the group had dispersed and she'd kissed her father good-night, she walked over to the bookshelves on which the tall volumes of the Babylonian Talmud stood. She found *Hagigah* and lugged it over to the table. It was a baffling riddle within a riddle, quoting a discussion between two rabbis thousands of years ago.

Ben Zomah was asked: May a pregnant virgin marry a High Priest. Do we assume that Samuel is correct, when he states that one can have intercourse many times without removing the physical characteristics of virginity, or perhaps this is unlikely. He replied: Samuel's position is unlikely, and we assume that the woman was artificially inseminated.

On the face of it, the lines expanded on the Biblical law that the High Priest, the Cohen ha-Gadol, was required to marry a virgin. Even in modern times, men by the name of Cohen and its derivatives were prohibited from marrying divorcees. But here, the question was raised whether a virgin was still considered a virgin if she'd engaged in intercourse, yet her hymen remained intact. As medieval as it seemed, such questions were used by modern-day sages to solve contemporary problems.

Back at the chalet, she settled down at the computer to find out all she could about the Beckmann Clinic in Antwerp. As she'd suspected, it specialized in fertility treatments— information she'd pieced together from the talkative Iris; Hadassah's childlessness and depression, Yoel's birth and the lack of subsequent children. She was convinced that *the Pregnant Virgin* was linked to the Levys. Yet, the leap from infertility to murder was great indeed.

CHAPTER TWENTY-FIVE

*M*AY *God and Freud forgive me.* Rachel knew she was about to commit the therapist's most unethical act; manipulating a patient for her own ends.

She knew Hadassah Levy always dropped by the minimarket at ten o'clock. Another sin; exploiting information gleaned in therapy. Sure enough, Hadassah was poking at the frozen fish. She was upholstered in dark green polyester, her head covered with a pancake hat, humming to herself as she fingered icy slabs of Nile perch.

"Hadassah?"

She turned around and her down-tilted eyes shone. "Rachel!" She grabbed her hand with chilly fingers. "It's positively *beshert* meeting you like this—I was going to phone and cancel our session…"

"Has anything happened?"

She smiled and lowered her eyes. "*Baruch HaShem,* we have a *simha* to look forward to amid all the tragedy and trouble."

"Yoel's wedding date is set?"

The woman positively glowed. "Yes, and you'll be one of the honored guests! It's thanks to you that I can feel happy."

Rachel drew closer. "I'm so glad!" Her voice dropped.

"Actually, it sounds unprofessional…*is* unprofessional…but I'd like to consult you about something related to Yoel's *simha*."

Hadassah giggled and covered her mouth. "*You* consult *me*! That's funny."

"Yes, it is." Rachel glanced around, to make sure they were alone. "And please keep it confidential, just like a therapist, especially from my parents."

The tiny eyes popped with curiosity. "You can count on me."

"Can I come over later before Mordechai gets home?" she murmured.

"I'll fix us lunch. One o'clock?"

"Terrific. And remember..," she placed her finger on her lips.

At one, she walked over to the Levys' cottage, isolated on a high ridge with a sweeping view of the sea and the crumbling Crusader castle on the peninsula below. The front garden was a showcase for Mordechai's horticultural skills, the preened and restrained mixed with the riotous and voluptuous, mosaics of color and stone. The house was whitewashed with red trim around the windows.

The smell of baked potatoes and roasted meat greeted her when Hadassah opened the door. The dining room table, covered with a plastic lace tablecloth, had been set for two. The dark wood paneling, the mahogany bookcases and sideboards gave the room a somber cast, the only source of light being the gleam of the candlesticks and the glare of sun and sky sweeping through the picture window.

On the walls hung paintings of Torah sages interspersed with modest photographs of Yoel: Yoel receiving a gold-embossed prayer book, Yoel holding a Torah scroll, Yoel at the Western Wall, his frank, rustic face looking straight at the camera.

"Make yourself comfortable," Hadassah called from the kitchen. "I'll be right there."

"Take your time." Rachel stepped over to a small photograph propped up against a crystal vase. A concrete hovel with a tin roof on a cluttered beach. A reminder of Mordechai's origins?

Hands encased in oven mitts, Hadassah bustled in and slid a pan of golden potatoes and a crisp roast onto straw trivets.

"You shouldn't have gone to so much trouble." Rachel tried to hide her dismay at the sight of the slab of meat.

Placing a tossed salad, pickles and a pitcher of orange juice on the table, Hadassah motioned for her to sit down in a chair facing the view. An eagle soared over the *wadi*, wafting on gusts of air before plunging sharply towards an unseen prey.

"No trouble at all. My husband needs a big lunch with all the outdoor work he does, and you must miss good home cooking after all that hotel food. And I enjoy a good hot meal myself. Not that I need the calories."

She patted her ample midriff. After mouthing the blessing over bread, she began slicing the roast while Rachel piled salad on a small plate.

"A hearty appetite shows how contented you are," she said. "It must be a relief having your son fixed up like that."

Hadassah's eyes misted over. "No one knows how complicated these things can be until you go through it yourself. Hand over your plate."

She ladled chunks of potato and thick wedges of meat onto Rachel's dish. Rachel avoided looking at the meat, concentrating on forkfuls of salads.

"To tell the truth," she lied, "that's the reason I wanted to talk to you." She squirmed in her chair.

Hadassah beamed. "Out with it. You can trust me. It's me who's the therapist now," she chuckled wiping her mouth with a napkin.

Rachel laid down her knife and fork and took a deep breath. "I've been thinking lately that…how can I put it? I'd like to meet somebody. I'm not getting any younger, and you have so many connections; maybe you could put out some feelers."

Hadassah bridled with pleasure and reached across the table for Rachel's hand. "*Baruch HaShem*! I've been praying for this. How can I help?"

"Tell me a bit about Yoel's *shidduch,* the procedures and so on. You once mentioned loose ends that had to be tied up?" She felt like the eagle swooping down on its prey.

Hadassah fiddled with the cutlery. "Yes, well. That's over and done with. There are always problems of lineage that the rabbis must examine, but with all due respect, they tend to go overboard with their nitpicking." She brightened. "That's not the case with you, of course. You're a good Jewish girl."

"I can imagine that strict rulings about lineage can ruin a

shidduch." She munched on a slice of brown bread.

Hadassah's mouth tightened. "Sometimes one rabbi, no matter how well-meaning, holds the power of life and death over a family's happiness, all in the name of Jewish law."

Her jaw grew taut and her soft eyes blazed. This was a mother who would do anything to protect her nest.

"Some rabbis are more understanding than others, I imagine, but it sounds unholy to have to shop around for a rabbi you like." Rachel's appetite plummeted as she took the plunge. An imaginary headline blazoned across her brain: *Psychologist shoves patient into deep depression.*

"Hadassah," she said softly, "for years you tried to get pregnant, but it turned out that the problem was Mordechai's." The woman's eyes stabbed with tears and her lips worked soundlessly. She fumbled in her apron pocket.

"Yoel isn't Mordechai's biological son, is he? Thanks to the Beckmann Clinic."

Hadassah bowed her head; her shoulders sagged.

Rachel continued. "The kibbutz was happy to finance the trip to Belgium, since everyone understood you two needed to get away together on a relaxing vacation. They'd been waiting for years for you to get pregnant."

"You don't know what it's like," Hadassah moaned.

Yes, I do. Rachel stifled the pain in her gut. "The clinic recommended artificial insemination. You both agreed, but you had no choice but to act according to the *halacha.* The sperm donor had to be a non-Jew to prevent the slightest chance of incest in the child's future marriage." Rachel glanced over at the photographs of Yoel's thatched hair and blue eyes. "And it was the vagueness of Yoel's parentage that caused major problems with the *shidduch,* wasn't it?"

Tears gushed down Hadassah's cheeks and she sat immobile, letting the tears stream down her neck and the front of her dress.

"It was Reb Elijah's ruling, wasn't it?"

When she finally spoke, the words erupted like a pent-up spring.

"No one knew about the treatments. Everyone was so happy for us; it never crossed people's minds that Yoel's conception was less than a miracle from the Almighty, which it was, it *is.* Mordechai was so overjoyed that he wanted to tell the Rebbe everything. The Rebbe raised him up from the dung heaps, shaped him and was father, mother, and sage all in one."

"For once I put my foot down. I forbade him to tell the Rebbe about the...conception. Who knew where such information could lead? Mordechai gave in then, but after the *shidduch* was arranged, he felt guilty. He couldn't sleep at the thought that he was betraying the Rebbe, that God would punish us."

Rachel handed her a fistful of napkins and she wiped her face and neck. She gulped down a glass of juice and filled up the glass again.

"He was obsessed. He just had to get Reb Elijah's blessing for the *shidduch,* to make sure the marriage would be kosher. He never dreamed the *psak* would be against us."

"On what basis?"

She sighed deeply. "On the basis of something in the Talmud called *the Pregnant Virgin*. May God forgive me; I never dreamed I'd hate the Torah." She buried her face in her hands.

"Go on."

Hadassah looked up. Lines of weariness etched her face and her mournful eyes were swollen slits. "The Sages debated whether or not a virgin could become pregnant...*oy*, the things they talked about! They said she could, if, let's say, she bathed in a ritual bath or pool in which a man had...you know...".

"Spilled his seed."

"Yes. Based on this example, the sages decided on the fine points of a child's parentage, which in modern times cover artificial ....you know..."

"Insemination."

"Yes, thank you. By the husband or by another donor."

"And in your case, the Rebbe adopted the strict rather than the lenient approach."

Hadassah reached for a napkin and blew her nose. "He told us that after checking all the *makorot*, the sources, he couldn't say Yoel's parentage was without blemish. He would have to notify the bride's family."

Her face twisted in anguish and she banged on the table with her fist. "Why is it important who donated the seed? *We* are his parents, Mordechai and I, we loved him and raised him and made him into the fine young man he is today, with

God's help and guidance. How could the Rebbe throw our future away, just like that?"

"But he didn't throw Yoel's future away. He was murdered first."

CHAPTER TWENTY-SIX

WHEN she heard Absalom's precise voice on his answering machine, she put down the receiver and crept away from the phone. *That's what cops do; they catch criminals. They don't sit by the phone waiting for your call.* She regretted having confided in him about her marriage and childlessness. It had ratcheted up her vulnerability to the extent that she already felt pushed aside by his job.

Never get involved with a cop. Heat rose from her neck and fanned across her cheeks as Miri's words echoed in her ears. She pictured the somber olive-green eyes and the serene core he seemed to inhabit. *Involved. Is that what I am?*

How cramped her world was and how meagerly inhabited: a hollow absence where Lydia had been, Malkie, grieving and preoccupied with six young children and Alona, now bubbling in the stew of suspects.

Miri, whose dance troupe was touring Germany and the Czech Republic, would have said, "Move your hide back to Jerusalem and get a life!"

The rigid formality of the sitting room kaleidoscoped around her and even the thought of whittling left her fingers inert. Air and movement was what she needed. Grabbing a light sweater, she stepped out of the chalet and turned right, away from the lawn. Pearly jasmine and the smell of the cowsheds drifted on the mild air. The only sound was the throb of the electric generator in the chicken run.

She headed out towards the circular road where Lydia had met her death. The mountains were humped against the black sky. As her blood quickened, her thoughts began to pound in rhythm with her strides.

Reb Elijah. He'd bound the community to him with morality of steel, yet had betrayed his most devoted followers. He'd vetoed Taleb's conversion, and cast doubt on Yoel's lineage. In both cases, the result was damning; erasing Alona's chances of a Jewish marriage, and thwarting the Levys' plan for crowning their *wunderkind* with a prestigious match. The sense of betrayal would be exponential, since Alona— like Rachel—had practically grown up at his house, and Mordechai, whom he'd resurrected from a life of criminality, worshipped him.

But were they—Taleb, Alona, Mordechai, Hadassah— capable of murder? Wily and twisted enough to kill an old man in a bloody ritual and implicate the unbalanced Shmaya Catz?

As she rounded a curve, she saw the lights of the Arab village flicker fitfully in the rising wind. Taleb. Since boyhood he'd known the Rebbe; the refusal to convert him would be the ultimate rejection. As for Alona, while physically unable to tie up an old man and slit his throat, she might well have a Lady Macbeth streak powerful enough to beguile her lover into it. Rachel knew her friend well—her egocentricity, her childish impulsiveness. The trysts in the dead rabbi's house indicated that the pair might be reckless and unconventional enough, and callous enough, to have committed murder. How much strength did such a killing involve? Reb Elijah was a dying old man, powerless to resist.

As for Mordechai and Hadassah Levy, like Taleb, they were robust and strong. Mordechai's violent tendencies—Lydia had once said he'd beaten up a pensioner outside the bank—may have boiled over at Reb Elijah's threat to destroy the future of his son. And Hadassah? The sheltered goody-goody who'd hooked up with the delinquent outsider? She could be a lioness when protecting her precious offspring.

Her fingers flew to the scar on her cheek when she considered Boaz Kashtan. Exposure as a ruthless sadist would smash his reputation as an enlightened peacenik. Had Reb Elijah threatened to reveal his part in Muna Rajoub's death? And if he had, why? As she knew all too well, Boaz possessed the petty vengefulness and necessary cruelty to snuff out a life and pin the murder on the eccentric son-in-law. An ex-officer, he had plenty of experience planning and executing operational details.

Breathing hard now, she sat down on a rock, gazing down into the *wadi*, pondering the threat Lydia had posed. Like Reb Elijah, she was a tribal elder with too many secrets. What revelations had she planned to spill at the Holocaust Ceremony? What precisely was her connection to Jacob Lifschitz? The three elderly victims were bound by tentacles rooted deeply into the past. Who had decided to sever them and why?

Paradoxically, the desire to return to her chalet was overwhelming; at the moment, its stilted embrace was her only refuge. She quickened her pace, menaced by shadows staining the road black. All at once, a slew of wild pigs clattered up from the *wadi*, ran across her path and vanished into the woods, jolting her heart into frozen terror. The hairy creatures had appeared silently from nowhere. How easy it was for a person to climb the mountainside and infiltrate the kibbutz. Above the pounding in her ears, she knew it wasn't outsiders she feared.

By the time she let herself into the chalet, she was breathing hard. She flipped on the light and downed a glass of cold water before tossing her sweater on the couch and heading for the bedroom to check email.

In mimicry of the *hassidic* doll, the wooden globe rested on her pillow, half-covered by the top sheet, a knife protruding from its gouged-out cleft.

* * *

The whoosh of tires stopped her compulsive pacing, round the sitting room and the kitchenette, avoiding the bedroom at all costs. She was hyped up on adrenaline like a runner at the starting line. Peering out the window, she put on the coffee pot and delved into the kitchen cupboard for a bag of potato chips.

Absalom stormed in without knocking, bringing a swish of chilled air in his wake. He looked disheveled, as if he'd fallen out of bed and grabbed a random pair of wrinkled jeans and yesterday's tee shirt. His facial scars were shadowy half-moons against the pallor of his skin.

"Show me."

"In here." As she pointed to the bedroom, her heart began knocking furiously inside her chest. She closed her eyes and took deep breaths. The last thing she needed was to have a panic attack, the core of her vulnerability, the secret he mustn't discover.

From the doorway, she watched as he leaned over the wooden globe and examined it closely. Straightening up, he took a handkerchief, ironed as usual, out of his back pocket and gently lifted the object out from under the covers.

He swiveled it around in his hand. "It's beautiful." Rachel recalled the sensuous folds of the wood, and then pictured the knife thrust into its core. A violation, a rape. The floor shifted sickeningly.

"I'm glad you appreciate my technique," she snapped, embarrassed that the globe revealed more about her than words could tell. Absalom rolled the thing into a plastic evidence bag.

His eyes retreated. "I'm not making light of what happened, or that some sicko didn't do this. I'm just saying that it's beautiful."

In the kitchenette, he pulled out a chair and crossed his legs. Only the sharp swipes at the bowl of potato chips hinted at a strong emotion.

"I'm sorry I lit into you like that," she said as she poured the coffee. "I know that you're trying to help me."

He nodded and the tense muscles in his jaw softened. "Tell me the latest in your private detecting. It might give us a hint at who did this."

Grateful to skirt the emotional quicksand, she filled him in on *the Pregnant Virgin* and what she'd gleaned from Hadassah Levy about Yoel's conception and Reb Elijah's *psak*.

He shook his head with incredulity, the hand clutching a potato chip suspended in mid-air. "You mean to tell me that a judgment that affects people's lives today is based on chitchat that took place between some old codgers…what…a thousand years ago in Babylon?"

"More like two thousand. And it wasn't chitchat," she said, feeling the hot coffee in her chest like a comforting fire. "That's how Jews around the world managed after the destruction of the Temple. While they adapted to the laws of the countries they lived in, their personal and religious lives were guided by the Rabbis."

"Judging by the runaround I'm getting, that's the way this place is run too. Without your rabbi to tell them what to say or think, they're flapping around like chickens in a barnyard. I can't get a straight answer out of any of them." He emptied his coffee cup and held it out for a refill. "Especially that slippery doctor of yours. He refuses to accept the autopsy report on Jacob Lifschitz."

Rachel laughed. "Slippery is the word. Ozeri can't stand my guts." She told him about her encounter with him and her suspicions about his drug scam.

"There's big money in that." Absalom snagged a fistful of potato chips. "What could be simpler? A closed community like this, most of them old and sick. No supervision whatsoever. We'll look into Ozeri, all right. My partner will press him to the wall. You've seen Yossi—a cement mixer with a good heart. Don't know what I would've done without him after…"

"After?"

His hand rubbed his left arm and his eyes grew remote. "It's not important," he said.

She shrugged. Tit for tat in the intimacy game. She jabbed at the potato chip crumbs that remained in the bowl. " Maybe Reb Elijah cottoned on to Ozeri's scam and threatened to go to the police."

"Giving him a motive for murder?" Absalom's forehead furrowed with skepticism. "Far-fetched, don't you think?"

"Depends what he has to lose." Rachel licked the salt off her fingertips. "I feel sorry for his wife. And he has six lovely kids. But he's not a very conscientious doctor. He never told me about Hadassah Levy's depression, and his files about my other clients are very slipshod. It smacks of an ego thing: acting the modest *kibbutznik*, yet making big money on the side, and using his status as a member of the Secretariat to gain respectability."

Absalom whistled softly. "And these are the religious folk among us."

She grinned. "I'll ignore that one." She was beginning to feel more at ease with him. And more secure. Perhaps a door to friendship was creaking open.

"I've got to get going. I want to drop your artwork off at the station. "He got to his feet, carrying their coffee cups. "I suppose one of these sinks is for dairy and the other is for meat." He chuckled. "This voodoo is beyond me."

When she took the cups from him, their fingers touched and she felt a brief sizzle. She turned her back and began rinsing the dishes. "I know someone in Jerusalem who's going to find out about Ozeri's background." *My psychiatrist.* "I'll email him tonight to remind him."

"Good idea." When she turned to face him, he was standing so close she could smell his clean spicy smell. His fingertip mapped the scar on her cheek. "How'd you get this?" His voice was hoarse.

She flinched. "It's not a pleasant story, but it's late and we're both tired. One day I'll tell you, but I want you to promise me? Scar for scar?" She gestured at his face, but didn't dare touch him.

His face relaxed in a smile, creasing his dimple. "It's a deal. Scar for scar."

At the door, he said, "I'll have a patrol car drive by here every couple of hours to keep an eye on you. We haven't cottoned on to Jacob Lifschitz's killer yet, but remember…he or she has access to cyanide."

CHAPTER TWENTY-SEVEN

THE next morning, the buzz of Mordechai Levy's lawnmower drilled through cotton-wadded layers of sleep, followed by the jangling of the phone. Rachel fumbled with the receiver and grunted a hello, only to hear a rolling Romanian accent on the other end of the line.

"Sorry to wake you, my dear, but I wanted to catch you before my first patient."

Dr. Nestor, her psychiatrist. She could picture the chair groaning under his weight as he lit a cigar, could almost taste the dry Jerusalem air streaming through his office window. She squinted at the bedside clock—seven-thirty and humid as steaming soup. The summer was not going to be kind.

"My head is all bunged up," she said, clearing her throat. "Never drink coffee at midnight." It was too early to examine whether it was the caffeine or her growing entanglement with Absalom that had kept sleep away.

"The brew doesn't affect me in the least," he said. "But I'll get straight to the point. I checked out your man last week. Sorry I didn't get back to you. Here's the gist."

The lawnmower rose to an insistent drone. "Reuven Ozeri, M.D." Nestor boomed, "premiered on this earth forty-eight years ago to a traditional Yemenite family from a moshav near Kiryat Gat, and soon became the pride of the village. Assiduous, self-disciplined, intelligent. However, his academic aspirations weren't recognized by any Israeli medical school, poor boy." The psychiatrist chortled. "Can't help thinking, damn psychiatrist that I am, that he's been compensating ever since. Did his medical degree at the University of Bucharest and worked as a surgeon at the city hospital. Did very well, I understand, private practice, big apartment—the usual in a place like that. He hobnobbed with *nouveaux riches* Romanian Jews. Didn't socialize much with Israelis, though."

"Probably needed the community services because he's religious." Of course Ozeri was of Yemenite origin; the elongated mocha-colored fingers and the carved features were a give-away. As for the thick-skinned ego he'd developed, she had to agree with Nestor's pop analysis—a simple moshav boy outracing his humble past.

"Tsk-tsk," Nestor chided, "Religious is as religious does. Your Ozeri was a bit, shall we say, remiss in his sense of ethics. Overzealous in his devotion to his private patients at the expense of the poor plebeians at the city hospital." He paused dramatically. "Because of his idiocy, a boy bled to death."

Despite the heat, Rachel felt a cold clutch in her throat. She was now fully awake. "Tell me."

"In his eagerness to treat Minister Mucky-muck or whoever it was, he placed the boy in the hands of an alcoholic intern. When the bleeding started, the intern had passed out and by the time Ozeri was located, the boy was dead."

"Was he ever put on trial? This monster is now a member

of Kerem El. He's treating patients, for God's sake." Her rage simmered. "My own parents!"

"I'll give you the short version, my dear, since my patient is due any moment. Romania was never exactly your average Anglo–Saxon democracy; corruption and patronage ruled. Nothing like a hefty bribe to the hospital director to erase all the charges from Ozeri's file."

"So how did you find out?"

"Now that Romania is a member of the EU, it's doing penance for the queasy sins of the past. I phoned a few colleagues from the old days. They were only too happy to dig up information about your doctor."

She almost spat. "He's not mine."

"My love, I've got to go. I hear the clunk of my patient's heels."

"Thanks," Rachel said, not sure what she was thanking him for. Now she had another suspect to add to the list. A particularly nasty one.

* * *

The first step was tracking down patients who'd bought drugs from Ozeri. She knew where to find one of them; in the treatment wing of the Hotel Spa. Hettie Trasker was a massage freak.

Rachel shoved open opaque glass doors into an air-conditioned haven. In the reception area, which featured modern oak and parquet floors, mineral water and fruit juice, matrons trundled along, veined legs peeking modestly beneath thick monogrammed bathrobes. Behind the reception room, an Olympic-sized pool gleamed like turquoise glass.

Datya, a slim twenty-something in a crisp white coat, sporting an ash-blond wig, presided over the treatment rooms. Twice a year, she flew to Brooklyn to purchase wigs made from natural hair, which cost twice as much as the plane fare.

After an exchange of greetings, during which she suggested that Rachel could do with a good blonde rinse, Rachel asked where she could find Hettie. Datya's manicured hand waved her in the direction of a room down the corridor.

The fragrance of incense and hot coals drifted through the open door, accompanied by a soundtrack of tinkly notes that sounded like droplets of water. Today, Hettie was pursuing her latest passion—the ancient art of Ayurvedic hot stone massage.

"Come in, Rachel." Larissa, the masseuse, greeted her in a throaty Russian accent. The eggplant-hued bouffant hairdo, pugnacious jaw and aircraft carrier build didn't exactly suggest the profound subtleties of Ayurveda. "You want Hettie?"

Rachel edged in through the door. "Sorry to barge in, but I have to ask her something about her health. It won't take more than a few minutes."

Larissa frowned and looked at her watch. "Now is good time as any. She have the hot stones. No more than five minutes, eh?"

"Thanks. I appreciate it."

The door closed behind her and Hettie squeezed out a reedy *shalom* from the massage table. She was laid out like a mummy, down to the toothless mouth and the wizened head swathed in terrycloth. A sheet covered her from the waist down. Flat stones snaked down her spine between shriveled bones that stuck out like chicken wings. A charcoal burner sizzled in the corner.

"I know I look like *shashlik* on a spit, but this is the only thing that helps my arthritis. And, *oy vey*, the bursitis I was telling you about…"

Rachel had no time for the litany of Hettie's ailments. She pulled over a stool and sat down to the left of Hettie's chin. The woman's face and body gleamed with oil.

"You once told me how much Dr. Ozeri's medicine helped."

The old lady's wrinkled lids closed. "A miracle, a *mechaya*. Can't get through the day or night without those pills. The doctor is an angel," she said, shifting her skinny body. "He's not like a regular health fund doctor, more like family. When I get nightmares, he's right there with my Dormiton. He has such a good heart."

So good he let a little boy bleed to death. "You told me they were very expensive." Rachel glanced at her watch. Larissa would be back any minute. "Did Dr. Ozeri ever explain why?"

Hettie sucked on her gums. "Because the medicine is at the cutting edge." She was clearly aping Ozeri's hype. "It hasn't been approved in Israel yet, only in America."

"Could I have a sample?" The request was absurd, and once again she was lying; prevaricating and betraying a patient's confidence in her. But—she thought bitterly of Reb Elijah—in this investigation, betrayal was the name of the game, it seemed. "I've had trouble sleeping myself and I'm at the end of my rope with exhaustion. If it works as well as you say, I'll go to the doctor myself, but in the meantime, this is a little experiment between us."

"Poor dear. I know this is a terrible time for everyone, even a therapist." She chuckled. "See my pocketbook over there next to my dentures?" She stuck her arm out in the direction of a side table. "There's a box marked Dormiton. Take as many as you need. I can always get more."

Rachel sped over and scrabbled through old tissues, coins and sucking candies until she found the rectangular box. She was just pushing a tablet through the silver paper as Larissa opened the door.

* * *

"The *chutzpa* of the woman," Ozeri muttered as he slammed the door of the Fiat Punto. Scratched and dented, the 1991 model was the only car left in the parking lot. And the air-conditioning had conked out, *davka* on this scorcher of a day. For years, he'd appealed to the Vehicles Committee to assign him a car for permanent use, but so far they'd turned him down. Because of their penny-pinching, he had to drive to Carmel Hospital in this ancient clunker.

The gear shift screeched as he thrust it in reverse. His jaw locked with tension. Finally, he coaxed the car down the hills and turned north onto Highway Four.

He felt as if the top of his head would pop off. Who did Rachel Shine think she was anyway? Who was she to make a man's life a misery?

That truck of a cop had shown up at the clinic two hours ago, one of the team investigating Lifschitz's so-called murder. Ozeri knew that it was a ruse; the old man had dropped dead of a heart attack—too much emotion and too much alcohol. The real reason the police were still hanging around was the Rebbe. That was clear now. And Rachel Shine had given them the ammunition. He'd heard that the head cop had been seen going in and out of her chalet. Bedroom ammunition, no doubt. He cursed the day he'd agreed to have her come to the kibbutz; she'd turned out to be a meddler, worse than Lydia had been.

A cement mixer rumbled onto the highway from Moshav Megadim and Ozeri leaned on the horn. Miraculously, the driver moved over to the shoulder and let him pass.

The heavy cop, Yossi-something, had heaved his body into a chair and flashed an idiot grin. "Mind if I ask you a few things, doctor?" After asking a couple of amateurish questions about Lifschitz's collapse at the gala, he got around to his real aim. The drugs. Ozeri had almost burst out laughing with relief. It wasn't about Reb Elijah, after all.

There are rumors going around, people are saying, there's probably nothing to it, doctor, but you know, we have to check everything out...blah blah. In short, doctor, are you selling illegally-imported drugs?

Just recalling the cop's words made him aware that fat drops of sweat were rolling down from his forehead, and he could feel patches of damp under his arms. He'd probably work up a proper stink by the time he reached the hospital. He prided himself on his fresh and natty appearance, especially at hospital staff meetings. It expressed self-mastery and competence. Damn this country! Even today colleagues did a double-take when they heard he was a Yemenite from a moshav in the south. As if he should be growing hothouse peppers like his parents, rather than practicing medicine.

Once again, he recalled the imbecilic grin that split the cop's face like a melon. *We've got the pills, doctor. They're on their way to the police lab as we speak.*

How did they get hold of them unless Rachel had put them on to something, had told them enough to suspect him of what, exactly? Sweat was pouring down his cheeks now, grit from the open window sticking to him like flies on flypaper. The Rebbe's face, gaunt and bloodless, floated through his mind, then Lydia, lecturing, hectoring. He remembered her death, Holocaust Eve, when he'd come late to the ceremony. His Haifa supplier had showed up late because of the heavy *khamsin*, their transaction whispered and hurried, behind the hotel.

He stepped on the clutch, switched to fourth gear and slammed the gas pedal to the floor. The car sputtered all the way up Freud Street. The last thing he needed now was for the damn thing to overheat. As he climbed higher and higher, he glanced out the window at the curve of the shoreline below and the endless turquoise sea. A faint breeze brushed his cheek. When he cooled down, he'd decide how to get rid of Rachel Shine.

CHAPTER TWENTY-EIGHT

THE parking lot was jammed. Despite the heat, crowds of hotel guests were strolling down the hill to the petting zoo; old people were draped on recliners, their faces soaking up the sun. Men were perusing holy texts while absentmindedly rocking baby carriages and young matrons were coaxing their children to eat slices of fruit and hard-boiled eggs that magically appeared from sandwich bags.

Yossi Gottwein wiped his forehead with a hammy hand. "This heat is killing me and it's not even summer."

Blinded by the white mosaic façade of the building, Absalom unfolded his sunglasses. "At least the hotel has bounced back. Three suspicious deaths haven't put off the believers."

Yossi snorted. "This is the only place where there aren't any drive-by shooters, that's why. You know where we'd be if it weren't for these murders."

Absalom nodded. They'd be out on the roads, counting bullet holes in still-warm flesh. God bless our boss, the bastard. "Let's go in."

Inside Gideon Mann's office, a frost bit into him that sank its teeth deeper than any air-conditioning. Absalom and Christina had visited such a room in a medieval Scottish monastery on their one trip abroad together. He remembered how they'd fumbled for the reassuring touch of each other's hands. Stark and minimalist the monk's cell had been, with no attempt to present a flesh-and-blood face to this world. Here, even the picture window that dominated the south wall was double-glazed, casting the room in gray. Beyond the smudge of hills, a pewter sea.

Gideon was dressed like a gentleman farmer, in jeans and a long-sleeved plaid shirt. A black skullcap hugged the curve of his skull, a contrast to the silver-blond hair. He held out his hand to the policemen. Despite the chill of the room, the hand was warm and vital.

"I wish I could say that you're always welcome here at Kerem El," he said, seating them around a steel-edged coffee table, "but under the circumstances, I'd sooner you stayed away."

"Three suspicious deaths in the space of six weeks don't make for happy hosting," Absalom said, "but I hope to visit at calmer times in the future." Gideon dipped his chin graciously and poured grapefruit juice into glasses heaped with ice cubes.

"Coffee and cake will arrive in a moment," Gideon said, flashing an unexpected smile that shed a thin ray of warmth into the room. "Please make yourselves comfortable. The cold drinks will be refreshing in this heat wave."

Yossi poured out glass after glass, yanked out a handkerchief and wiped his sweaty neck. "It's boiling out there."

Absalom steered the conversation away from the ritual exchange of pleasantries. "Though we've been briefed by

Thaddeus Kamienski, we'd like to hear more about the Trust."

Gideon nodded and crossed his legs. "Certainly. The Trust entitles Polish Holocaust survivors to two fourteen-day vacations per year at the cost of four thousand dollars per person for a two-week stay." Gideon reached for the computer printouts on his desk and handed them to Absalom.

"Eight-thousand dollars per client a year." Absalom whistled softly.

"Thaddeus is a generous benefactor and shrewd investor. Believe me, what the Trust pays the survivors is a pittance compared to his financial assets."

Yossi was scribbling on a pad. "And what do the guests get for all those dollars?"

Gideon's hand gesture was leisurely as if waving away a fly impudent enough to enter his space. "You can see for yourselves. Aside from the peerless setting and fine mountain air—not today, of course—the guests receive luxurious rooms, gourmet food, cultural activities, and a whole range of health treatments. Plus, there's a doctor on the premises full-time."

"We know," Yossi said, meeting Absalom's eyes. "Ozeri. I've talked to him."

Gideon reached into his shirt pocket and pulled out a pipe. "I hope this doesn't disturb you. It's my one vice and my office is the only place I feel entitled to indulge."

"It's your office." Absalom shrugged. At least the ascetic Gideon Mann has a vice, he thought. The woodsy smoke made him think of cozy fire-lit rooms, of him and Christina, naked, in front of the fireplace at a Scottish inn.

"About these health treatments," Absalom said, quoting from the printouts. "Massage, Reiki, acupuncture, chiropractic care. Are they covered by the Trust as well?"

"Yes. The guests pay per treatment, or if they prefer, for a treatment package, which is billed to the Trust."

Absalom sipped his grapefruit juice, still undiluted by the ice cubes. This place doesn't even melt ice, he thought. "Does the Trust pay the hotel directly?"

"It's all here in black and white. We supply detailed receipts for services rendered and are reimbursed by the Trust."

"I suppose this can be verified."

Gideon smiled. "I once told Thaddeus that he was more German than the Germans as far as paperwork was concerned. He didn't appreciate my sense of humor." He guggled a mock bottle of vodka and mimicked Kamienski's accent. "'There is no humor in the Holocaust,' he said."

So there was a nasty side underneath all that polish. Absalom felt a perverse need to peel back the man's layer of *sangfroid*. "Do you think there's humor in the Holocaust?"

An infinitesimal blankness clouded the gray eyes. He pulled on his pipe. "Are you being deliberately offensive, Chief-Inspector, or has the heat addled your judgment? My parents' entire families perished in the camps. My remark to Thaddeus represented a gentle teasing among old friends."

Even under attack, Absalom thought, there's no heat in him, just a glacial retreat. There was a moment of silence, broken only by Yossi thrumming his pen on the pad.

Absalom gave a transitional cough. "Let's get back to

Jacob Lifschitz. What do you know about the source of his considerable income?"

"Nothing. He lived very simply. Of course, he bore a terrible burden."

"His son."

Gideon sighed. "I never asked how he could afford it. It was a very painful subject."

"And how about you, *Adon* Mann? How would you describe *your* financial situation?"

He had to admire the man's self-control. The gray eyes bore into him with undisguised dislike, yet he barked out a jovial laugh. "Chief-Inspector Brill," he chided, "I'm a *kibbutznik* living on a monthly budget, just like my fellow members. My wife is a highly educated woman whose skills the *meshek* recognizes by allowing her to work at the Technion, but her salary, benefits and pension all go to the kibbutz. If you are as thorough as you seem to be, you'll discover that I lead a very modest life-style. My wife and I rarely go abroad. We don't own a car, but drive kibbutz vehicles."

Yossi pushed his eyeglasses higher onto his nose. "So everyone's the same out here."

Gideon made a tilting movement with his hand. "Theoretically, yes, although there are slight differences, like in any society, but the fact I run the hotel doesn't entitle me to more benefits than anybody else."

As he leaned back in his chair and sucked on his pipe stem, a patch of sunlight picked up the threads of gold in his hair.

Alona Golan, the woman who'd fallen apart at the gala,

entered carrying a tray of coffee and cake, which she set down on the table.

If she sensed tension in the room, she gave no sign. "No need for introductions, right? You've seen me at my worst. How do you guys take your poison?" Gideon winced, perhaps at her choice of words.

"Black with sugar, "Yossi said. He stared as she bent over to pour the coffee.

Absalom took the opportunity to study her. Though dressed in a discreet long-sleeved white blouse, long skirt and black pumps, there was something desperately hyper about her, as if she were about to spring into outer space. As she handed him his cup, Absalom noticed that her eyes were jungle-cat green.

"Thanks for taking such good care of my friend," she whispered as she bent down to hand over his coffee. Her lips broadened in a sensuous smile. "I hope she's taking care of you, too: there's nothing like mutual...investigation."

Absalom sat stony-faced. She was a real *mispar,* that one, impulsive, not to be trusted.

"I'll leave you men to it," she said, gliding out the door and waving to Gideon. He responded with a languid raising of the hand.

"Nice woman," Yossi commented, munching on a piece of sponge cake. "Adds class to this place."

Absalom shot him a warning glance. *Don't parade your stupidity in public.* Lonely, virginal Yossi, goggle-eyed at the sight of a sexy woman. Sometimes he wondered whether his partner had the stability to be a policeman. "His urges gallop away with him," Rachel had pointed out when she'd described how he'd nearly choked Shmaya's teenage lover.

"There's one more question I'd like to ask," Absalom said, catching Gideon's gaze over the coffee cups. "Did Jacob Lifschitz have any enemies?"

Gideon puckered his brow. "The very thought seems absurd." He puffed on his pipe and watched the smoke disappear in the recesses of the ceiling. "On the other hand, he was very active in the Pomorzany *Landsmanschaft;* he was the head of the organization, in fact. Who knows what grudges may have festered throughout the years."

"That's a very good tip, *Adon* Mann. Sometimes the past jumps up and grabs us by the throat." Absalom rose and offered his hand.

Gideon walked them to the door. "Feel free to come again. When this horrible time is over, maybe you'll spend Shabbat here as our guests."

"With separate pools for men and women?" Yossi guffawed, "Not my style."

Laughter all around. "One more thing," Gideon said as they stepped into the corridor. "Try and keep out of the heat."

After the interlude in that arctic room, there was nothing Absalom wanted less.

CHAPTER TWENTY-NINE

ACHEL strode down the hill in the late afternoon after the heat of the day had dissolved and the sun slanted across the mountains in a soft buttery haze; the scent of pine mingled with loam and the ghosts of decaying leaves.

Though she'd spied the police Toyota parked at the hotel, she hadn't heard from Absalom. Her heart gave a little skip at the thought of his unblinking gaze and rare smiles. There was no getting around it; she liked him. She was attracted to him. Yet he'd revealed so little about himself. For all she knew, he could be a cross-dresser or shoe fetishist. The fact that he was a cop meant nothing; policemen were drawn to deviance like mosquitoes to a swamp.

Shrugging off her reverie, she noticed that she had walked as far as Jabal-a-Zeit and her thoughts whirred back to Alona and Taleb. She hesitated, then crossed the road to the stony path that led to the entrance to the village, passing the Moslem cemetery where low gravestones were strewn helter-skelter in the yellow grass. At the crest of the hill, hastily constructed concrete houses were jumbled together. Dotted here and there was the occasional whitewashed villa, festooned with oriental arches, bows and frills, but those were the exception, the property of the village *mukhtar* or prosperous contractors who worked for customers in Haifa or Zichron.

The original Zeita residents had fled here in the 1948 war. She wondered whether it was fertile turf for Boaz Kashtan as he canvassed support for his quirky plan. The village was spotlessly clean; every veranda sported a plastic bucket, mop and floor rag; no garbage-strewn alleyways or open sewage. As she wound her way up to the main square, consisting of the elementary school, the mosque, and a general store with a Diet Sprite sign in Arabic, she caught sight of Kerem El on the opposite ridge just up the hill. How fragile and fragmented it looked, the houses resting on cement stilts at the cliff's edge. Her throat constricted with longing and fear.

We're all transients, running from place to place hoping to find an anchor, but wherever we go, the ground rumbles beneath our feet.

She recalled the ruptured doll on her pillow and the wooden globe gouged out with her whittling knife, yet here she was, pursuing danger; she realized she had reached a milestone in the quagmire of the panic attacks.

A boy, no more than five or six with a soccer ball tucked under his arm tugged at her skirt. He looked up at her with eyes the color of peppercorns. She kneeled down and ruffled his hair.

"*Min beddek?*" he asked.

"Taleb Mahajna."

He pointed to the right of the mosque and skipped away in the direction of the schoolyard. The Mahajna compound comprised two villas surrounded by a hedge. She walked up to the main house and clapped the hand-shaped knocker.

The stately middle-aged woman who opened the door could only have been Taleb's mother. Below a paisley headscarf glass-green eyes nested beneath wrinkled lids. She wore a dun-colored *abaya* that reached the floor.

"*Salaamtek. Wen Taleb?*" Rachel asked.

"*Naim,*" she said suspiciously, but escorted her into a cavernous living room, not much smaller than the lobby at the hotel, the floor as shiny as an icy lake. Painted turquoise against the Evil Eye, the walls were lined with sofa beds heaped with blankets and pillows, like a dormitory. The only decoration was a large needlework tapestry of the Dome of the Rock that dominated the wall above a long sideboard.

In the face of the formidable woman with the ramrod spine, Rachel's Arabic failed her. "Could you please tell him that Rachel is here?"

Her son might be napping, but centuries of Middle Eastern hospitality would never allow her to leave a guest cooling her heels on the veranda. Nodding, Taleb's mother motioned toward an overstuffed chair, but not before raking her eyes over Rachel's loosely-fitted slacks, blouse and cardigan. Her face softened with approval. In the tentative alliance between the religious mountain communities, there were two points of agreement: faith in the Almighty and the modest dress of their women. No belly tops and mini-skirts would corrupt the alleyways of Jabal-a-Zeit. With her provocative sexiness, Alona would never be accepted here, Rachel thought; it was her status as war widow that barely won her acceptance at Kerem El.

Boisterous cries of children filtered through the lace-curtained windows and rays of sunlight shimmered along the waxed floors of what seemed like endless corridors. Rachel tried to collect her thoughts and concoct a strategy. Assuming Taleb knew that Rachel was aware of his affair with Alona, how could she goad the stolid handyman into an outburst that might lead to a confession of murder?

Taleb's mother descended the stairs followed by her son, who was buttoning his shirt and flattening the sleep spikes in his hair. The older woman headed toward the kitchen where sounds of water running and the whoosh of a gas burner indicated that refreshments were being prepared.

Taleb grasped Rachel's fingers in a knuckle-crushing handshake. She stepped back and appraised her friend's lover, the wary intelligence in his eyes and the dignified splash of gray at the temples. In another era, in a different society, such charisma would have assured him a place among the movers and shakers.

"*Mabruk*," he said, gesturing for her to resume her seat, while he reclined on a sofa bed piled high with red, green and black embroidered cushions which Rachel recognized as traditional Palestinian village weaves. He reached for a box of hand-rolled cigarettes and a lighter on the shelf behind him, lighting up with great concentration, then exhaled swirls of acrid smoke.

"This is an unexpected surprise. The last time you paid a visit was when you were about thirteen. Your parents brought a group of Americans to study the conditions in the village.

They were angry, but nothing much was done except raise money for a pocket playground."

His tone was genial, but the bite in his words was new. Taleb was doing his duty by receiving her, but she was not welcome here. Alona had told him everything.

Rachel nodded at the expansive room. "Considering the way your family lives, they could finance a few pocket playgrounds of their own."

He smiled and leaned against the cushions, rubbing a tassel between his fingers. "My family has done well. Sixty years ago we were homeless refugees. If you're interested, I'll show you the house we left behind in Zeita. My great-grandfather planted the lemon tree in the garden. Now it belongs to.." He mentioned the name of a famous orchestra conductor.

"Are you still bitter about '48?"

He stared at the ceiling where smoke rings were circling in the air. "The bitterness is always there like the day after strong alcohol. Some injustices are never really forgotten. Or forgiven."

Taleb's mother was moving softly in the kitchen and the aroma of coffee snaked through the house. Dusk was closing in and a chill advanced through the room.

Absentmindedly, Rachel touched her facial scar. "Did you ever meet Boaz Kashtan or was he before your time?"

Taleb shot up, his body rigid. Hate bubbled behind his eyes as he swore in Arabic. "Why in the name of Allah did you mention him?"

Her heart leaped and her fingers tensed around the arms

of the chair. "Whew! What did he ever do to you?"

"Take my word for it; he's poison." He flopped down on the sofa bed, then snapped off one of the tassels with a sharp rip.

At that moment, his mother entered, carrying a copper tray with a *finjan* of coffee and porcelain bowls of nuts and dried fruit. She kept her gaze lowered and placed the tray on an olive-wood table inlaid with mother-of-pearl. Despite the tension that radiated from her son, she didn't glance up at him, only padded silently out of the room.

Taleb had used the hiatus to smooth out his features, slipping into the gears of hospitality. He poured the coffee into tiny cups and handed one to Rachel; it was black, sweet and laced with cardamom. Rachel made sure to keep her hands busy, shoveling almonds and raisins into her mouth, but her mind pumped on. What had caused Taleb's volcanic reaction? And if she dared bring up the subject of the murders, Taleb could wring her neck the way he'd demolished that tassel and no one but his mother would be the wiser. Only the boy with the soccer ball was witness to the fact that a Jewish lady had been traipsing through the village. She felt as vulnerable as the day he'd glimpsed her naked in the chalet.

Relax. It's Taleb. You've known him for years. Yet the mantra was far from soothing. She couldn't trust anyone.

"Sorry about that."

"I'm the one who should apologize. There was no way you could know that the man's name is forbidden in this house." His voice was genial, but the cords across his knuckles bulged as he flexed and released his fists. He was looking at her the

257

way a cat eyes a mouse, a target for amusement, twisting the rope, waiting to see how she would broach the real reason for her visit.

She reached for a clump of cashews, trying to keep her tone casual. "May I speak frankly?"

"Please do."

"Do you remember the day you came to hook up my computer?"

He nodded, eyes wary under heavy lids.

She warmed the tiny cup in her hand, more confident now. "We talked about the Rebbe's murder and I asked you how Shmaya could've killed him. Do you remember what you told me?"

Taleb stubbed out his cigarette in a nest of peanut shells. "Every man has a boiling point. I still believe that."

"Good, because I've never forgotten it. Especially after three murders."

He shifted to the edge of the sofa. "What are you talking about?"

She sought out his gaze. "Lydia was pushed off that cliff. The police are convinced she was murdered."

" Poor woman!" He lounged back against the pillows.

"Then, there was the old man who collapsed at the gala, Jacob Lifschitz. He died of cyanide poisoning. The police figure both he and Lydia knew things they shouldn't have."

"A tragic coincidence," he murmured.

She took a deep breath. "Actually, I came here on account of those murders."

He glanced at her attentively and lit up another cigarette.

"I've seen a lot of boiling points lately, like Alona, for example. She told me about the two of you."

"Our relationship is a private matter," he said sullenly, darting a glance toward the kitchen.

Rachel crept toward the edge of the precipice. "She's a good friend of mine. If she's in trouble it's my business too."

His features twisted. "What kind of trouble?"

She flew off the cliff, hoping her wings would stay aloft. "She told me how furious you were because the Rebbe refused to convert you." She leaned towards him. "Don't kid me. Do you really intend to marry Alona?"

"Shut up."

"And killing the Rebbe—whose idea was that?"she taunted, rising to her feet. The curtains billowed in the wind. "Who was the brains and who was the muscle? And Lydia—you had to make sure she didn't blab about Reb Elijah's murder. Well, she told me."

He lunged for her, but tripped over the coffee table, scattering nuts over the floor. As she raced through the door, she heard a woman's cry from deep in the house.

She ran down the alleyway, hit the village square, and fled through the cemetery, sliding on the rough pebbles. The air had turned dry and cold, piercing her lungs. Dusk shrouded the mountains except for a shimmer of sunset lingering above the sea as she headed for the road that led up to the kibbutz. She slowed her pace and trudged uphill, Taleb's roar echoing in her ears, his powerful frame, like a panther crouched to attack. She clutched her sweater about her, then swung her arms back and forth to get warm. Aside from the headlights from the occasional car swerving around the bend, the road was deserted.

What had she done? She wasn't impulsive; she was analytical and reserved. Suddenly, she recalled the story of the *dybbuk,* the spirit that took over a woman's body and stuck— *davak*—to her insides until a holy man exorcised the demon. She'd acted like a woman possessed. Why?

When she heard the grinding of an engine behind her, she moved over to the guardrail to let the vehicle pass, but it continued dogging her closely, bathing her in strong headlights. She turned and shaded her eyes from the blinding light. With a roar, it sped straight at her, heading in the direction of the guardrail. Terrified, she looked down at the black chasm below cut by outcrops of sharp rocks. Her mind tumbled amid the noise and the light and her fear, but in a split-second of clarity, she clambered over the rail and clung to it with all her strength. Her legs were dangling in mid-air, she thought her arms would break and she sobbed out one last prayer. The truck ploughed into the guard rail, ramming it again and again. Suddenly, it backed up, made a U-turn and drove down the mountain.

Her heart was thumping wildly and she started to shake. Arm muscles trembling, she found a foothold in the side of a rock and slowly pulled herself over the railing again, only to collapse on the shoulder of the road.

She stayed there, clutching the railing, until the blackness of the night took over. The stars beaded the sky with clusters of light. The hoot of an owl and the scurrying of creatures in the underbrush broke the stillness. Gradually, she got to her feet and started to limp up the hill.

CHAPTER THIRTY

IT had become a nightly ritual; to stow away the stodgy image and slip on clothes that had flair. Like tonight; mocha-colored slacks and a sleeveless fawn top with an auburn scarf knotted around her neck, echoing her red-gold hair. She'd applied make-up and sprayed on her favorite perfume.

Who am I kidding, dolled up like this? Taleb hadn't phoned her in two days and ignored her messages. Alona looked desolately around the living room, furnished in golden tones, with blonde wood and an authentic Chinese rug. On the shelves that lined the ceiling stood Peruvian pottery that belonged behind museum glass.

Money, money, money had been her chant since Nimrod's death in the skies over Lebanon. As a twenty-two-year-old war widow, she'd paid her dues in full; the black spaces of loneliness and the burdens of national commemoration. Financially, she took good care of herself. A discreet bank manager funneled her widow's stipend into a private bank account, far from the clutches of the kibbutz.

When she and Taleb had started their explosive affair, money had been replaced by sex, and then incredibly, by love. But things had come full circle and she was back to the jingle *money, money, money,* like the old song. Damn Taleb and his stubbornness. With her money they could buy freedom, taste the world's delights and settle in an enlightened country. There was no one to stop them now.

Now that the heat of day had melted, she stepped out onto the veranda with her cell phone and a cigarette. A figure limped toward her in the darkness. She switched on the light.

Rachel's face glimmered white in the darkness, and she looked as if she'd climbed out of a sewer. Dirt matted her hair and smeared her blouse and slacks. The gash in her leg from the night of the fire had split open and blood was dripping onto her shoes.

Alona reached over, hugged her, then stepped away. "You haven't done anything to yourself." Her snappy tone disguised the fear that Rachel would never totally bounce back from what Alona called "the trauma disease." Her friend's return to life had kicked in only since those goddamn murders. It wasn't natural.

"What happened?"

Rachel shuffled off her arm and dragged her leg up onto the veranda. She sank into a chair and took off her shoes. "Your boyfriend."

"Taleb?" Black ice slivered through her belly.

"He tried to kill me."

The words clanged inside her head, blotting out Rachel's voice. She felt herself drifting away, hovering outside the cacophony of sound.

"Do you understand what I'm saying?" Rachel was shaking

her arm.

"I need a drink."

"No, I need you sober. I love you, Alona and I don't want him to hurt you. He's done terrible things." Tears thickened her voice as she stroked Alona's face.

Alona felt the ghost self floating further away, receding from the pain. Taleb loved her; he had proven it. He would return to her.

And then, Rachel's mouth was moving again and sounds were coming out, this time about Boaz Kashtan, of all people. No, she wasn't normal. Maybe she should go back to her shrink in Jerusalem.

"Alona, listen." Rachel was pleading now.

The cigarette. She needed a cigarette. "What?"

"I have to know. It's connected to all the murders. Your boyfriend went wild when he heard Boaz's name. Why?"

Alona tried to grasp the unraveling thread "All those deaths," she muttered. "Boaz did something terrible to Taleb's family. Because of him, his cousin in Gaza died."

* * *

"You did *what*?"

Absalom reeled as if bludgeoned. He grabbed Rachel's arm so forcefully that her sneakers skidded on the esplanade. A jogger with a speckled bandanna and a droopy midriff slowed down as he chugged past.

"Everything all right, lady?"

Rachel flashed a wobbly smile. "Fine, thanks."

She relished Absalom's grip on her sleeve, but he gave it a strong shake and let go.

He practically shoved her over to an outdoor café where he plunked her down in a plastic chair. Eyeing her as though she'd bolt, he eased himself into the chair opposite, disbelief suffusing his gaze. "The handyman tried to kill you."

Bubbles of laughter exploded in her mouth; she felt giddy. "It's the first time I've seen you like this, so…engaged." He was wearing his uniform for once, navy pants and light blue shirt, gun. His official appearance clashed with the lines of concern that slashed his face.

"'If that's some kind of shrink term, you bet I am. A crazy impulse makes you go and accuse Taleb Mahajne of murder." He shook his head. "It makes no sense."

"It doesn't." She shrugged and smiled at him.

He stared. "What's so amusing? He nearly killed you. Show me." She rolled up her sleeve and exposed the underside of her arms. He whistled softly, then pulled out his cell phone. "I'm bringing him to the station for questioning. Now."

"Don't."

"The guy tried to kill you."

"He'll only deny it. The whole thing happened only ten minutes after I'd left the village, and I can't swear it was his truck. Besides, his mother will claim he never left the house."

He laid the cell phone on the table. "Why the smug grin?"

Withdrawing her arms, she let him fume as she glanced out over the sea. Under pearly skies, it looked white as ice.

Was it time to confide her bewildering sense of elation?

"Rachel, don't avoid me."

She returned to him and sighed. "I did something stupid and dangerous and I feel great! Let me try to explain the dissonance."

"Dissonance. Go on." He sat stony-faced, his arms folded across his chest. For once, his stiffness liberated her rather than drove her into retreat or anger. She felt the powerful whir of her heart.

A teenage waitress with braces on her teeth sensed the atmosphere, threw two menus on the table and scuttled off.

"Fries and coffee," Absalom called out.

"Now that I'm on the telling end, instead of the listening end, it's awkward." She gave a little laugh. " I'm not sure I'm doing the right thing."

Other than a brief twitch of his lips, he remained motionless. Surfside cries and odors shifted in and out of her consciousness, as the severed head of the suicide bomber filled her mind. She told him about the suicide bomber, the squeaky sound of her shoes on human flesh, about her post trauma and her hospitalization, about Dr. Nestor.

"And then," she said, "when I thought I was over it, the flashbacks started."

During her recital of events, the fries and coffee had arrived, but he didn't touch them, just sat immobile with his palms on the chair, almost catatonic.

But she was suddenly starving and she reached for the fries, ramming them into her mouth, as if trying to stem the flood of words. "Then, Taleb nearly attacks me, tries to run me down and what happens? Rather, what doesn't happen? No panic attacks. My life was in danger, yet I coped; no, more than that, I saved my own life. I was brave." She thought of the wooden globe and its sensuality. Something inside her had begun to bloom.

"Look," she said, leaning forward, her hands flying in all directions, "I'm a person who lives a lot in my head and in other people's emotions. All this thinking and analyzing has its place, but for once, I realized that I could be impulsive and daring." She added. "Like now."

The sun had sunk lower on the horizon and people were streaming to the open-air podium for folk dancing. Joggers stopped to watch, towels slung around their necks, while kids on bicycles threaded among them. Her feet itched to dance.

She turned to him. "Don't you have anything to say?"

He reached across the table and took her hand. "No."

"Take a French fry," she said, her throat closing up. "You haven't touched a thing."

"No." He began stroking her wrist with his finger, like feathers dappling her skin. She gaped at their hands, both slim with long fingers, both thatched with scars. Her body softened and she felt a throb of desire. She didn't dare look at him.

Luckily, a blare of music caused them to swivel around to face the dancers, who were executing a complex Yemenite dance step, swirling around and pounding their heels in sharp movements to the rhythm of a *darbuka*. A salt breeze blew in from the sea, ruffling hair and lifting skirts, while onlookers clapped their hands to the music.

A figure in white hovered at the edge of the crowd, staggering from the direction of the beach, a gold lame bag hanging from her shoulder, smoke dragging from the cigarette she clutched in her hand. Something about her snagged Rachel's memory. She peered more closely and when their eyes locked, flares of panic soared in the woman's eyes.

By the time Rachel had got to her feet, the woman was stumbling on backless stiletto heels, shoving chairs out of her way, ducking behind the café and homing in on the parking lot. Ignoring Absalom's shouts, Rachel sped after her, sidestepping a flabby man in a bathing suit walking his dog. By the time she reached the parking lot, the woman had disappeared among the sea of cars.

Absalom rounded the corner of the cafe and put his arm around her shoulder. He was out of breath. "What was that all about?"

She wiped perspiration from her eyes. "I just saw a very frightened woman."

"So you just took off after a stranger? Rachel, you're getting.."

"No, no." She stared at the parking lot, willing the woman to reappear. "She wasn't a stranger. That was Emanuela, Lydia's niece."

He shook his head. "This bravery of yours is making me thirsty. I need a beer."

CHAPTER THIRTY-ONE

DEAR *Miri—*

I can't believe that you're back! I need wisdom, fast and strong.

Remember Taleb's attempt to turn me into road kill? And Alona's spacey reaction? Well, that's only the beginning.

Absalom asked me to meet him at the beach where I told him all about Taleb, etc. He went ballistic—for him, that is—and I opened up the whole can of worms: the suicide bomber, my PTSD, the hospitalization, the works.

Did I make a mistake, dumping my ultimate secret? He sat there like a Father Confessor from the movies, not saying a word, which only encouraged me to spill more; how empowered I felt by the Taleb incident ("incident?" He tried to kill me!), the rush when I realized I had coped and saved myself without walls falling in or ants marching up my scalp.

Afterwards, we had an intimate mini-second when he took my hand. Before I could decode the romance/friendship components, who did I spy on the beach but Emanuela, Lydia's so-called niece. The minute she spied me, she ran—but not before she threw me a look of sheer terror. I ran after her, but lost her.

If Absalom ever thought I was normal, he must think I'm

totally screwy after yesterday.

What's your take on all this? Love

Rachel—

As the saying goes, you made your bed, now sleep in it! My gut feeling? The cop will run. Intimacy is not for him. Just as well; I told you—never get involved with a cop! But I'm glad for YOU that you came out strong from this Taleb thing. Attempted murder as therapy.

Who are we kidding? You're mixed up with some crazies over there. Why don't you come back to J'lem and your ever-loving me? Besides, I bought you something from Germany. Love, Miri

She tried not to let Miri's analysis wrestle her down. Even if she'd scared Absalom off, at least she had rediscovered a kernel of her old self. Still, that night she'd picked up the phone to invite Absalom to a movie, but got his answering machine. Vaguely disappointed, she decided to delve more deeply into the black hole of Lydia's past. There were too many unsolved riddles and Emanuela's coincidental appearance on the beach and the look of terror on her face demanded more research.

David and Hana Cherniak lived in one of the original houses set on a spacious plot filled with gnarled fruit trees and a huddle of cats crunching their way through a pile of fish heads. Even from the front garden, Rachel could hear the blare of the evening news.

After sharp stabs at the buzzer, the volume dropped a few

decibels and Hana answered the door. Wreathed in a chignon of white hair, she was lean and tall, like Rachel. A beatific smile seamed her baby face.

"Rachel, what a lovely surprise! Come in, come in. We were just having tea and cake." She turned toward the living room. "Dovidl!"she shouted, "It's Nate and Aviva's little girl."

David Cherniak lumbered out to join them, leaning on his cane. Shorter than his wife, all width and bulk, his paunch was split by the belt around his middle, creating two pillows. His balding pate was fluffed by wisps of white, most of which was covered by a gaily embroidered skullcap. His eyes radiated the shrewdness Rachel remembered from the *gemara* class.

He cackled with pleasure. "Come in, girlie. Sit down and eat a little something."

Hana had bustled off into the kitchen to fetch additional goodies, while Rachel followed David into the living room. Just as her parents' place was fossilized in the 'sixties, the Cherniaks' décor had never emerged from the austere fifties, when stick-legged furniture and nubbly orange upholstery were the rage. The T.V. was covered with a lace doily, as were the backs of the sofa and armchairs. David sank down ponderously on a leather recliner, clearly a new acquisition, while Rachel perched on the edge of a chair whose wooden arms were scraped clean from years of use.

"Hope I helped you with *the Pregnant Virgin*," David twinkled.

"More than I'd hoped." Thinking of the Levys, she grimaced and leaned back on the thin layer of foam rubber beneath the orange upholstery. Hadassah Levy had ducked out of therapy, beaten down by Rachel's knowledge of Yoel's origins. "You and Hana are the oldest *haverim* here, and I need to ask you for other kinds of information. You won't object talking about old times, would you?"

"At our age, what else is left except our memories?" He folded his hands over his paunch. "What do you want to know?"

"About Lydia, for one."

The blood vessels that mapped his nose purpled and a startled expression swept across his face. "Lydia? What's your interest in her, girlie?"

"Ever since I was little, she was very special to me, but she was always close-mouthed about her own life. Now that she's dead, I need to know." She threw him a shamefaced smile. "Sometimes I think it's an obsession."

"Lydia, eh?" David chuckled softly. "Quite a woman, very unique indeed, who came to a premature and terrible end, God bless her soul."

Hana wobbled into the room, ferrying a tray and plied Rachel with tea, *mandelbroit*—toasted cake studded with nuts and dried fruit, and a slice of wicked Black Forest cake.

"So it's Lydia you want to hear about. Well, you came to the right place." She gave her husband a kick in the shin. "There was a time I was convinced that you and Lydia...you know. She was what used to be called "a free thinker.""

Her husband sputtered denials and turned to Rachel. "Hana always believed that Lydia and me...you know," he said, echoing his wife. *Sex, the great unmentionable, at least on Kerem El.* Rachel speared a slice of *mandelbroit.*

"I came across an old photograph of her. She was very beautiful."

"After Mengele got through with her, she was less beautiful,"Hana said grimly, pouring tea out of a china pot. "That's how she became crippled—from his experiments."

Rachel's throat went dry and she gulped down some tea. Lydia had been tortured by the Nazis, yet she'd remained gutsy and full of wry humor.

"What about before the war?"

David brushed crumbs from his paunch. "Her ancestors were captured by the Romans and brought over to Italy from Judea as slaves. They became silversmiths for various emperors."

"You don't have to go that far back."

Hana interceded. "Yes, he does. Her aristocratic past explains a lot about Lydia: her chutzpa, for one thing, and her belief that she was always right. She never doubted her place in the world, which caused her to do some foolish things."

"If it weren't for those foolish things," her husband retorted, "we might all be dead."

Rachel's ears perked up. Now they were getting to the nub of things. "Tell me."

David leaned back again in the recliner. "Like many refugees after the Holocaust, Lydia was sent to a British DP camp on Cyprus where she was treated for her medical problems. There she met up with our agents who were smuggling illegal immigrants into Palestine."

"How could Lydia swim to shore?"

Hana snorted. "There was nothing Lydia couldn't do. Somehow, she made it to shore from the immigrant ship. Some man was involved, most likely."

"Hana, you should be ashamed!" David admonished. "Don't speak ill of the dead."

His wife shrugged. "It's not speaking ill of the dead. Thanks to Lydia's affection for men, as you said before, we're alive and well today."

"Tell me that part." Rachel was intrigued.

"Well," David continued. "This was 1948 and Lydia got caught up in the War of Independence, like all of us. She joined the Hagana, which used her on many important missions due to her fluency in so many languages and her many, shall we say, human attractions."

"A spy," Hana volunteered succinctly.

Her husband nodded. "Lydia risked her life on many occasions, getting involved with a number of cutthroats, one of whom was the *mukhtar* of the village down the road— Zeita, which belonged to the Arabs then."

Hana whispered, "She became his mistress."

"I knew him," David continued the tale with the crisp delivery of a military man. "He was one of the most fanatic Jew-haters in the village, which enjoyed a steady supply of weapons from Kaukji's gangs. His hobby was taking potshots at Jewish convoys traveling the road, especially buses filled with civilians."

"But he had one weakness," Hana continued. "Tell her, Dovidl."

He dunked a slice of *mandelbroit* in his tea. "Beautiful women. One after the other, he discarded them like dirty handkerchiefs; wives of British officers, Jewish whores. Until he met Lydia. Naturally, their meeting had been plotted by the Hagana with Lydia as bait."

"A crippled femme fatale?" Rachel cried.

"Ahhh!" He waggled his finger. "Which proves that you didn't know the Lydia of those days. Despite her...what's the word these days?...disability, the wheelchair and all that, no man could resist her. She had a special way of captivating men, a kind of black magic."

Hana threw him a warning look. "Dovidl!"

David erased the fleeting look of wistfulness that had drifted across his face. "Yes, well. Within a short time, Lydia had become his mistress, was wined, dined, and even assigned a special room, a kind of seraglio, in the *mukhtar's* villa. From this strategic position, she became privy to many secrets: information about weapons and planned attacks, all of which she transmitted to Hagana headquarters in Haifa."

"What did the villagers think of his liaison with a Jewish woman, especially during wartime?"

Hana waved her hand dismissively, and shoved a slice of cake her way. "Oh, a fling with a Jewess didn't count for anything much. It didn't threaten the family unit."

Rachel felt a pang. *Alona, Alona.*

Hana went on. "Besides, he was the *mukhtar*, the tribal

leader. He could do whatever struck his fancy."

Rachel swallowed a bite of cake. "You said that Lydia saved your lives?"

David shifted in the recliner. "One night, she overheard Ali and his men plotting an attack on Kerem El. We were isolated here on the mountain, most of the men had been recruited by the Hagana, with only women and children left to defend themselves with a couple of rusty Czech rifles.

"Somehow, Lydia communicated this information to the Hagana, down to the exact date and time of the attack. Two hours before it was to take place, the Hagana attacked Zeita and killed Ali's men."

"What happened to Ali?"

"Oh," David said casually, "We slit his throat. After we paraded his body through the village, there was general panic and the villagers fled up here to the hills and hid in caves."

"Which was the beginning of Jabal-e-Zeit."

"Exactly. The Hagana took over the original village until the end of the war."

"When it became the artists' village."

"You know your local history, all right," David grinned.

As she munched, Rachel thought of Lydia: her snappy black eyes, her acerbic comments on human nature, her love of books and cooking. What had caused her reticence about her heroism? Humility? The desire to put her past behind her? And what had she decided to reveal before her death?

"Did anyone ever discover that it was Lydia who had betrayed Ali and the village?"

David fell silent, a look of sadness crossing his features. "It became general knowledge, especially when she vanished just before the attack and stayed away from the area until after the war."

"Where did she go?"

"I don't know. She had friends in the center of the country." Hana added, "Men friends."

Jacob Lifschitz? Could they have known each other from the DP camps? Rachel remembered the barbed wire in the missing photograph. She checked her watch. Her hosts were drooping. "I have another question, and then I'll let you go. Are any of Ali's descendents alive today?"

David answered readily. "They all are, up in Jabal-e-Zeit. After almost sixty years, the old grudges have faded and there are friendly relations between us and them, as you well know. In fact, you know Taleb, the handyman?"

Rachel nodded, her heart skipping a beat.

"That Ali—he was Taleb's grandfather."

CHAPTER THIRTY-TWO

SINCE her visit to the Cherniaks, Rachel had endured restless nights, in which Taleb crouched at the hub of a web, whose filaments reached Boaz Kashtan, his cousin's murderer, and Lydia, his grandfather's betrayer. Eager to share what she'd learned with Absalom, her enthusiasm dwindled when her messages remained unanswered.

Miri was right; he was running scared. What a fool she'd been, exposing her rawest secrets, and interpreting his Buddha-like silence as something deeper than inarticulate dumbness. His interest in her was that of a cop investigating a few murders, and he saw her as nothing more than a fertile source of information.

She cursed the memory of spontaneous combustion she'd felt the moment he'd stroked her wrist. *Idiot, idiot, idiot.* Hoisting the shopping bag onto her shoulder, she sensed a surly pride at her decision to return all the potato chips she'd bought to the mini-market. *Let him choke.*

Battling a headache, Rachel ignored the dew-laced morning, which only mocked the curtain gradually sealing off her heart.

The tension hit her as soon as she pushed open the door. Knots of tight-faced *haverim* whispered in the aisles, the men in their dark blue work clothes, caps and high boots. Why weren't they out in the banana fields or with the dairy herds? *Someone's dead. Or there's been a terrorist attack.*

Detaching herself from the clot of women near the vegetable bins, her mother raced in her direction, her snood crooked on her hair, and her plump flesh trembling slightly beneath layers of saffron-colored robes.

"Baby," she whispered breathlessly, "have you heard?"

Rachel braced herself on the rim of an eggplant carton. She shook her head.

"Terrible news, just devastating." Aviva pawed her daughter's arm. "It's the doctor. He's been arrested. The police took him away late last night."

"Ozeri?" Rachel felt disbelief flood through her. "Dr. Ozeri?"

Aviva nodded, her head bobbing up and down like a marionette. "They say he's been selling medication that expired or was watered down or something. It can't be true. Why, there's no doctor as dedicated as Reuven." She wiped her forehead with her tunic. "Gideon's down at the police station now arranging bail. Poor Orly and the kids!"

Through her mumbled platitudes, Rachel felt a blade as sharp as the guillotine she'd plunged down on Ozeri's neck. He'd been worse than sleaze, had caused the death of a little boy and lied about it and wormed his way onto Kerem El with phony recommendations. But he'd built a life here with his wife and six nice kids. On the other hand, he was scamming patients—Holocaust survivors, her parents. And if the Rebbe had dug out this information and threatened to turn him over to the police, the doctor might've gotten rid of him. As a result of her blabbing to Absalom, that creep, she'd sealed Ozeri's future.

She blurted out. "Maybe it's true."

Aviva's hand flew to her mouth, "God forbid! Don't even say it. Your father thinks we should change all the *mezuzot* on the kibbutz, and I agree."

"As if the plastic cylinders we hammer onto our doorposts cause all our problems." Irene Mann put her arm around Aviva's shoulder. Dressed for work in a neatly tailored lime-green suit and low-heeled sandals, she was doing the early morning shopping. Fresh rolls, brown rice and fruit yoghurts. No potato chips for the health-conscious Manns, Rachel thought.

Aviva shook off her arm. "Don't be flippant at a time like this, Irene."

Irene hooked a curl over one ear. "If not at times like these, then when? I'm just as shocked as you, Aviva, but superstition isn't going to help Reuven."

"Has Gideon phoned?" Rachel asked, calmed by the woman's steady common sense.

"About half an hour ago. The *meshek* will post bail and he'll be released. After all, he's a respected doctor with no criminal background." She sighed. "He won't be able to work, of course. I feel so sorry for him and his family."

Aviva wiped her eyes. "No rabbi, no doctor. What'll happen to us?"

Irene patted her hand. "We'll cope just as we always have." She turned her eyes towards Rachel. "This means you'll stay on longer, I hope. We'll be needing you more than ever." She smiled. "Not that you'll want to go running back to Jerusalem, from what I've heard."

Aviva's ears pricked up. "What have you heard about my daughter?"

Irene tapped her manicured fingers on the shopping cart. "Oh, a little birdie told me she was holding hands on the beach with a certain policeman."

Rachel didn't know whether she wanted to smack Irene, or hug her for the glow that lit up Aviva's face. "Is that so? Why do I have to hear this from someone else?"

"Believe me, *Ima*, there's nothing to hear." Turning her back, she picked up the shopping bag and hurled the bags of potato chips onto the shelf one by one.

* * *

The news of Ozeri's arrest was on everyone's lips. Even Malkie and Auntie Bracha, sticklers about *lashon ha-ra,* were dissecting the charges against him when Rachel dropped in to help with the kids. In the absence of her whittling—Absalom had taken her knife and the globe to the police lab and hadn't returned it—*bastard*—playing games with toddlers on the lawn and helping Malkie change diapers proved to be effective therapy. In the evening, when Malkie had taken off to Haifa for a women's Torah class, a step forward towards her rehabilitation, Rachel stayed on to put the kids to bed, .

By the time she returned to the chalet, she was sweaty and exhausted and the sadness that she'd kept in all day began to seep through her like a sluggish infection. Before climbing into the bathtub, she checked her messages. Just one from Miri wondering where *she'd* disappeared to. Nothing from Absalom.

Lying in bed, she was aware of how much the silence of the night pressed against her and fed her isolation. She missed the raucous Jerusalem traffic sounds, the boisterous cries of vendors in the *shuk*. What remained for her on Kerem El? Not the murders, surely. Images flickered through her mind: Taleb's truck bearing down on her, the lolling head of the Rebbe doll, Boaz Kashtan's whiplash rage. Let Detective-Inspector Catatonia solve them. If Ozeri had been arrested during the night, Absalom must have been there and if he hadn't bothered to see her, it meant only one thing.

Another sleepless night awaited her. She tried visualizing a happy end to the Absalom fiasco. She approached a bridge opening into a field of golden wheat. Beneath the bridge, in the fetid darkness, lurked Absalom, a grotesque, misshapen troll. She ran across the bridge, arms outstretched towards the sun, and the troll broke into pieces.

She must have fallen asleep, because the thumping sounds caught her in a dreamlike state. Her heart raced yet every muscle felt paralyzed. Someone was moving through the chalet. She tried to make out what the intruder was doing: the scrape of a chair, the sounds of water running, but to no avail.

Should she dare use the phone to call for help? Pretend she was asleep? That was the safest thing to do. What she hadn't counted on was the sudden infusion of anger in her limbs. Shoving the blanket aside, she reached for her robe, and swung her feet onto the carpet. Her gaze swept the room for a weapon, cursing Absalom once again for failing to return the knife. Her eyes fell on the scissors from the art therapy group; she retrieved it from the top of the bureau and clasped it in her fist.

She filled her lungs with air, ran into the kitchenette, screamed out a war cry and hammered the light switch.

Yossi Gottwein blinked at the sudden flash of light. As his hands flew up to shade his eyes, she saw they were dripping blood.

CHAPTER THIRTY-THREE

SHE screamed, this time in earnest when she saw the kitchen cupboards and tile floor spattered with blood. Yossi Gottwein sank down in a chair, clutching his scalp in crimson-stained hands, a moan emerging from his lips.

Once the banging in her heart subsided, Rachel felt as if she'd stepped into a surrealistic painting. The pristine sitting room, fresh fruit in the crystal bowl, elegant chairs set around the coffee table like ladies at a tea party, and adjacent to it, the kitchenette with gobbets of blood on the kitchen floor, and the flabby cop sobbing with his head in his hands. Rachel focused on the blood, waited for the walls to cave in and for her knees to buckle. Other than the pounding of a pulse in her head, she remained clear-eyed and steady.

An overturned plastic bowl had contained the blood. Yossi's eyes peeked out through blood-spattered glasses. "It's not what you think." He gurgled a laugh. "Chicken livers from the supermarket." He splayed his chunky fingers in a gesture of appeal. "I never meant to hurt you, Rachel, only to scare you."

"Thanks so much." She took a seat, careful not to tread in the blood, which was drying now into rusty blotches. "You have a lot of explaining to do."

"Maybe I can get cleaned up first?" For the first time, he appeared to have absorbed what he'd done. His gaze swiveled around the cupboard doors, the floor, coming to rest on his hands.

"No, first you talk. I'll get you some water, though." *And coffee for me. You don't deserve it, you worm.*

She stood up and poured water from the cooler into a plastic cup. No crystal goblets for him. As he slurped it down, she spooned coffee grinds into the percolator.

"I feel weird, you know," he said, wiping his mouth, "Even glad you caught me. This isn't the real me, Rachel. I'm a nice, easy-going guy."

Sure. Breaking into my chalet, pouring blood all over my kitchen. A peach! She clanged the percolator onto the stovetop and lit the flame.

"Okay, okay, that seems hard to believe. But…give me a minute. I shocked myself just now. I have to take it all in." He dropped his head into his hands once again.

She spit out the words, thick with sarcasm. "Right. It wasn't you. Something got into you and made you do it."

"Yeah, something like that." He looked at her gratefully. "You *are* a good shrink."

Rolling her eyes with disgust, she poured her coffee and sat down again. What a police force. A catatonic misfit and now, this clown. "This isn't a therapy session, Yossi. You owe me an explanation. And if it doesn't wash, I'll report you for breaking, entering, vandalism…"

His features sagged. "Maybe you'd be doing me a favor. I'm

not sure I'm cut out to be a cop. But first hear me out." He took a deep breath. "It's about Abs, my partner. And you."

She closed her eyes and took a sip of the coffee, grateful for the pain that seared her lips. "What about him?"

"Let me back up a bit. The first time I saw you in the courtroom my eyes nearly popped out of my head. You see," he looked up at the ceiling, "you look so much like Abs' old girlfriend, Christina." His gaze swerved towards her. "The hair, the eyes, your figure."

"I don't believe this," she said.

"Sounds crazy, but it's true. You see, he and Christina, this Danish girl, lived together for a long time. He was happy with her, very happy."

Rachel closed her eyes, trying to concentrate on the coffee and not on her heart, which was sinking like an elevator.

"But," Yossi threw his arms in the air in a helpless gesture, "one day she leaves. Has to take care of her sick mother, she says. Goes back to Copenhagen, leaves him hanging in the wind, promises she'll come back. Then, nothing. She's staying there, she says. You can imagine what it did to ol' Abs." He shook his head.

"Just what *did* it do to ol' Abs?"

He paused and looked at her quizzically, as if finally registering her caustic tone.

"Sent him way, way down. If I were a shrink like you, I'd call it depression. His body looked hammered, you know, like a car wreck." He leaned forward. "Then, when he came out of it, the Paradise happened."

"What do you mean?"

His voice rose impatiently. "You never heard of the bombing over at the Paradise? How d'ya think he got those scars all over his head? And his arm all broken?"

The coffee cup clattered into the saucer with such force that the tissue-thin china broke into shards. Tears stung her eyes.

Yossi scrambled to his feet. "Don't take it so hard. It's only a lousy cup."

"It's valuable," she wailed, tears streaming down her cheeks. Her whole body convulsed in pain. How could she survive this agony, these losses, both Absalom's and hers? The fragile bond that had begun to take root was stronger than they had both imagined. Why had he kept mum about the Paradise when she'd exposed her own trauma?

Yossi clattered about the kitchen, muttering about rags, a dustpan and a mop, in charge again now that a woman was crying.

She sniffed. "This is a hotel, Yossi. There are no cleaning things here. Use those paper towels." She lifted her head and pointed to the marble counter. Her eyes felt bruised and her hair was glued to her cheek, yet she had to hear more. Hear it all.

"Okay."

He soaked reams of paper towels, scrubbing blood off the kitchen doors. "Yossi," she yelled. "Rinse those towels in the meat sink! Right-hand side." She couldn't believe it. On one of the worst nights of her life, her kosher instincts were kicking in.

"Anything else?" Exhaustion was overtaking her, yet Yossi seemed hopped up with energy.

"Yeah, a lot. As I was saying, Abs was caught in the Paradise, got out of hospital and then who shows up at the station one day? You." He aimed a finger at her. "Bang!"

She closed her eyes at the memory; how the cops at the station had gaped and nudged each other and how nasty Yossi had been. And she'd thought he was getting back at her for Dima. He was protecting Absalom.

"I could see he was all stirred up," Yossi continued, "and how he kept coming back here about these murders. I knew he was cooking up excuses to see you again, even when he didn't know it himself. Y'know what I'm driving at?"

She nodded. "You knew him better than he knew himself."

"Bingo!" he said, chucking the bloody paper towels into the bin. "Then, there was the night of the Polish gala when Lifschitz was killed." He tore off another ream, moistened it and began tackling the floor. Rachel got the impression that he was ducking his head in order to avoid her glance.

"You were shaking like a kitten, your eyes rolling up inside your head."

She flinched. "Don't remind me."

He looked up at her. "You wanna know what happened, don't you?" He grinned. "Besides, it's shrink time. I'm in the confessing groove."

"Go on." She glanced out at the night layering into grayness. Wind from the east keened through the window and the curtains flared. A cock crowed. A new dawn. *My God!*

How will I drag myself through this day?

"As I was saying, you were out, sliding from the chair, and what does Abs do? Picks you up in his arms like Mr. Romeo himself. That did it. Yossi, I figured, you gotta stop this or Abs is gonna get kicked in the teeth by love *again*."

Instead of elation at the memory of those strong arms around her, she felt dulled. He was only interested in her because she resembled his old girlfriend. It had nothing to do with her at all.

"The doll with the broken neck put it into my head. Absalom brought it to the lab to test for fingerprints. He was fuming, told me how scared you were, cursing the bastard who did this to you. So," he grunted as he got to his feet, "I decided to scare you good and proper, and send you packing all the way back to Jerusalem."

"Thank you, Yossi. How did you manage to do that?"

He poured dishwashing liquid on his hands and started soaping them. "I came by one day—you've gotta be careful about locking your door, you know." He gave her a reproving look below his glasses, then shook his hands dry. "I saw that wooden thing you carved and stuck the knife in deep, turned it round and round."

Rachel knew she should feel something, but she didn't. So much for her moment of sensuality, her openness to life. How fitting that this moron should've been the one to defile her beautiful globe. What a bitter joke.

"I'm sorry, Rachel," he said simply and hung his head. As comical as he looked, with the sparse hairs nesting on the red scalp and his ungainly body, she was touched. At least he was genuine, which was more than she could say for his partner, with all his ironed suavity. He might be nuts, but he was a loyal friend. She didn't have the heart to ruin his career. Besides, the less contact she had with cops the better.

"Friends, Yossi?" She wearily extended her hand.

He shook it with vigor. "That's how Abs would want it."

Absalom again. "Where is he? Who arrested Ozeri?"

Yossi grimaced and shrugged. "I did. Abs is away, but I don't know where. Ron—he's the superintendent—said that he'd asked for leave and Ron granted it." His features blurred with embarrassment, clearly hurt that his partner hadn't included him in his plans.

"In the middle of a murder investigation?"

He sat down. "I asked Ron about that very thing and he said something weird. 'I owe him one.'"

"What did he mean?"

Yossi scratched his head. "Something happened between them a long time ago before I came along. They used to be partners, Abs and Ron, and all of a sudden, Ron gets promoted and Abs freezes him out. He never told me why."

"And you have no idea where he is?" She felt irritated with herself for asking.

Yossi shook his head. They were silent for a while, listening to the wind rattle the trees. A soft yellow paled the sky above the mountains.

Rachel got up and hugged the robe around her. "It's morning, Yossi. How about a cup of coffee?"

CHAPTER THIRTY-FOUR

IF the maid had wondered about the rust-colored smears on the floor, Rachel wasn't aware of it. For most of the day a dreamless sleep had seized her, and when she awoke to the afternoon sun streaming through the shutters, she knew what her decision would be.

She showered, put on fresh jeans, drank coffee and took stock of her possessions. Tonight she'd tell her parents she was returning to Jerusalem, and tomorrow she'd notify Malkie, Alona and her remaining patients. For the first time in ages, she turned on the television and sat through an idiotic sitcom. She felt like a miniature ship in a bottle, unreachable and protected by glass. Outside, the afternoon sounds of chattering young mothers and whoops of children rose and fell.

The phone rang. *Keep calm. It's your mother, Alona, a wrong number.* She steeled herself against the possibility that it might be the one person she wanted to speak to most of all.

But it was a woman's voice, faint and hoarse. "Is this Rachel?"

"Yes, it is."

A brief silence. "This is Emanuela, Lydia di Rossi's niece?" She wheezed.

Rachel's heart lurched, adrenaline racing. "Oh, hello."

Another silence, longer now. "I have something for you, something really important. Don't tell anyone."

"Can't you give me more information?"

"No! I…no. Don't ask me again." She paused. "It's about my aunt's death."

Rachel's body was taut with concentration. "Of course, whatever you say."

"Tomorrow at five?"

"Where?" She reached for a pad and pencil.

Emanuela was speaking rapidly now, the words tumbling over one another. "You know the old quarry near the Arab village? Be there at five."

"Aren't you being a bit dramatic?"

"No, believe me, I'm not. I'm scared stiff…" Her voice rose in panic.

"Okay, Emanuela, I'm sure it's not as bad as you think, whatever it is. But I'll be there."

"Remember, five o'clock. And keep your mouth shut about this."

Her response was cut off as she hung up. For a moment, Rachel wondered whether this frightened woman was the same hard-bitten chain smoker with the bleached hair. She'd seemed scared enough when she'd spied Rachel on the beach. What had changed from the time she'd corralled her into mailing Lydia's books?

Automatically, she punched in her parents' extension. "*Ima*, it's me. Sure, I'm fine. Do you remember that Irene said a little birdie had seen Absalom and me on the beach?"

Aviva chuckled. "I suppose you want to know who it was."

"I do. Just this once, don't ask me why I want to know. Just tell me."

"All right, Miss Snippity-Uppity. It was Gideon. He was jogging on the beach that day."

After hanging up, Rachel made sure the door and windows were locked, turned on the air-conditioner and closed the shutters. Her gaze fell on the unmade bed, the half-filled glass of water on the floor. Like a sleepwalker, she wandered around the chalet, while she tumbled through a chasm that ripped her world apart.

Since childhood, she'd smelled that scent. It conjured up lazy wood smoke curling through mountain air, yet not until Aviva's words, did it meld with the indefinable odor that had lingered in her room the night she'd found the doll with the broken throat. The insight had only taken a shift in a brain cell or two, the soft landing of stimulus on gray matter. It hadn't been the sight of Rachel that had terrorized Emanuela, but Gideon. Why?

Bracing herself for a panic attack, she opened the refrigerator and poured a glass of cold water, then dipped a clean dishtowel into the icy liquid and wrapped it around the back of her neck. The chill galvanized her thoughts into coherence.

Gideon Mann. Her childhood was infused with the comforting sight of him puffing on his pipe, his gray eyes crinkling with humor and good sense. Her parents' best friend, the godfather at Michael's circumcision ceremony so long ago.

Now she had no one. She wanted desperately to confide in Absalom, but he'd vanished from her life. Briefly, she thought of Yossi Gotwein, but he was too oafish and volatile.

She ripped the towel from her neck. The panic attack hadn't materialized. She knew what she had to do. Go it alone.

CHAPTER THIRTY-FIVE

B Y the time she set out for the old quarry it was after four-thirty. She was going to be late.

Waving to the guard at the gate, she rushed down the hill to where the road forked in the direction of the quarry. The mountains basked in the slanting rays of the sun and a faint breeze carried the scent of the hardy wildflowers that still held out in the face of the early summer heat. Few cars passed on this remote stretch so she was alone, her breathing harsh and shallow, anxiety fluttering beneath her skin. Why was Emanuela so afraid? Why had she contacted Rachel? Why the need for secrecy? And above all, why was Rachel pushing on so recklessly? This time, she refused to speculate on her motives. Something real was happening and she was on her way to meet it head on.

When she reached the quarry, she was breathing heavily and paused to lean against the stone slabs hewn out of the mountainside. On weekends, it was a popular meeting place for hikers setting out on the many trails that snaked through the nature reserve. A pebble-strewn parking area led to the fringe of forest beyond, but it was empty. The only sounds were the faint songs of birds twittering in the trees.

Where was Emanuela? Foolishly, Rachel had forgotten her

mobile phone, not that she knew the woman's number. She realized that Emanuela had no way of notifying Rachel if she'd be late. She began to pace.

"Emanuela?" she shouted, feeling ridiculous as her voice echoed through the hills.

A faint rustle caught her attention. Gideon Mann emerged from the woods, jingling a bunch of car keys in his hand. When he saw her, he grimaced ever so slightly.

"Rachel, I want you to come with me." He held out his hand, but she turned and walked quickly away. He grabbed her arm.

"Please." His voice was firm.

"Why?" she demanded, whirling around to face him.

"Just do it," he said quietly. Then she saw the gun in his hand and her legs turned to jelly.

"What are you doing? Where's Emanuela?" she stammered.

He gestured towards the woods with the gun. "Do as I say and I'll explain everything."

As if in a paralytic dream, Rachel stumbled ahead, away from the solace of the road, of the quarry, deeper into the woods. Hidden among the trees stood a navy blue Pontiac. Among the irrelevancies buzzing through her brain was the thought that this wasn't a kibbutz car.

As if reading her thoughts, he said, "It's mine. It has its uses. Get in the front seat."

Opening the passenger door, he nudged her in and solicitously locked her seat belt. *This is Gideon, taking me to the fun fair in Haifa, buying me pistachio ice cream, buckling my seat belt, taking me home to my mommy and daddy.*

Except that it wasn't Gideon. This stranger was looking at her through sliding eyes. As he slipped into the driver's seat, she could smell his wood smoke pipe tobacco clinging to his clothes. He'd put the gun in his belt, underneath his jacket.

"Don't even think it," he said, as he turned on the ignition. He turned to face her. She felt swallowed up in his metallic eyes. "I push one button on my mobile phone, give an order and Emanuela gets a bullet through the head."

To her shame, Rachel let out a sob. "Why are you doing this?"

As he backed out onto the highway, he said, "We're in for a leisurely drive. There'll be plenty of time to explain."

Backtracking, he drove past the turn-off to the kibbutz, and as she gazed longingly up at the red-roofed houses hugging the mountainside, she wanted to shout, jump out the window, and will her body to float out of the car and upwards towards her parents.

Gideon's eyes were on the road. She turned to glance at his profile, his gray eyes, straight nose and sculpted chin. Somewhere was the Gideon who'd lifted her up to the highest rung of the jungle gym. She mustn't lose sight of that, but manipulate it to her advantage.

He turned south on the old road to Tel Aviv, lined with the banana fields and kibbutzim that skirted the seashore. At the Fureidis junction, he turned left again. They were heading east, away from the coast. The traffic was heavy on the new road, and as they sped along past the Yokneam Mall, a truck came alongside, laden with cages packed with live chickens on their way to slaughter. Even the chickens stared down impassively at her.

It was only at the green bowl of the Jezreel Valley that Gideon visibly relaxed. He shifted in his seat and fumbled for the pipe in his shirt pocket, which he stuck in his mouth unlit.

"One of the qualities I've always liked about you, Rachel, was your inquisitiveness."

"I'm flattered."

"Except that it doesn't suit you as an adult. Your meddling has seriously interfered with my plans."

She wiped her sweaty palms on her jeans. "Am I supposed to apologize?"

He chuckled. "I've made my share of mistakes. Telling Irene that I saw you at the beach, for one."

She stared out at the softly rolling hills that cupped the ancient valley which armies had criss-crossed for thousands of years. Now it was pastoral, dotted by kibbutzim.

"I'm allowed to ask a question, aren't I?"

"Of course. As I said, your curiosity has always impressed me."

"How did you know about my so-called meddling?"

He overtook a tractor that was rumbling ahead of them. "Modern technology is truly marvelous. It doesn't take much to hack into the kibbutz computer network. Or to listen in on your phone extension." He tsked-tsked. "All those emails to your friend...what's her name...Miri?...were extremely detailed. Tracking your progress made me understand what a danger you were becoming. I had to scare you off."

It all clicked into place. "The Rebbe doll."

He briefly took his eyes off the road and twinkled at her. "Very clever, I thought at the time. Now I'm not so sure. It sucked that policeman deeper into your life."

Absalom. Her heart dived. She'd never see him again, would never be able to berate him for abandoning her. Never…anything. Tears rose in her throat.

"What do you know about me, Rachel."

She looked straight ahead. "As it turns out, nothing at all."

He chomped on his pipe. "You're not far wrong. I'm not really alive, you see."

"What are you talking about?"

"A small Holocaust flickers inside me, with a crematorium warming my gut. Its ashes choke my throat."

Rachel wanted to flatten him. "So you're a poet, now." But she was intrigued. This might just be the last story she'd hear in her life. "What do you mean about the Holocaust part?"

"My father called himself The Death Man, his task in the camps being to extract the gold teeth from the mouths of corpses. He'd been a smelter before the war, in a little town called Pomorzany in Poland. His young wife and baby were murdered at Auschwitz. I have their picture on the desk in my office."

She recalled a photograph of the couple with the blond baby in their arms, snow-capped mountains in the background.

"They were his true family. I wanted to be that little boy, not the shadow boy I grew up as. That's why my parents never had any more children, to cherish the memory of that little boy. My mother worked in slave labor camps during the war, and so she remained for the rest of her life—a slave to my father. She was his shadow wife, just as I was a shadow son. I hated my parents for turning me into a fire-and-ash person. Imagine the silences. Silence when my mother made us ersatz coffee with milk in the mornings with bread and jam, silence when she made avocado sandwiches for school, silence served up with schnitzel and potato puree for lunch. She was a slave, an automaton."

They kept heading east. The green fields whipped past, tractors, combines, sprinklers dancing in the fading light.

Gideon continued, as if in a trance. "As for my father, he was Gray Man; gray hair streaked with white, gray trousers, the gray shirt of a laborer. Even his face had a gray pasty color. The way he looked mirrored what I felt inside—ash. He worked as a smelter in a small workshop with his best friend from the camps, Yankele Lifschitz, a boyhood friend from Pomorzany."

"Jacob Lifschitz," she whispered. "So you killed him too."

"All in good time," Gideon chided. "First, I must clarify things about Yankele and me. He was the only adult who'd ever shown me any warmth. He'd take me to the beach, even to a movie once. But his great tragedy was his only son, Ari. You know all about that."

She nodded.

"So in the close circle of shadow children, I became Yankele's substitute son also."

Rachel blurted out. "What about religion? How could a religious person do the things you've done?"

Gideon sighed and glanced to the left where a jeep was trying to overtake them. "My parents spoke Yiddish and grew up in religious homes in the *stetl*, but lost their faith during the war. My father said that God turned his face aside and let the Germans kill his lovely young wife and innocent son. Then, God turned him into an animal which yanked gold teeth out of the mouths of Jews. Yankele, on the other hand, never lost his faith, even when Ari was born. He felt that God's purpose was carried out through the suffering of small souls."

Though he'd avoided her question, she let him talk. *Maybe that's the smart thing to do. Just let him talk.*

"Yankele took over my religious instruction, took me to *shul* and taught me how to understand the *siddur* and the services. He even paid for my bar mitzvah lessons. Being active in the National Religious Party, he arranged a scholarship for me to study in yeshiva."

"It was my first time away from home, you understand. I made friends, the teachers and rabbis showed an interest. I was quiet and spoke in a low, reasonable voice, never yelling or horsing around. It turned out that I had a good mind, reflective, logical, suited to Torah study. I also had a head for figures and my teachers suggested I study accountancy."

Rachel couldn't restrain her sarcasm. "And you always did what the rabbis told you, right?"

But he was lost in a world of his own, his hands easy on the steering wheel, the pipe clicking through his teeth.

"I found comfort in religion. It soothed the small crematorium in my gut. It gave me boundaries and guidelines. I'm not sure I found God, but I found religion. When I was at yeshiva, my mother died of a cancer that ate her from the inside out. The last time I saw her, she'd become the walking dead on the outside, too. A skeleton with a hank of hair and the smell of putrefaction already emanating from her body. Her death left me cold. Literally. Though she died in the spring when winter was already over, my hands and feet stayed cold for months."

"That was when one of the teachers suggested I start running. It would help my circulation, he said. So I ran. Every morning I ran. The cold went away. The blood rushed through my body and I felt invigorated. More alive and less dead. I've been running every since."

"And you're running now, running from the deaths you caused." Rachel glanced out the window at the big green sign marked *Jordan 20 kms* in thick white letters.

He smiled broadly. "I have an affinity for death, you see. In the army I was the one who identified the bodies, pulling them out of burning tanks, bundling them onto stretchers. I thought of my father in the camps, handling the corpses the same way, with the same affinity. It was the first time I ever felt empathy for him."

"What happened to him?"

"During my second year in the army, he died of blood poisoning. Ironic, that both my parents died from something endemic within them. Like a fetus, they carried death inside them and passed it on to me."

They reached the Beit Hashitta interchange and Gideon veered off to the side road that bypassed the town of Beit Shean. The narrow road curved through a forest of date palms, as the landscape turned tropical.

"So," she said, "Why did you do it? Don't tell me it was because of your deprived childhood."

He briefly glanced at her. "The killings? Isn't it obvious? In order not to be found out, of course."

She shook her head. "You've lost me."

He sighed, as if he had the tiresome job of explaining something to a mental defective. "It was Yankele who gave me the idea. He'd starting obsessing about Ari's future. Who would provide for him after he died? The idea that the boy would be uprooted from his familiar surroundings and be put into an inferior facility tortured him. He confided in me. How could Ari's upkeep be assured in perpetuity? It would take money, lots of money."

"At first, my thoughts centered on how to help Yankele achieve the peace of mind he so deserved. It was also a mental and financial challenge for me, a professional challenge. As to how to perpetuate the fraud, it was Yankele who provided me with the means."

"The Pomorzany *Landsmanschaft* and the Kamienski Trust," Rachel murmured, gazing out at the violet landscape. The mountains of Jordan were looming hulks against the darkening sky.

"Clever girl." Gideon gave her a sideways smile of approval.

"The Trust entitles the members of the *Landsmanschaft* to treatments at the spa of their choice. As the organization's president, Yankele would push our hotel as an ideal venue. Indeed, the members loved every moment of their bi-annual vacations at Kerem El."

"How lovely. If you're going to be ripped off, why not enjoy it?"

Gideon clicked his tongue. "No need to be so cynical. Anyway, the Trust handed over the money to Yankele who was the liaison with our hotel. No one questioned the padded fees or the inflated rates for special treatments."

Disgust consumed her. "It never bothered you that you were cheating Holocaust survivors? You're almost as bad as the Nazis were."

"Don't talk that way to me. Show some respect." He scowled.

It was then she realized how crazy he was and that she'd better keep her mouth shut if she wanted to get out alive. But then, he was confessing everything, which could only mean one thing. He intended to kill her.

They'd turned south on Route 90, the road that cut through the Jordan Rift Valley. To the left was Jordan, to the right, a few kiosks and a small village called Rehov, "Street." Rachel's mind clung to that strange detail: one of the last things she'd mull over was the anomaly of a town named Street.

Gideon glanced over at the mountains of Jordan and the pools of light flickering from villages there. "About a year ago, when he was approaching eighty, Yankele began getting attacks of guilt. Ari's future was assured, but Yankele's place in the world to come didn't look very promising. Before he died, he wanted to confess. For both of us. This jarred me. His obsessiveness was taking over again. Nothing I could say would deter him, not even the fact he'd have to return the money he'd salted away for Ari, and it all would've been for nothing. By the time it went through the courts, he said, he'd be dead and he would have found a foolproof way to squirrel away the money for Ari's care."

"So you killed him."

"Patience, patience," he chided. "It's hard to describe how I felt at the thought of Yankele confessing. My family, reputation, freedom, money would all be destroyed. I would end up like my father, the walking dead, rotting away in prison, old and rejected when I got out. I would become the shadow man, the gray man. Yankele was beyond all reason. I knew I had to put a stop to him."

He slowed down and carefully parked at the side of the road, took out his mobile and looked at her with his strange eyes. He punched in a number and lowered his voice.

"We're almost there."

Apart from a few cars, they were alone on the road. Since the Second Intifada, very few cars drove through the Jordan Valley. He gripped her chin with his fingers and swiveled her head towards him.

"Listen carefully. Half a kilometer from here, there's a checkpoint. No nonsense, do you hear? One sign, one sound, Emanuela dies."

She nodded. He'd been clever, had chosen the laxest checkpoint between Israel and the territories. No soldier would look twice at a car with Israeli plates, a driver with a skullcap and a woman in the front seat wearing modest jeans.

Spotlights signaled the checkpoint. An Israeli flag fluttered above the concrete structure. Two soldiers yawned, glanced into the car and waved them through the zig-zag barriers. She tried desperately to catch their eye, willing them to stare into hers and notice some sign.

Gideon picked up speed. "We're almost there." His profile was etched in the dark glow of the dashboard. All of a sudden, she saw the winking of the signal light turning right. She looked out the window and saw the sign in Hebrew and Arabic. *Bardalah.*

Her heart plummeted. They were leaving Israel and heading for the Palestinian Authority.

CHAPTER THIRTY-SIX

THE paved road ended at the outskirts of Bardalah, after which they bumped along a dirt track that led through fields of dried grass; aside from the headlights, bucking and weaving ahead on the rough patches, darkness enveloped them like black cream.

All at once serenity cloaked her; the calm of complete surrender. There was nothing she could do; she was going to die. Her mental calculator clicked out the possible ways—strangling, stabbing, shooting. She chuckled out loud. She'd ruled out poisoning unless Gideon had doctored his pipe tobacco.

"What's so amusing?" Gideon was concentrating on the road.

"Nothing I'd want to share with you. Besides, you're the big talker."

Her sarcasm was lost on him, his ego too pumped up by the chance to share his exploits at last. "Where was I?"

"Jacob Lifschitz's guilt." Rachel still couldn't think of the man as Yankele.

"Of course. Yankele's overburdened conscience. He boasted that he'd written out the details of our scheme, including bank account numbers, and had given it to two people—Reb Elijah and Lydia."

She shifted in her seat. Yankele had lied about the written confessions; they didn't exist, but they'd precipitated three murders. However, she didn't intend to share that with the psychopath driving the car.

"The Rebbe I can understand, but why Lydia?" She knew from the Cherniaks, but wanted to keep him talking.

He turned off the air-conditioner and rolled down the windows. The pungent smell of animal dung and wild sage filled the air.

"They met at a DP camp in Cypress after the war, where they became lovers."

"The photograph!"

He grinned. "Good girl! Needless to say, I got rid of it after the Holocaust ceremony."

"After you'd killed Lydia, "Rachel said bitterly.

"Yes…well, to make a long story short, after arriving in Israel, Yankele went to Kfar Saba and Lydia came up here to work for the Hagana. At a certain point she went underground and hid out in his apartment. They never lost touch."

She swallowed hard over the swollen lump in her throat. "If it isn't against your principles, could you tell me…did Lydia say anything before you threw her over the cliff?"

He laughed. "She spat in my face and let out some juicy curses in Italian. But I'll say this for her—she was gutsy to the very end. She knew I was going to kill her, you see."

Rachel understood her. He was planning to kill her too, and she had nothing to lose. She could say or do anything.

"You started the fire, didn't you."

He nodded. "The *khamsin* played right into my hands. Hot ash is a fine incendiary device in that arid wind. The dry brush on the mountainside caught fire immediately."

"Making Lydia's cause of death unidentifiable." She laughed.

"Am I amusing you?"

Rachel sighed. "I was just remembering how you pulled me up the hill and out of the fire. You were my savior at that moment." A cramp seized her foot, and she flexed her instep. "Why did you save me if I was such a meddler? You could've let me burn?"

Gideon tousled her hair and she threw off the touch of his palm. "I'm not a complete monster, Rachel. I've known you since you were born. Besides, people would remember my heroism instead of wondering where I was when Lydia was killed."

"So I was a convenient alibi."

"You can look at it that way, yes."

The pitted road smoothed into tarmac and they began climbing up into the hills. Every now and then, a donkey brayed or a dog barked from an isolated village. To the west, the lights of Afula stained the sky red. Gideon pulled over and stopped the car. He unbuckled his seat belt and glanced at his watch.

"We still have time. Want to hear the rest?"

"May I?" She gestured towards her seat belt. Holding the gun in one hand, he undid the clasp in a swift gesture. Then, he lit his pipe. She thought she'd choke on that wood smoke smell.

He leaned back lazily in his seat, sucking on the pipe. "The Rebbe was a different kettle of fish, however. His sermon left me no choice. It was clear that he knew everything. That morning in *shul* he gazed at me with those fiery eyes. Like a smelter's oven."

"I had to lure him to the shul on Saturday night, make him feel that I was prepared to do the right thing. The dust storm played into my hands. No one would be wandering about. And if anyone saw me, I'd be out jogging, right? I phoned the Rebbe, telling him to meet me in the *shul,* that I'd thought it over and had something important to tell him. I'd already changed clothes, knowing I'd get his blood all over me." In the glow of the pipe, she noted a faint tic of distaste.

"What did you do with the bloody clothes?"

He crowed. "The *matza shmura oven,* of course. I threw the clothes in the flames."

The logic that had ticked away in his mind chilled her. "You murdered our Rebbe."

Gideon waved the gun at her. "What would anyone else have done in my position?"

Rachel wanted to throw up. "Incriminating Shmaya was a brilliant touch."

He smirked. "I knew he always showed up in *shul* earlier than the rest of us and was bound to discover the body. Poor fellow. So obviously the fanatic, a true borderline personality."

Unlike you. You crossed the border a long time ago.

"It was very simple, really," he continued, puffing his pipe and glancing at his watch again.

Rachel didn't want to hear any more, certainly not his boasting about how the Rebbe went to his death like a trussed-up animal. She sat in silence, listening to the crickets gnash the air with rasping feet.

"How does Emanuela come into it?" she asked.

"I needed her thanks to that stubborn Lydia. Till the end she refused to tell me where she'd hidden Yankele's document." 'Emanuela' is someone I knew from the old days. She still had affection for me, so she agreed to play the part of Lydia's niece and rifle through her stuff until she retrieved the document. Her real name is Yaffa, by the way."

"And you're prepared to have her shot."

He shrugged. "I've traveled so far no one can stand in my way. Not even you, Rachel."

She persisted. "You'd killed two people by the time you brought Emanuela into the picture. Why didn't you search Lydia's house on your own?"

"It's precisely because I'd come so far that I didn't want to jeopardize my achievements because some idiot on guard duty might see me and ask questions."

They sat in a strangely companionable silence. At that moment, she felt God closer to her than ever. He had brought her to this juncture. Why, she'd never know.

"What about God, *Thou shalt not kill*? What about mass betrayal: your wife and kids, friends, my own parents. What was it all about? Money? I can't believe that."

He fingered his pipe. "You don't understand, do you? I thought you were a therapist." He eyed the darkness and sighed, "Of course it wasn't money. It was need, the need to be filled—with power, control—the need to satiate the growling crematorium in my gut."

"That's psychobabble. You've become a monster."

He looked at her gravely. "In a way, yes. Like Moloch, the Canaanite god, who could only be propitiated by babies hurled into the flames of his belly. I'm a walking dead man, fueled by the need to be satiated."

At the faint hum of a motor, he sharpened his gaze and ordered her out of the car, brandishing the gun.

"Ah, just on time."

A van stopped fifty feet from them. In the headlights, Rachel couldn't see the driver, but after the slam of the passenger door, he drove away. Muffled footsteps came towards them and a tall shape sauntered over in the darkness.

It'd never occurred to her that Gideon had an accomplice. Though he'd used other people along the way—Yankele, Emanuela/Yaffa—he'd always done his killing alone.

A familiar voice drifted towards her. "Did she give you any trouble?"

Gideon addressed Rachel directly. "Not at all. She's a good listener, that's her job."

The voice came closer. "You're crazy. You told her everything?"

"She won't be in a position to tell anyone a thing."

The man walked around to Rachel's side of the car and

held out his hand. She smelled liquor on his breath.

"Taleb."

"Rachel," he said formally. She ignored his outstretched hand.

"I thought you had better taste in friends."

"Friends are a luxury." He spat on the ground.

"So is love, I guess. Alona really believed that the two of you had something special." Despite the terror in the pit of her stomach, the image of Alona, all radiance, filled her mind.

He walked past her and opened the trunk of the car. He put a firm hand around her arm and gave her a slight tug. "Get out of the car and into the trunk, Rachel."

She pulled her arm away. "Tell me one thing. The day of the Holocaust Ceremony; the stomach poisoning was an excuse, wasn't it? Where were you really?"

In the dark, she barely discerned his features, but she saw them sag. "No harm in telling you." He glanced at Gideon, who nodded. "I've been helping Gideon for a long time now in return for more money than I ever would've seen if I'd hooked up with Alona. And fewer problems. I have friends I can count on. Gideon needed them. It's no problem." He dragged her over to the back of the car where she gaped at the black, airless space, as plush as a velvet coffin. "Now, get into the trunk."

Gideon walked around from the other side. "Come on, climb in like a good girl, otherwise Taleb will lift you up and throw you in." His voice was cajoling, yet strict, like a gentle disciplinarian.

"What do you intend to do with me?"

Over her head, they exchanged glances. Taleb shook his head imperceptibly.

Ignoring him, Gideon spoke in the same dreamy yet didactic tone he'd used to tell his story. "Like Taleb said, he has friends, in this case Palestinian friends that burn luxury cars from inside Israel. Like this Pontiac, let's say. After stripping the car, they pour petrol on the chassis and set it alight. In the end, all that's left is ash and twisted metal—totally untraceable. There's a lively wind tonight. I think that you will burn very nicely, Rachel."

Taleb stepped towards him. "Gideon," he said, "don't."

"Taleb," Rachel said with all the force she could muster, "Do you think he'll stop with me? He'll kill you too."

Gideon let out a snort of disgust. "Taleb and I have our agreements which are none of your business. Get into the trunk. Now!"

Though she saw the glint of metal in his hand, she fixated on the glowing embers of his pipe. The fires of Moloch, the crematorium, the *matza* oven, her own death by fire. She was propelled by one thought—to extinguish the conflagrations.

She lunged forward and smashed her fist into the pipe perched in the corner of his mouth. He bellowed with pain as the pipe stem rammed into the back of his throat. Exhilaration ripped through her even as she heard the blast of the gun and pain seared her hip.

Gideon yelled and Taleb grabbed her and shoved her into the trunk. The last thing she saw before the lid crashed down was the prayer beads dangling from his waistband.

CHAPTER THIRTY-SEVEN

RACHEL breathed black. Her eyes opened and squeezed shut into dense and airless black. Her right hip sizzled with pain and blood crept down her thigh. Beneath her cheek, carpet fibers smelled of overripe oranges.

Though squashed in a fetal position, she was able to jiggle her fingers and toes, keeping the circulation going, for what purpose, she had no idea. Soon she would be dead. The car moved onto tarmac and rode smoothly and fast on what felt like a good road. She swayed back and forth in her enclosed sac.

Scenes from her life did not flash before her eyes. Instead, there was completion. She prayed intensely. Prayers exploded full-blown in her head. *Shma Israel..The Lord is our God, The Lord is One. Life is good. Keep my family safe, guide them through. Thank you God, for not giving me children.*

She was lulled by the soothing bump of the tires, the gnawing pain in her hip, which was the only sensate part of her. She lay in a puddle of blood and prayed she'd bleed into unconsciousness before the rasp of the match, the stench of petrol, the blast of the explosion, the wave of heat, the flames eating her flesh.

The car was speeding. Every now and then, the road curved

and then straightened again. Dimly, she realized that it was a bypass road, like the one that led to her brother's outpost, a road where Jewish settlers traveled. A hunting ground for terrorists.

From a distance, she heard a car approach, slow down and then stop, engine idling. All at once, staccato blasts from a rifle rocked the Pontiac; the car shuddered, lurched sharply to the right and, in a cascade of shattering glass, crashed into the mountainside. The impact hurled her body into the back of the trunk.

Footsteps crunched on shards of glass and came up to the car. Two muffled voices speaking Arabic. She heard the click of a gun followed by two shots. The Pontiac jumped twice. Footsteps running away, and the revving of an engine. The other car zoomed off.

Rachel lay in a vacuum of silence. Her hip thrummed and her neck, skewered against the back of the trunk, felt as if molten filaments were goading the top of her spine. Blackness folded into blackness as conscious thought seeped away. She was being swept into a dark river whose waters swirled her in a cold embrace and tugged her down, down into a void where only hollow echoes filled her ears.

A mosquito droned through the echo, whining louder and louder, whooping, shrieking her into consciousness. An ambulance? Like a boring rerun, her ears picked up the sound of engines, car doors slamming, thuds of running footsteps, men shouting, in Hebrew this time. Why didn't they let her sink into that cold ebony river? Why couldn't they leave her alone?

They were surrounding the Pontiac now. She felt the slam of a palm on the car and heard the scrape of metal. They were so close to her, she could hear their urgent voices. Something about terrorists, a drive-by shooting. She wanted to crawl out of her lair and crumple at their feet. Not a soul knew where she was; she had to let them know she was alive. She started screaming, emptying her lungs with shrieks. With her right hand, she pounded on the roof of the trunk. The voices faded away.

"No, No!" she wailed, filling the void with her cries. Remembering how her body had tumbled with the movement of the car, she jerked every muscle and limb to rock it. Maybe they'd notice. She continued to shriek, writhe, pound the trunk with her thrusts. Her strength ebbed, surrender crept back. Thankfully, she dipped her toe in the ebony river, then slid in. Cool water lapped against her thighs, kissing the gash in her hip. Miraculously, all the pain evaporated into mist and she closed her eyes. She floated down the limpid water.

They were shouting now and slamming on the trunk. A seep of cold air drenched her face as the trunk shot open. Then, more shouts, in Hebrew this time. "Bring a drip!" "Get a blanket over here!" And then the medic's voice leaning into her, "It's all over," before carrying her towards the ambulance.

She didn't look back at the car crumpled against the mountainside, nor did she ever get a glimpse of the blood streaming down the shattered windshield. She never laid eyes on Taleb's ruptured face, or the crater that had once held Gideon's brain.

She simply turned her back.

CHAPTER THIRTY-EIGHT

"Iᴛ's been a nightmare for my family and for our community. To think we'd nurtured a snake, the apex of Evil…"

But Aviva didn't say "nightmare," she said "nightmeah." Her Brooklyn vowels, coupled with the English Lit. vocabulary she touted whenever she tried to make an impression, blared out from the T.V. Small and stout, a maroon beret on her head, she flung her hands out towards the reporter from the English news. From the edge of Rachel's hospital bed, her real mother nodded emphatically, as if agreeing with every word her taped image said.

Rachel's right hip throbbed, so she shifted onto her left side. "So you think she makes sense, the mother of the victim?"

"Shut up, you!" She smacked Rachel's knee, then stroked it lovingly. "Glad to see that your chutzpa has bounced back."

Nate poured her a glass of lemon soda from the bottle on the bedside table, inserted a straw, bent it and handed it to his daughter. "We're mighty grateful to God." He eyed the television screen. "Those reporters just won't give up, will they?"

She sipped her drink, savoring the ping of bubbles in her nostrils, as Miri leaned over and arranged her pillow. "Why should they? You've been the hottest item in the news for a week. The kidnapping, the drive-by shooting of the bad guys, gross fraud, exploitation of Holocaust survivors...."

"You bet." Aviva slid off the bed and turned off the program, which had switched over to the afternoon children's shows. "I forgot to tell you. Uncle Irv called. He and Claire saw you on the CBS Evening News. And," she added, raising an eyebrow meaningfully, "you even made the New York Times."

Rachel tried to smile. She knew that her parents' bravado covered layers of pain. Their bucolic reality had been shattered and once again, their daughter's life had hung by a thread.

"At least something good has come out of all this." Miri flitted around, arranging a fresh bouquet of flowers in a mayonnaise jar. "Malkie has decided to ask the Rabbinical court to grant her a divorce. Knowing for sure that Shmaya didn't kill her father gave her the strength to make the break."

"Poor Shmaya has been transferred to an ordinary psychiatric ward," Aviva said. "He'll be spending a long time there, I'm afraid."

"Maybe it's for the best." Her meeting with Dima seemed to have taken place in another lifetime. Though most of her secrets could be told, Rachel knew there were a few that were better buried forever.

Her hip felt like glowing coals. The bullet had gouged out flesh and the stitches from the surgery bit into her skin. She repressed a groan.

Nate dashed over to her. "How about one of those painkillers?" Without waiting for an answer, he thrust a fat capsule into her palm.

She swallowed the pill, knowing that the pain, her parents, Miri, the festoons of flowers that studded the room would melt into mist once the medicine took effect. She remembered the surrender she'd craved in the blackness of the trunk.

"Am I disturbing you?" Absalom stood in the doorway, holding a plastic bag. He was dressed in civilian clothes, pressed jeans and a white tee shirt.

"Of course not, come on in." Her mother padded over to him on bare feet, and took his hand, leading him, dragging him to the easy chair next to the bed. "Sit down next to Rachel."

Miri coughed. "Hey, didn't the doctor want to talk to you about Rachel's recuperation?" She jerked her head towards the door. "I need to go anyway."

Baffled, Aviva stared, then scooped up her sandals. "Yeah, yeah, sure."

"You don't have to rush out barefoot, *Ima*." Rachel said, "And Miri…come back later, huh?"

Miri winked. "Can't keep me away."

Aviva slipped into her sandals. "Absalom, you hold the fort here. We'll be right back." Nate gave her a slight shove out the door.

"No need to hurry, no need at all," Absalom waved. "Now," he said, opening the plastic bag. "We can indulge."

He removed a Styrofoam box from the bag and the steamy tang of French fries filled the room.

"Hmmm," she said and wriggled higher up on her pillow.

The pain in her hip had dulled to a low ache.

He ripped open a packet of salt and sprinkled it on the chips, then passed her a wad of napkins. They munched in silence for a minute or so.

"How do you feel today?"

"Greasy with chips. Heavenly!"

Every day he drove to Hadassah Hospital to visit, a two-hour drive each day. A couple of times, he had picked up her brother Michael on the way. They were getting to know each other.

"He's okay," Absalom had said, pokerfaced, "for a religious guy."

A few days after her operation, he'd explained his vanishing act.

"I convinced Ron to let me fly to Warsaw to examine the records of the Kamienski Trust. I couldn't let you know, since I suspected that you were being tracked. The minute I caught onto Gideon's involvement, I phoned Ron from Warsaw to have Gideon picked up, but he'd already grabbed you at that quarry." His eyes bored into hers and he squeezed her hand. "The flight back from Warsaw was hard. I knew that he'd killed three people."

He gave himself a slight shake. "Thaddeus was shocked when he discovered the extent of the embezzlement—the paper trail that led from forged receipts to the Trust and back to Gideon's various bank accounts in Tel Aviv. He had nothing but sympathy for poor Jacob Lifschitz."

The night of Rachel's kidnapping, the police had blown

open a hidden safe in Lifschitz' Jerusalem apartment in which he'd stowed a confession, complete with bank accounts, dates, places. The clue to Gideon and Jacob's scam in the Rebbe's possession was the photograph of the ancient Polish cemetery, which turned out to be in Pomorzany. Emanuela's search for a similar confession among Lydia's papers proved fruitless.

She bit through the hot, doughy fries, savoring their salty flavor. She felt mirthful, dopey, loose-tongued.

"How's Emanuela?" she asked, staring at the golden glow that seemed to hover around Absalom's head.

He said, "Your eyes are swimming. You'll want to sleep soon. Yaffa, a.k.a. Emanuela, came to visit you here, don't you remember? All that blond hair?"

"Oh, yes," she replied, sinking more deeply into the bedclothes. "She escaped, didn't she?"

Absalom took the box of chips and placed it on the bedside table. "Gideon's accomplice was a small-time hood Taleb had scraped up from somewhere. The minute he heard the news about the confirmed killing on that road and realized that Gideon and Taleb were dead, he let her go. He's in jail now, awaiting trial."

"Hmmm." She concentrated on licking her fingers, sucking off all the salt.

Absalom reached for a tissue and wiped her fingers dry. "Boaz Kashtan wanted to come by, but your parents vetoed it. Instead, he came to see me."

"All that blond hair," she giggled.

He smiled, the dimple snagging his cheek. "He's a charmer,

all right. Tried to convince me that he'd turned over a new leaf, had paid his dues to society—he sat in prison for three years because of the Rajoub atrocity—and that he'd never hurt a soul. It was important for you to know this about him; said you'd know what he was talking about."

"I can't remember." Her voice was drifting above her head. Absalom's voice droned on through a long tunnel.

"...he'd trashed Lydia's cottage, he was so filled with rage against the kibbutz. He played the miserable childhood card."

Rachel snuggled down into the pillows. "What about Alona and Irene Mann?"

Through a blur, she noticed his grimace. "Both women were questioned very thoroughly. Irene didn't have a clue about the kind of person her husband really was, attributed his strangeness to his Holocaust background. She's aged ten years, hasn't been able to face anyone. As for Alona, she wrote you a letter. She's decided to leave the kibbutz altogether and to move to Tel Aviv to start a new life."

"Taleb wasn't so bad," she murmured, watching the ceiling revolve above her bed. "It was Gideon who was the baddie." She was floating now amid the muted hospital sounds of creaking wheels and laughing nurses.

"You're blabbing." Absalom put his hand on her cheek. She placed her hand over his and slept.

AUTHOR'S NOTE

Although this book is set in the Mount Carmel Nature Reserve, it is a work of fiction that in no way reflects the peaceful and generous people who live there.

I am grateful to those who devoted time and effort to bring this book to life. To Evan Fallenberg, my manuscript consultant, who has always believed in my writing. To my first readers—Rosi Ben Yakov, Laurie Bisberg, Lilian Cohen and Carole Gotlieb—whose perceptive comments always hit the mark. To The Three Writers—Sally Drucker, Barbara Kroll and Chava Romm—whose professional tinkering helped me get to where I wanted to be. To Pardes Publishing, for their care and guidance.

Finally, I wish to thank my husband, David, love of my life, for his support and patience.